HARAPPA 2

The Fall of Shuruppak

Shankar N Kashyap

ALCHEMY

First Impression in 2014

ALCHEMY PUBLISHERS
4767/23, Pratap Street, Darya Ganj,
New Delhi: 110 002

is a registered trademark of Mehras
and is licensed for use to Alchemy Publishers.

Distributed by
MEHRAS BOOKS PVT. LTD.
38 A, Akshoy Kumar Dutta Sarani,
Second Floor, Kolkata–700 006

4767/23 Pratap Street, Darya Ganj, Ansari Road
New Delhi: 110 002

ISBN: 978-81-927491-3-6

Cover design by Sambaran Das

Layout by Bit Blits Digital Workstation

Content

Foreword

That there were trading links between the Harappans and the Middle East (such as Egypt, Mesopotamia and Elam) for several millennia has been well established for a long time now. Merchants have travelled between the large port cities of Lothal and Dholavira in India and Mesopotamian ports such as Dilmun, Ur and Uruk in antiquity. Harappan seals have been found in Mesopotamia, Egypt, Dilmun, Susa and other places in the west. Dilmun was known to be a staging post for ships sailing between Sumer, Harappa and Dholavira. Recent excavations have shown that the port in Dilmun shipped copper in both directions. Sage Vasishta is said to have travelled over the seas to the thousand-pillared temple of Varuna in Susa. He migrated to the southern slopes of Mount Arbuda after his spat with Sage Vishwamitra, according to the scriptures.

Arbuda Mountain (Mount Abu) was a large snow-capped mountain on the southern fringes of the Aravalli hill range. There is now evidence of the mountain peak having collapsed on itself due to prehistoric tectonic activity. This flattened the top of the mountain, giving us the structure we see today, with a substantial plateau of about ten square kilometers and the city of Mount Abu. The Vedic scriptures tell us that the god Indra flattened the Arbuda Mountain when he fought the serpent demon called Arbuda which lived in the mountain. He is said to have hit the serpent with a 'great slab of ice' and, in the process, flattened the peak of the mountain. At the end of the Last Glacial Maximum about 12,000 years ago, the melting of the ice of the Himalayan glaciers played havoc with the geography of the region. Sage Arbuda Kadraveya is said to have lived in these mountains. It was he who described the technique of extracting *somras* from the *soma* plant.

The epic of Gilgamesh tells the story of the semi-mythical king/sage, Sage Ziusudra (Utnapishtim)and the great flood in Mesopotamia. Gilgamesh is considered part God and part human. He fights the wild man of the forest, Enkidu, and wins. Gilgamesh makes friends with Enkidu and brings him into his city, Uruk. They become very close friends and travel to the cedar forest to fight the demon, Humbaba. They are cursed by the demon as he lies dying and they return home with his head on a stake. On return to Uruk, Enkidu falls seriously ill. Sumerian physicians try to save him, with no success. They succeed in relieving his pain but cannot save him.

Gilgamesh is distraught at the death of his friend, Enkidu. Against the advice of the elders and royal priests, he sets off in search of Sage Ziusudra in the middle of Apsu to get answers to his questions and get solace for his tormented soul. After a difficult journey fraught with mythical monsters and scorpion men and lions he reaches Apsu and asks the sage the secret of immortality. The sage puts him to test, trying to make him stay awake for six days and seven nights, but Gilgamesh fails. The sage tells him to go to the bottom of the ocean to get a plant which will make Gilgamesh young again. The plant is stolen by a serpent on his way back home. He finally realises the futility of all his quests and learns his lesson

This is a story based on the travels of the Harappans to the Sumerian cities of Ur, Uruk and Shuruppak. Recent archaeological excavations have shown that a fire destroyed the city of Shuruppak around the third millennium BCE. Evidence has been found of at least two floods affecting the cities of Ur as well as Shuruppak. Approximately, the dates of these calamities are around the middle of the fourth millennium BCE and the beginning of the third millennium BCE. The story of the famous archaeologist Sir Leonard Wooley finding evidence of the Thirty Days' Flood in the ruins of Ur is now well known. It was touted as evidence that the biblical flood really happened, until further investigation showed it to be localized flooding in the cities of Ur, Kish and Shuruppak. The story of flood in the Epic of Gilgamesh is very similar to stories of mythical floods in most religions. Similar, but not identical. There are certain basic differences as to how and why the flood was caused. The basic plot ingredient, a hero saving mankind and animals from the devastating flood by building an ark, is the same in most religions. In Hinduism, Manu is considered the savior of mankind with the help of Vishnu who takes the form of a fish to help him.

The Aryan invasion theory has now been pushed into the dustbin of history. There is also evidence of inhabitants of India migrating to countries as far away as Afghanistan, Iran, Syria and Turkey. The Rigveda tells us about the five sons of King Yayathi who go on to populate the world – Yadu, Turvasa, Druhyu, Anu and Puru. One of his descendants, Bharata goes on to expand the empire and the ancient name of India, Bharat, is derived from him.

Recent excavations at the ruins of Ur have shown what may have been the birthplace and house of Abraham, the father of three major world religions – Judaism, Christianity and Islam. The story of how Abraham led his people out of Mesopotamia to Canaan and the famous 40-year journey across the desert by Moses to the promised land is now considered historical rather than a fairy tale or a myth.

Characters and Places

Upaas – Upaashantha Angirasa, a physician of Bharata

Shushun – Prince Shushun, Prince of Elam

Parthava – free-spirited Harappan soldier

Lopa – wife of Upaas

Sage Shunahotra – Chief of Harappa

Sage Vamadeva Gautama – sage and composer of the Rigveda

Sage Arbuda Kadraveya – sage of Rigvedic times

Sage Vasishta – sage and composer of the Rigveda

Sage Ziusudra/Utnapishtim – Sumerian sage of the flood myth

River Buranuna – Euphrates

River Hidekal – Tigris

River Gihon – Karun

Budii – Avestan Magus

Shu-Ilishu – Sumerian translator

Nisaba – wife of Shu-Ilishu

Ur-Nanshe – King of Lagash

Gilgamesh – Emperor of Sumeria

Enkidu – friend of Gilgamesh

Ambhasika – Meluhhan living in Sumeria

Upar-Tutu – ruler of Shuruppak

River Ulaja – dried-up tributary of Euphrates

Zubi – Zagros mountains

Ursanabi – ferry man of Ziusudra

Siduri – tavern keeper at the Apsu

Journey to
Arbuda Mountain

They had been watching the camp for a while now. The campfire was dying out, and the sleepers were beginning to move. One of them had walked across to the thick grove at the edge of the clearing and disappeared for a few minutes behind the trees. Parthava began to fidget when the man refused to reappear for quite a while and it took a stern stare from Shushun to keep him down. We were well-hidden behind a huge rock on top of the hill. With the sun coming up behind us, the men at the camp in the clearing at the foot of the hill would never be able to see us with sunlight streaming into their eyes. Shushun had chosen this spot well. Parthava counted seven of them sleeping around the dying fire. That meant five of them were unaccounted for from the day before.

It had been an eventful day. They had taken us by surprise. Our caravans were trudging around a corner in a narrow gorge, when the first of the bevy of arrows hit the wagon at the back. Lopa was fast asleep inside the caravan while Pindara was driving the four bullocks attached to the caravan. We were leading the caravan in front, on our horses. The spare horses were trailing at the back, including Lopa's Elamite horse. When the first arrow hit the wagon, Parthava's immediate reaction was to turn his horse toward the door of the caravan where Lopa was sleeping, with his bow drawn and loaded. There was a scream at the head of the caravan. Pindara had been hit, sitting high up in front of the caravan. He was writhing in agony and nearly fell off the seat, saved only by the leather lead of the bullocks caught on the seat post. Soon, there was literally a rain of arrows thudding onto the caravans at a furious pace.

"There are too many of them. We have to make a run for it. If we can reach that copse ahead, we could get some cover," Shushun shouted. I jumped from my horse onto the seat of the caravan in front to take the reins from Pindara. I knew that Shankara, my favourite horse, would just follow me wherever I went. I took the whip from the side of the seat and flicked it on the sides of the four bullocks pulling the caravan. As the whip cracked next to their ears, the bullocks ran as fast as they could. Their speed made the caravan sway wildly and rather dangerously. There was a curve around the gorge and it was a good place for an ambush. We could not see the riders very well because they were shooting from behind the boulders which were strewn along the ridge at the top of the gorge on both sides.

I could see the copse Shushun had spoken of, at the end of the curve not too far away now. Not a place for the faint-hearted, I thought. Parthava had jumped onto the steps on the side of the caravan and was now emptying his quiver with great enthusiasm. It would have been a miracle, however, if any of his arrows had hit any of the raiders. There was no sign of Shushun in all this mêlée. Where could he have gone? It was not like him to miss a skirmish or a confrontation of this sort. He relished the thought of unfair battles. We could not hear anything over the loud thuds that the arrows were making on the sides of the caravan. The swaying caravan was also rattling quite loudly. The raiders must be behind us now, and it won't be long before they catch up with us, I thought, getting increasingly worried. I was trying to hurry the bullocks as hard as I could and had precious little time to worry about anything else. After what seemed to be an eternity, we reached the safety and darkness of the copse with dense vegetation and tall trees. But I dared not stop. I could hear Parthava swearing in his dialect, which I could not understand, at the back. The thudding of arrows reduced and stopped soon after we reached the copse. I could feel the sweat pouring down my face and drenching my white cape.

"Stop! Upaas, stop," Parthava was shouting at the top of his voice, to be heard over the din of the rattling caravan. I don't know how long he had been shouting because I found him holding fast onto his horse almost next to me, waving his arms wildly, asking me to stop. He must have gotten back onto the horse once the arrows had stopped.

"It is okay to stop now, Upaas. I don't think they are following us," the sweet voice of Lopa tried to reassure me. She was carrying her bow with a few arrows ready to be shot in her right hand. She was a sight for sore eyes. She looked beautiful and calm in her white dress with not a crease out of place. One would have been forgiven for thinking she was out for an evening stroll, going by her calmness. She must have fired a whole bunch of arrows because her quiver was half empty. "You handled the caravan very well. I am impressed."

"Thank you. Poor Pindara appears hurt," I said, and turning to Pindara who was lying still on the floor near the seat, said, "How are you, Pindara? Let me have a look at you."

"I am not too bad, Master Upaas. I have been hit on my left shoulder."

As I turned him around, I could see an arrow buried into the back of his left shoulder. The staff of the arrow head was distinctly curved; this was typical of the Nagas. And if it were the Nagas, I better get the arrow out quickly as they usually had poisoned tips. I turned to Lopa and said,

"Can you please get me my instruments and medicine bag from the caravan? Parthava, can you please get some clean water from the stream quickly?"

Lopa was back with the two bags in an instant. We managed to get Pindara off the caravan on the ground and laid him face down on the grass. Lopa kept talking to him all the time in a soothing voice.

"It will be fine, Pindara. You have the finest physician of all Bharata looking after you."

Pindara smiled weakly but did not say anything. I tore off the cloth he was wearing over his shoulders to expose the back. Luckily, the arrow did not seem to have gone in too deep. I could still see one edge of the triangular tip of the bronze arrow. There was a slow trickle of blood from the wound. I knelt on the ground and put my ear next to his chest to listen to any air escaping from the entry wound of the arrow. I breathed a sigh of relief when I could not hear any such thing. No air was escaping the wound. I hoped that the arrow hadn't penetrated his lungs. I asked Lopa to make him chew on some poppy paste.

"Pindara, I will have to take this arrow out quickly before any poison gets into your body. If you chew on that paste Lopa has given you, it will numb the pain."

"Thank you, Master Upaas. I am grateful for your help."

"No, Pindara. Thank you for steering the caravan through all those arrows," I said and started working on the arrow. I applied the poppy paste around the edges of the wound and gently pulled out the arrow. I had my ears close to his chest and my hand ready to seal off the wound if there was any air escaping from the wound. There was no such thing.

Again I breathed an enormous sigh of relief. By this time, Parthava had run back with a leather satchel full of water from the stream. I cleaned the wound, applied some neem paste to it and bandaged the wound with some padding. Parthava had seen numerous such injuries during his time in the Harappan army. He quickly fashioned a sling to support Pindara's arm.

"That looks quite professional. Well done, Parthava."

Shushun had crept up behind us, obviously without our knowledge. He looked slightly dishevelled, and his clean silk robes were mud-stained.

"There you are, Shushun. Where had you been? We were getting worried about you," I said.

"I wanted to see who our attackers were and why they were attacking us. When I saw you had the situation under control, I went back to check. They were some rogue bandits from near the base of the Arbuda Mountain. I am afraid there are still some Naga tribes who have not accepted the rule of your Sage Shunahotra," Shushun replied. "They are holed up in a camp on the other side of the western ridges of the gorge not very far from here. There are twelve of them in the camp and some of them have been injured by our arrows. But they will be back, and this time they will be more careful. They probably did not realise that there may be an armed response to their attack."

That worried me a little. "What do you think we should do? Should we negotiate with them? What do they want?"

"I am afraid the Nagas don't negotiate. They only take what they want, and that is—everything in our wagons. We have the advantage of speed because they don't have any horses. So we should be able to surprise them and find them unprepared. They know we are only four people. They would not be expecting us to attack them." Shushun was actually smiling when he said that. "We can ride up to the northern end of the gorge where a rough path goes up to the top of the western rim. We can leave the horses at the bottom and climb it. Night time for the Nagas is sacred because their snake gods are active during that time. We can surprise them if we get them at sunrise."

He appeared to have worked out the plan exceptionally well. We waited for nightfall before setting off. Lopa agreed to stay back and look after Pindara after several protests by Pindara. There was a full moon, and we kept to the eastern side of the gorge to stay within the shadows until we reached the northern end. The 'path' Shushun had described turned out to be a stiff climb over several large boulders and a treacherous, steep scree.

The darkness did not help. By the time we reached the top, there were several scrapes on our knees and elbows and a couple of close shaves with accidental deaths by stepping on dangerous paths carelessly. We had to walk with our bows and quivers full of arrows strapped to our shoulders, which made it harder. The moon had lit up the top of the ridge and we had to hide under a large outcrop on the side of it. We kept watch in turns—more to make sure that we did not roll off the ridge than to protect us against the attackers. We had prepared ourselves just before sunrise and slipped over to our vantage point with a battle plan.

Parthava was getting worried about the 'missing five' from the group of Nagas at the camp. "I wonder where the other five are," he wondered aloud.

"Three of them are hidden just on the other side of the camp and two of them are below us. We cannot see them from here. We can deal with them later," Shushun said. He had obviously been remarkably thorough with his search the day before. "Remember our plan. First arrows are crucial to cause confusion and scare."

We drew out our 'specials' from our quivers and loaded the bows waiting for the sun to rise. These had phosphorus mixture tips which would go off on contact with fire or any kind of friction. As soon as we saw the rays of the sun hit the camp, we let loose a volley of the specials into the campfire. When the first of them hit the fire, the explosion was rather spectacular and almost blinded us even from that distance. The noise was tremendous and enough to strike terror into anyone. Each of us had shot five of these specials at the same spot and stopped to see the effect. As the smoke cleared, we could see four of the seven lying still without moving, in unnatural angles. The other three were running in different directions. That is when I saw the three scouts from the far side of the camp jumping up and running away from the campsite.

"Ignore those scouts. Concentrate on those at the camp and keep an eye out for the scouts on this side of the camp. I'll take the one on the left." Shushun was firing as he spoke and I could see one of the Nagas running wildly off to the left drop.

"I'll take the one on the right," Parthava also shouted and fired at the same time. The one in the middle had run behind a large boulder on the far side of the camp. That is when one of the scouts from below us ran into view. I took careful aim and let loose two arrows in quick succession. The second one hit the target, and I saw him fall, with some relief. Shushun was already aiming for the second scout and shot three more arrows. He appeared to hit the scout's leg as we saw him stumble away, limping away fast to hide behind the boulder with his compatriot.

It suddenly became dead quiet. The three forward scouts from the far side of the camp had obviously scampered at the first sign of trouble. There were only the two hiding behind a large boulder at the edge of the clearing, one of whom would not be a threat, injured as his leg was by Shushun's arrow.

"I think we should go in there and finish them off," Parthava gushed.

"No. We will wait and see what they do," I replied. "I think we should give them a chance of surrender or escape." I was hoping that they would escape rather than surrender because it would be really difficult to carry two prisoners with us all the way during the rest of our journey to Arbuda Mountain. Shushun must have read my mind since he turned around and said,

"They won't be a burden, Upaas. We can leave them at the ashram of Sage Vamadeva Gautama. I remember you telling me that his ashram was not too far away from here."

"Of course. It cannot be too far away now. By my reckoning, we should be able to reach the ashram late this afternoon if there are no more obstacles. We can leave Pindara at the ashram to recuperate, and he can catch up with us later on."

It was decided that we would approach the two survivors and offer them a chance to surrender. I was quite surprised by how easy it was, and the two Nagas appeared to be very happy to surrender to us. The man with an arrow stuck in his thigh was even more grateful when I took the arrow out and gave him some poppy paste to chew. Once he was bandaged, we set off, climbing down to the valley floor, and our horses, with the two prisoners in front. It was tricky going down the steep, boulder-strewn slope while keeping an eye on the prisoners at the same time. However, they did not appear to want to escape and gave no trouble. Parthava insisted on tying their hands once we were on the ground. He took the wounded Naga to ride on the back of his horse.

As we approached our caravans, which were well-hidden within the copse, Lopa came out from behind one of the trees with her bow at the ready. She was a sight for sore eyes after a night on top of that ridge and the little fracas we had just had. I jumped off my horse and ran towards her. She must have been watching the road with some anxiety for as soon as she saw me, she dropped the bow and came running towards me and threw her arms around my neck. I held her in my arms for a long time until Shushun coughed politely and said,

"I think we should get a move on if we have to reach the ashram before nightfall."

I could see Lopa's face go bright red, and as I turned around, I could see both Shushun and Parthava grinning from ear to ear.

"And the two of you can stop grinning like idiots. I am sure both of you have work to do." I feigned annoyance. Turning back to Lopa, I said, "We now have two wounded people with us. It may be better if we keep both of them inside the wagon for the trip up to Sage Vamadeva's ashram."

"It would be more comfortable inside our caravan than inside that wagon. I will ride my horse like the rest of you," Lopa insisted.

She would not hear any of the protests from me or Pindara. I had learnt long back that it was almost impossible to get Lopa to change her mind once she had made it up. Pindara was distraught to see Lopa riding a horse while he was comfortable inside the caravan. He kept quietly objecting all the way up to the ashram.

So it was that all of us were on our horses while the wounded Naga and Pindara rode inside the caravan. The road started to climb gently, and the forest became denser as we progressed. The road became narrow until it petered out into nothing but a rough line amongst gorse bushes. It must have been soon after our lunch break that the mountain came into view. It was breathtaking, to say the least. We were at the top of a small rise where the trees were sparse and the majesty of the mountain became more obvious. A thick, green carpet of dense forest lay beneath us, spreading over as far as our eyes could see. In the distance, the majestic Arbuda rose up into the sky like a giant craggy seashell. The base of the mountain was quite broad and merged into the smaller, rolling hills on either side. The top of the mountain was covered by a thick white cloud which gave the impression of it being turbanned by a white cloth. Halfway up the mountain, thick, grey mist encircled it like a coarse girdle. The sun was behind us and the sunrays bounced off occasional boulders bejewelling the mountain sides, which were rather shallow at the bottom and gradually became steeper after the mist wore off. There was dense vegetation on the sides with occasional streams winding down in gentle curves all the way down to the bottom. I could count at least four streams from this distance.

The sight of the mountain was mesmerising and we were spellbound for a long time. As we looked back onto the carpet of the forest below, we could see smoke. It was twirling slowly up, very near the place we were standing, staring at the mountain. It was Parthava, who had been to the mountain before, who broke the silence saying,

"That is Sage Vamadeva's ashram. We better get there before sunset, before they start their evening hymns. The sage does not like the prayers being disturbed."

Parthava had been driving the caravan and the wagon had been tagging along. He poked the bullocks on their sides with the whip and they hurried along down the path towards the ashram. We stood there for a little while longer, taking in the beauty of the mountain before following him on our horses. Lopa, who had been quiet for a while, suddenly said,

"That is a beautiful mountain, and it looks so peaceful there. Heaven must look like that. No wonder Sage Vasishta has his ashram there."

I smiled at her and replied,

"Well, I have not seen heaven. But it sure looks remarkably peaceful from here. Not too long ago this whole area, including the mountains, were a stronghold for Dasyu rebels until Sage Shunahotra defeated them. They used to attack the camps and yajnas of rishis, regularly killing and maiming and looting. Only sages like Vasishta and Vamadeva were left alone because they were too powerful for the Dasyus. Just a few years ago, it would have been impossible to come here without an armed escort." Lopa looked quite shocked. "Parthava was with the Bharata army and Sage Shunahotra at that time. He can tell you stories of the terrible deeds of the rebel Dasyus."

"I can imagine them to be quite gruesome. No, thank you. It looks so peaceful now. I know why the *rishis* want to come here for their ashrams."

We reached Sage Vamadeva's ashram well before sunset. As we approached the ashram, I could see deer and goats grazing peacefully outside the ashram. There was a makeshift fence of bamboo sticks but that was hardly to be called a boundary. It did not protect the ashram from any real danger. Several vines grew on the fence; it was almost green and wonderfully fragrant. The branches of the mango trees in the garden drooped to the ground, heavily laden with fruit. The pomegranate trees were full of blossoms besides having the juicy, red fruit hanging from their branches. The pomegranates were so enormous and heavy that a few of the delicate branches had snapped. There was a small stream running through the ashram from east to west, dividing it into two. One bank of the stream was covered with numerous banana trees. The stream appeared to be in a permanent shade by the huge trees on either side, and the water appeared crystal clear.

As we approached, the deer stopped grazing and looked up at us. Instead of running away scared, they just went back to grazing again as if they knew that we would not harm them. Lopa was so impressed that she wanted to get down and stroke them. We stopped near the entrance to the ashram and were watching Lopa stroke a little fawn, when a soft voice said,

"Welcome to our humble abode, strangers. After you have finished washing yourselves in the stream, I will bring some refreshments to quench your thirst." It was a young *shikshu* not much older than my little brother Satakratu, wearing the *anga vastra* and a *rudraksha* necklace around his neck. He had a soft and innocent smile and looked very peaceful.

"I will take you to see Sage Vamadeva once you are refreshed. We have been expecting you for some time. My friends will take care of the wounded. It may be better that the prisoners stay here under guard."

And he was smiling all the while he was talking. I was not entirely surprised. By now I had come to think of these things as normal for the powerful sages. They seem to know about things before they happen. But it was a shock for the others. Both Shushun and Parthava were staring open-mouthed at the young apprentice in shock. They both looked at me with a question mark on their faces. Lopa appeared to take it in her stride. She obviously had seen this before with other sages.

Some more apprentices showed up and took Pindara and the wounded Naga inside with them. Parthava was moving the caravan to one side of the ashram when another apprentice walked up to us to take our horses.

"Let me take your horses to our stable. I am sure they could do with some water and food."

We went down to the stream and washed ourselves. The apprentice took us to a little pergola next to a large mango tree and filled our cups with a delicious drink he poured out of a large earthen pot.

"It is a *panaka* made out of a little *soma* and some fruits in the ashram. It refreshes and rejuvenates you. It is extremely refreshing and gets rid of your tiredness from your bodies," he said. It certainly did do that. It was cool and clear with a musty, fruity smell and had a light brownish tinge. I could feel my body ache all over from having continuously ridden the horse for several hours - getting rid of the gnawing pain in my joints. I could see both Parthava and Shushun were suitably impressed with the drink as well.

"Please come with me. I will take you to the sage. Don't worry about your injured friend. They will be taken good care of," he said with a smile on his face. As we followed him inside the ashram, both Shushun and Parthava had numerous questions, and they started to whisper,

"How did they know we were coming? How did they know we had wounded people and prisoners with us?" It was Shushun who began first. "Back home in Elam it would be extremely suspicious. Has someone been watching us?"

"No, Shushun. Stop being paranoid. These sages are extremely powerful. Among other things, they can see things happening far away. You just follow my lead in the presence of the great sage," I replied.

Lopa smiled, turned to Shushun and said,

"There is no need to whisper, Shushun. They can hear everything we say, it does not matter how softly you say it. They can even read your mind."

"It is truly astounding. I wish I could learn such things from the sages."

"They have endured lifetimes of penance and dedication to achieve this. It does not come easy. Several people have tried and failed, and some have perished in the attempt," Lopa replied.

We were walking along a grassy path with flowering plants on either side. There were several thatched huts on our way with no doors. We could see men and women moving around everywhere with smiles on their faces without wasting their breath on words. Some were carrying water from the stream in large earthenware pots. The sage's hut was the largest in the compound with a porch in front of it. That is where he received us.

There was a large *agni kunda* in front of the hut where apprentices were getting ready for the evening prayers and *yajna*. The sage was quite short, compared to others in the ashram but immense in stature. He had tied his hair into a bun with rosary beads to hold it in its place. His forehead was smeared with ash, he had a small white beard and the rosary he wore hung down on his bare chest. I could not attribute his aura to anything extraordinary in his appearance but his face was glowing and he looked ever so peaceful. The smile on his face was genuine as he welcomed us.

"*Hari Om tat sat.* You are welcome to our humble ashram."

I prostrated myself in front of him and touched his feet with my fingertips. Lopa and the others followed me.

"*Dheerghayushman Bhava.* Please rise, my children. . I hope the little *shikshu* has given you some refreshments."

"Thank you, O great Sage Vamadeva. I am Upaashantha Angirasa, and I bring greetings from Sage Shunahotra and my father Kapila Angirasa," I replied, still on my knees. I could see the rest of the group kneeling in front of the sage.

"Please sit down and make yourselves comfortable. Please pass my greetings to your father and the great Sage Shunahotra. I have sent a message to Sindhu and soldiers will be here soon to take care of the prisoners. Your cart driver is being looked after by our physicians as we speak. He should be good as new in no time. I believe that you are on your way to Sage Vasishta's ashram?"

I was surprised at the wealth of information he appeared to have regarding us, but did not say anything to that effect.

"Yes, sir. Sage Vasishta has invited my friend Shushun here to visit his ashram," I replied. He then turned to Shushun and said, "Oh yes, Master Shushun. A special welcome to you. It is right that you are travelling incognito. A prince of the Elamite empire is a target for all kinds of people for power as well as treasure.

Your *prana* is too powerful. You should learn to curb the *prana*. It is visible to anyone with the slightest power."

We were all sitting on straw mats at the side of the porch and the sage was sitting on a small tool in front of the doorway.

"Thank you, great Sage. I feel truly humbled in your presence. I have heard of a sage in Sumer who can teach me how to curb my *prana*. I am hoping to go to Sumer one day to find him," Shushun replied.

"Yes. I have heard of the great Sage Ziusudra. He lives in the abyss you call Apsu, and it is difficult for mortals to find his abode. Best of luck to you in your quest. It is not quite safe for travelers in the forest; Sage Shunahotra has asked me to send two of his soldiers along with you for the rest of the way. They will be here in a day or two. I recommend that you leave your caravan here and ride your horses the rest of the way. It would take you at least a week to reach Vasishta's ashram if you take your caravan. You can cover the same distance in a couple of days on horseback. I suggest that you rest at Sage Kadraveya's ashram on the way. It will make your journey tolerable," Sage Vamadeva replied. "In the meantime, please rest here in our ashram. Shikshu will take you to your hut. If you will excuse me now, I have to prepare for our evening prayers. You are welcome to join us if you are interested."

With that, the sage stood up and went back into the hut. The little *shikshu* appeared at the porch as if by cue again, with the smile that never faded from his lips.

"Please come with me. I will show you your quarters." He turned around and started to walk briskly towards the back of the hut. We went past the large communal kitchen where cooks were busy cooking for the whole ashram. The smell of the freshly-cooked *ghee* and spices wafted through the air and made us hungrier than before. Some food would do us good after having eaten dried bread and fruits for so long. It was nearly six weeks now since we had left Harappa. He took us to a pair of huts away from the kitchen.

"I will leave you here now. If you want to join us for the prayers, please come in front of the sage's hut in half an hour. The food will be served just before the sun sets in the dining area near the kitchen. I bid you goodbye for now. *Namaskar*," he said with folded hands and left. As soon as he left, there were a thousand questions from both Parthava and Shushun.

"Who is Kadraveya? You had never told me about his ashram being on the way," Shushun asked me.

"He is a *nagarshi*. He is one of the very few Nagas who have achieved the status of being a *maharishi*. He simplified the technique of making the sacred *somras* and wrote a detailed account of it. It used to be a complicated process in the past with lots of hits and misses. A lot of *soma* plants were being wasted. Nagas, historically, have kept themselves aloof from others. We are all wary of their magical powers. I am not sure of the reception we will get in his ashram. I am not even sure we will be able to find the ashram. I had hoped to bypass his ashram. Now we have to visit it. I have a suspicion Sage Vamadeva has already sent a message to him, and I don't want to incur his wrath."

"He cannot be all that bad if he is a *maharishi*. I would like to meet him. I am sure we will learn something valuable from him," Shushun continued.

Parthava, who was listening to us all the while, piped up. "I have been involved with the Nagas in the past. They are tenacious fighters and they can do magic none of us have seen before."

"Well, it is settled then. We will have to stop at Kadraveya's ashram on the way. It will only be a day's ride to Vasishta's place from his ashram."

Shushun wanted to listen to the prayers, and the four of us went to the altar when the prayers began. The sage was leading the prayers and Vedic hymns were being chanted with such passionate calmness that it had an almost ethereal quality about it. It was in pure Sanskrit, and the clear diction of the sage and his apprentices made it easy for Shushun to follow the hymns. It was impressive to see all of them sing the hymn in identical diction and in one voice. The prayers started off with offerings to Agni, followed by their offerings to Soma and finished with an obeisance to Indra. Shushun was surprised to note that the hymns essentially meant that they were all one and different forms of Indra. He had quite a few questions for the sage at the end of the prayers.

"I was moved by the prayers, Sage Vamadeva. May I ask you some questions about them?" Shushun said to Vamadeva, in his usual impeccable, unaccented Sanskrit.

"I am very impressed by your command of Sanskrit, Master Shushun. Your Sanskrit has no trace of the Elamite slang that we normally hear," Vamadeva replied. "Please go ahead and ask anything you want. I will try to answer them to the best of my ability."

"Thank you, sir. I have had excellent Meluhhan teachers

during my childhood," Shushun continued. "Your prayers teach about various gods as different forms of Indra. Does it mean that you believe in one God?"

"You are asking me a fundamental question, Master Shushun. Our scriptures say that God is omnipresent, he is in everyone of us and that he is universal. It is up to us to interpret him in any way we want," Vamadeva replied. "I know you have several gods in your religion. Our scriptures say that all gods, regardless of creed, colour or race, are the same, and they are all different forms of one supreme being. It is a pity you are going away shortly. I hope you might stay for a few days on your journey back. I also have some questions about your scriptures."

The discussion was interrupted by the *shikshu*.

"Forgive me, Sage Vamadeva, but dinner is ready to be served," the shikshu said, bowed his head and withdrew.

"Come and taste the humble offerings of our ashram." The sage turned and walked towards the kitchen. Dinner was being served in a clearing in front of the kitchen, under the shade of a large peepal tree. It was getting dark. Several torches had been lit and placed around the clearing. I could see a few deer and a couple of peacocks hovering around the corner. The food was served on plantain leaves by young men and women of the ashram.

It was a simple affair with boiled rice, barley bread, vegetables and pickle followed by a sweet dish I had not tasted before. I could see Parthava really relishing his meal. He took a second helping.

We were tired after the long journey, and the heavy meal at the end of the day meant we were literally dead to the world till we woke up next morning. The soldiers arrived two days later and took charge of the prisoners. They were going to wait till the wounded Naga felt better. We spent the time wandering around the ashram and outside in the forest.

I took Lopa for a long ride in the forest along the stream one afternoon. I had been asked to "Stick to the stream" so I wouldn't get lost. The forest was, as Lopa put it, "Heaven on earth". We had spent a couple of hours wandering about aimlessly, enjoying the bountiful fruits of the forest. Once all four of us went on a small expedition and came back with satchels full of strange-looking wild fruit.

Pindara was being looked after very well by the *rishis* of the ashram. When we went to say goodbye, he was already up on his feet and looking a lot better than the day before.

"It won't be long before you are fully recovered. You can join us at Sage Vasishta's ashram when you are fit to do so," I said. Pindara would have none of it. He was raring to go.

"I am feeling much better now, Master Upaas. I have recovered fully. You need me to keep an eye on your back," he insisted. I could see that he was still in quite a bit of pain. He winced every time he moved his left arm accidentally in the sling. It took all my persuasive skills to make him agree to stay in the ashram till the *rishis* said he was well enough to ride a horse.

There was no sign of the sage when we left the ashram later that morning. The *shikshu* brought us cloth satchels full of dried fruit and nuts for our journey. He was still smiling when he waved us goodbye. The *shikshu* gave us directions and left us with a cryptic remark to our query on directions to Kadraveya's ashram,

"The ashram will find you, don't worry."

The journey to Kadraveya's ashram did not take us long. Sage Shunahotra had sent two soldiers to accompany us for the rest of the journey. As we went along a curve on the road winding up the mountain, we were faced with a valley entirely covered in mist. We could not even make out the path in front of us. Shankara neighed suddenly and refused to go any further. He had never done that before without a reason. I got down to investigate and walked gingerly forward into the dense mist with the two soldiers on either side of me. It was a complete white-out, and I could not see anything beyond my fingertips. There was a humming noise in the background which I could not place. When I turned around, the two soldiers had disappeared. My heart started to get heavier as I inched forward and it nearly skipped a beat when I heard a hissing sound. It was the country of the Nagas! The forest would be full of snakes. I reached into my scabbard to draw the sword out and called out to the others,

"I cannot see a thing. The place is crawling with snakes. Better stay back."

I lifted my sword, ready to defend myself. The hissing continued from a different direction. I started to flash my sword wildly in all directions without actually hitting anything. This was useless; I must stop panicking and think. I stood still for a minute and stared intently in the direction of the hissing. I wished I had learnt the art of seeing *prana* like the sages. Then I thought I saw several snakes hanging from the branches in front of me and was about to take a swipe at the nearest one when a voice said, "There is no need for that, Master Upaas. You are amongst friends."

A Naga appeared in front of me from nowhere. He was quite tall, fair-skinned, clean-shaven and had his long hair plaited and tied in a bun at the top. He held his hand out with an open palm which showed the markings of a king cobra's head. "Come, follow me. You are safe."

He turned around and started to walk into the dense mist. I quickly followed suit.

"Wait, we must get my friends. They are behind me."

"Don't worry, Master Upaas. They have been taken care of," he said, and kept walking. There was not much I could do but follow him because I was totally blinded by the mist. He obviously could see where he was going better than me. The mist suddenly started to lift, and bright sunshine hit my eyes. The light was so bright that it hurt my eyes. As I shielded my eyes against the glare of the sun, I could hear the dulcet tones of Parthava,

"Don't tell me you have been fighting the dragon without me?"

A mighty odd sight I must have been, with my left hand covering my eyes and the unsheathed sword in my right hand. I quickly brought the sword down and said,

"How did you guys get in front of me?"

"If you had not dashed off headlong into the unknown, our friends here would have shown you the way as well," Parthava continued. I could see both Shushun and Lopa trying to control their giggles unsuccessfully.

"You might very well laugh now, but this was the reason I did not want to come here."

Luckily, the Naga apprentices were not anywhere around us. It was not long before the two soldiers joined us again, led by a Naga apprentice. Sage Vamadeva had been right again: the Naga ashram had found us, we hadn't found it. We were actually standing at the gates of the ashram of Kadraveya. We were welcomed at the gate by a *shiskhu* similar to the *shikshu* we had met at Sage Vamadeva's ashram. The ashram was remarkably similar to the one we had left a couple of days ago, except for the numerous serpent idols, and there was a large hut near the back of the ashram where they appeared to be working with plants. On closer inspection, it turned out to be the *soma* plant. There was a small nursery where the saplings, in various stages of their growth, were kept. I could also see some contraptions for extracting the juice.

My apprehension was soon put to rest by the expansive welcome of Sage Kadraveya later in the day. He turned out to be quite tall and rather skinny, with long flowing hair neatly plaited and tied at the top and a broad white ash mark on his forehead. He was clean-shaven just like the rest of the Nagas in the ashram. His jet black eyes pierced into people; he never missed a thing. His eyes exuded peace and a gentleness which belied his impressive stare. Like Vamadeva, he knew everything about us. It was rather unnerving for Shushun to have these sages read his mind. He was still not used to the extraordinary powers that these sages possessed.

"Welcome to our humble ashram. Please make yourselves

at home. I have some good news for you. Your friend Pindara
is improving rapidly and he was allowed to ride his horse this
morning which he did quite well. He should be able to travel in
a couple of days to meet you."

Our stay at Kadraveya's ashram was as pleasant as our stay at
Vamadeva's. The Sage spent time explaining to us the intricacies
of *soma* extraction and different techniques for getting different
types of *soma*.

"You still need the *soma* plants from Mount Mujavant and
water from the sacred river Sarasvathi for the major *yajnas*. I
am afraid the plants grown elsewhere are not good enough." He
went on to explain the different types of *soma* plants grown in
different regions of the country.

"It should take you one whole day to reach Sage Vasishta's
ashram. I suggest you rest well tonight and leave at daybreak."

The discussion ended abruptly and he left us looking at his
back. It was rather unnerving, to say the least.

Gilgamesh

She had done her best to clean up her insatiable lover from the forest to bring him to the court of the Lugal, Gilgamesh. She had used the best oils and soaps to get him cleaned up and had dressed him in the best robes. She could barely remember the first week, which they had spent in passionate lovemaking with this beast of a man she had found chasing the beasts of the forest outside Uruk. Her knees went weak every time she thought of him: tall, heavily built, muscles bulging at the seams, covered all over by thick black hair. She was still not sure what his face looked like because it was covered by a thick moustache and a beard. They had moved into the shepherd's camp after that. Enkidu was given the job of a night watchman for the camp.

Enkidu had taken to the people of the camp. The women and children adored him. There was excitement in the camp because the chief's daughter was getting married. He came to Shamhat's hut one day looking rather serious.

"Shamhat, you must bring Enkidu to the wedding."

"I will certainly, chief. Why are you looking so serious? It is a happy occasion," Shamhat replied.

"The Lugal has threatened to use brides outside the city as well. You know I cannot fight him."

"What is this? Why is the Lugal using the bride?" Enkidu, who was sitting quietly, barked.

"Gilgamesh, the Lugal of Uruk, has been using the brides on the day of their wedding in the city and no one can stop him. He is too strong. They say he is half god and half human. Now he is threatening to do the same outside the city," the chief explained.

"That is stupid. I am stronger than anyone else. I'll look after him," Enkidu had growled.

True to his word, Enkidu had challenged Gilgamesh to a duel on the wedding day.

"I will not let you defile a woman you have not won in combat," Enkidu had shouted at Gilgamesh, blocking his way to the bride's chamber.

"I am the strongest man in the world. You are just a coward, preying on weak women."

Gilgamesh had laughed and tried to brush Enkidu aside.

"Go away, wild man. I am not some beast of the forest that is afraid of you. I will stamp you out like a little insect. Get out of my way before I disembowel you."

The fight had been long and gruesome. But Gilgamesh was obviously more talented in the art of fighting and despite his brute strength, Enkidu found himself on the floor with Gilgamesh's foot on his throat. Gilgamesh was out of breath and had difficulty speaking.

"I will give it to you, wild man. You fight well. With some training you can be as good as me. Come join me and we can rule the world."

Turning to Shamhat, he had said, "Bring your man to the court tomorrow" and had left without going into the bride's chamber. Enkidu was not so sure about Gilgamesh. It had taken Shamhat a lot of persuasion to get him to agree to come to the city.

"The city is full of nice things and the luxury there is unimaginable. You will be like a Lugal," Shamhat had implored him.

"I have everything I want in the forest. Why should I go to the city?" Enkidu was adamant.

"The Lugal lives there and you can be the Lugal if you want to," Shamhat had persisted. "You have been sent to me by the gods and you are no less than a Lugal."

Enkidu finally gave in the next day and agreed to go with her to the city to meet the Lugal called Gilgamesh. They had travelled to the city and Shamhat had spent a whole day sprucing Enkidu up to get him to meet the royalty. Enkidu was hugely impressed with the massive walls that surrounded the large city of Uruk. The city was bustling with people, carts, chariots and horses. The paved roads were wide and traders were selling their wares all over the huge city. There were numerous temples and large brick houses on either side of the roads. Enkidu was dumbstruck at the size of the ziggurat which dwarfed the rest of the city and large temples for the gods of the city.

"There is the temple for the sky god An, at the top of the

ziggurat. We can climb to the top tomorrow," Shamhat had said, seeing him staring at the building.

There were several boats plying the canals everywhere within the city, nearly as many as the number of main roads. Soon they were at the huge promenade which stretched as far as the eyes could see with a row of colossal round pillars on either side of the promenade.

Enkidu had never seen anything like that before in his life. The Great Court stood at the end of the mall, an imposing brick structure with immense cedar wood doors. The soldiers guarding the doors appeared to know Shamhat and they did not have any problem getting into the court. They pulled back the tall brass-tipped wooden spears to let them pass. The doors led onto a dark passage. There was another set of doors at the end of this dark passage. The two burly guards who paced up and down in front of the doors silently let them enter. No questions were asked.

The hall of the royal court was massive, with a high ceiling and arched windows at the sides. The torches on the walls burned furiously despite there being quite enough light outside to make the hall appear bright and airy. The smell of burning oil mixed with the fragrant incense sticks lit at the foot of the tall goddess Inanna at the end of the hall was rather heady. Officers of the court, guards and citizens thronged the sides of the hall. There was a priest standing near the statue waiting for Gilgamesh to arrive. Shamhat thought of standing right in the middle of all these people, in a place where she knew Gilgamesh could not help but notice them. Just as the crowd was beginning to get restless, the trumpeteer announced the arrival of the king with a sharp blast followed by the drum roll. The drums continued beating as Gilgamesh walked in through the doors and marched up to the podium at the end of the hall. He was wearing his royal robes for the occasion and looked radiant. As expected, he noticed Shamhat and Enkidu as soon as he reached the podium and turned around.

"Your Majesty, my friend Enkidu is here, as you had commanded him to be," Shamhat said, bowing her head down to the king.

"Please come, my friend, and stand with me".

The officers and the ministers looked at the beast of a creature walking across to the side of the king with astonishment. Enkidu swaggered across the hall to Gilgamesh and embraced the king. Everyone present there gasped. 'How can this wild ruffian embrace our Lugal, an incarnation of god?'

And that is how it started. A true friendship without any ambitions or expectations. Friendship between a royal and a savage, an incarnation of God and an incarnation of brute force. They came from two different spheres of existence. The two of them became inseparable. They went everywhere and did everything together, much to the annoyance of the courtiers. They hunted together and Gilgamesh learned new tricks of trapping animals from Enkidu. One day, as they were returning from a hunting trip, Gilgamesh turned to Enkidu and said,

"We must fight the demon of the cedar forest, Humbaba. That will give us strength and the entire world will bow to us."

"You surely will be the master of the world then. The two of us can easily beat the demon," Enkidu replied.

But when Gilgamesh's ministers heard of the plan, they dismissed it.

"The cedar forest is a long way and it will take you away from the country for a long time. What will happen to the country? Who will be the Lugal if you are killed?" lamented the ministers and the chief priest of the ziggurat of An.

"I will not be killed. When I am with Enkidu, I am invincible. I will leave instructions for you about how to rule the country until I get back."

Gilgamesh would not listen to any arguments and decided to take his mother's blessings before leaving for the cedar forest. His mother Ninsun welcomed him and asked the sun god, Shamash, to protect him from the demons of the forest. She embraced Enkidu and said,

"You are like my son. You are strong and very powerful. You must look after your brother, Gilgamesh, in the forest."

Both Gilgamesh and Enkidu left Uruk the next day and headed north towards the forest. They traveled for several days crossing rivers, streams, valleys and mountains. They would camp at night on mountain passes to be away from wild beasts of the forest. As they went closer to the cedar mountain, they could hear the demon, Humbaba, bellowing and growling at night. It was as if the demon was expecting their arrival. The bellowing got louder and more menacing as they came closer to the mountain. Gilgamesh nearly chickened out of the adventure,

"That sounds ominous, Enkidu. Are you sure we can beat this demon? I am afraid."

"Of course we can beat him. He cannot match our combined strength. Don't let his growl frighten you," Enkidu replied. "We have to get past the guardian of the cedar forest, Huwawa first. Leave him to me."

"Who is this Huwawa? Is he another demon?"

"No. He looks after the cedar forest and generally keeps an eye on who can enter and more importantly who leaves, if you get my meaning. I know how to deal with him. Leave him to me."

Next morning, as they were about to enter the cedar forest, Huwawa stood in their way. He was a giant of a man. He looked almost like a wild beast.

"You cannot enter the forest without my permission. What is your work in the forest?" he growled.

"Ha, Huwawa my friend, don't you remember me? It is me, Enkidu. And this is my good friend, Gilgamesh. We have come to fight the demon Humbaba."

Huwawa looked at both of them and started to bellow with laughter. He could not control himself. "You puny humans, you have come here to fight the greatest beast the world has ever known? He will eat you for breakfast."

"That is enough, Huwawa. You don't know who you are talking to. Between the two of us, we will not only destroy the demon, we will destroy your forest as well if you don't let us pass," Enkidu growled at him. "Gilgamesh is the son of Shamash, the sun god. He can burn your forest down in a minute. Don't make him angry."

Huwawa was confused. He thought, 'How can this puny human be the son of Shamash? Well, if he is, I don't stand a chance'.

"You are the son of nobody. I will rip your guts out and feed them to the birds. I will be waiting for you if you ever get out of the forest..."

Huwawa went on cursing Enkidu and avoided looking at Gilgamesh. He was still rambling on when Enkidu pushed him out of their way and the two of them went past him deep into the forest looking for the demon. They did not have to go very far before they were confronted by the demon himself. He was a frightening sight even for the bravest. He was tall, dark and built like a bull, with bulging bloodshot eyes, thick, matted hair covering his whole body, long claws caked with clotted blood, nostrils flaring with every breath, strong teeth protruding out of the corner of his thick, red lips. and saliva dripping from the corners of the mouth. He appeared to be wearing a thick, spiked leather armour on his chest. It was enough to strike terror into the bravest of hearts. He was growling as he spoke,

"How dare you puny humans enter my forest? You'll do for my dinner tonight."

And he started to guffaw loudly. It was more like a screech than a laughter. It was Enkidu, who replied,

"Beware, you demon. You don't know who you are speaking to here. I am the strongest man in the forest and this is Lugal Gilgamesh, son of Shamash the sun god."

That did not seem to make any difference to the demon. He just growled menacingly and screeched at them, blowing fire on them which singed Enkidu's beard. He then lunged at Enkidu with his open claws. He managed to hit Enkidu's face and there was blood pouring out every where. The claws had gouged out a fair amount of skin from his face. It enraged Gilgamesh to see blood pouring out of his friend's face. He lifted his mace and attacked the demon with a ferocious sweep at his head. The demon ducked and managed to get out of harm's way. But he could not avoid Enkidu's fist which had buried itself in his stomach and winded him. However, he was soon back on his feet and attacking both of them. The fight went on for a long time and just as Gilgamesh thought they were losing the fight, Enkidu had the demon by his throat and shouted at Gilgamesh,

"Quickly, get your spear and aim at the bottom of his chest." Gilgamesh suddenly remembered Enkidu telling him of the demon's vulnerable spot. He quickly grabbed the tall brass-tipped spear he had dropped on the ground when the fight had begun and thrust the tip into the demon's chest from underneath. The demon wailed loudly and started rolling on the ground, writhing in pain. The wailing did not stop and he started to curse Enkidu,

"You have betrayed the beings of the forest. You were one of us and you have sided with these humans. The humans are no good. They will destroy the forest and then the world. I curse you for your betrayal. You will die a painful death. Mark my words, you don't have long to live." The cursing and wailing went on for a long time and eventually stopped with a loud gasp.

Huwawa, who had been watching the battle all along, said,

"You will die of those wounds, Enkidu. The demon's claws are poisonous. No one can save you now." And Huwawa laughed.

Gilgamesh looked at Enkidu and said, "I will not let anything happen to you, my friend. I will get the best physicians in Sumeria to treat you."

Huwawa guffawed and said, "That is what you think. His poison and curse will be the end of Enkidu."

"You malicious creature, for that, we will destroy your cedar forest," Enkidu growled at him. The two of them set about pulling down the huge cedar trees and destroying the rest of the forest by setting fire to it. They used some of the wood to build a boat. Enkidu cut off Humbaba's head and unceremoniously stuck it on a stake in the middle of the boat. Gilgamesh was watching him without any questions,

"We'll have to show people his head or they may not believe us." Enkidu replied to Gilgamesh's questioning smirk.

They could see the forest burn as they sailed down the Buranuna river with the cedar trunks. They could hear Huwawa's wailing for a long time until they turned a curve in the river.

"I'll build a gate for the city of Uruk and a door for the royal palace with this wood," Enkidu said, touching the wounds on his face. Gilgamesh had cleaned the wounds with water from the river and applied a poultice on it. It was a lot quicker getting back to Uruk and they were at the city gates within days. The ministers and the chief priest of the ziggurat were at the jetty near the gate to welcome Gilgamesh. As the boat came to the edge of the jetty, there were cheers from the huge crowds when they saw the head of the demon stuck high up on the stake on their boat. Both of them were welcomed as heroes. They were taken to the palace in a chariot, being cheered on by the crowds who lined the streets all the way up to the palace. This was all strange to Enkidu, and he found it rather disconcerting. Gilgamesh's mother, Ninsun was at the palace gates to welcome both of them. She hugged Gilgamesh as he stepped off the chariot and said,

"Welcome home, son. I have been counting the days since you were gone. "

"Thank you, mother. There was nothing to worry about as long as my friend Enkidu was with me. He looked after me all the time," Gilgamesh said, beaming from ear to ear. Turning to the ministers, he continued, "And what news of the country?"

"Hail, great Lugal Gilgamesh, the emperor of the whole of Sumeria. You are now the most powerful man in the world, Your Highness. You have destroyed the powerful demon and destroyed the cedar forest which harboured all the demons."

"Please get the best physicians in our country to treat my friend Enkidu. He has been injured by the demon, Humbaba. And hurry. I want him seen today."

The ministers rushed off and sent for the royal physician. The royal physician was a short, bald and rotund chap who was breathless as he rushed into the palace. His short grey beard bobbed up and down as he spoke. He was a jittery character and kept looking at the emperor all the time. He obviously did not want his head chopped off!

"What seems to have happened, Your Highness?"

It was Enkidu who replied. "That demon, Humbaba, scratched my face with his claws. I have been told it is poisonous. But I am fine."

The physician frowned at this information and said,

"Hmm... let me have a look at this."

He asked Enkidu to sit down on a chair and started to clean off the poultice Gilgamesh had applied. The scratches had turned red and there was greenish pus in the wounds. Beads of sweat appeared over the physician's forehead as he examined the wounds in detail. He kept muttering under his breath as he fussed over Enkidu's face with lotions he had brought in his bag. It was difficult to hear what he was muttering. It sounded like, "This is no good. I am surely going to lose my head over this wild man's face. He is surely going to die and I will be put to the sword."

After what seemed an eternity, Gilgamesh could not control his curiosity any longer and said,

"What is the matter? What are you muttering about? Speak up. Can you cure him or not?"

The physician sensed the anger in the Lugal's words and started to sweat profusely.

"Yes, Your Highness. I am sorry, Your Highness. But, but..." His voice trailed off again.

"You are muttering again. Speak up, man."

He started to stutter even more at this and it was difficult to understand what he was saying.

"You see... This is a serious injury...the poison... the demon ... no medicine...," and again the words trailed off.

"Are you telling me that you cannot cure my friend Enkidu?" Gilgamesh shouted. Everyone could see that the physician was on the verge of breaking down and crying. His mother Ninsun intervened calmly.

"You don't need to worry, master. Tell us exactly what is wrong." He turned to the royal mother and said in a steadier voice this time,

"Your Highness, the wounds have been caused by a demon of the forest. No physician in Sumeria can treat this wound. I have heard that Egyptian physicians and Meluhhan sages can treat this."

"Do you know if there are any such men in Uruk at present?" Ninsun continued.

"There are no Egyptians, Your Highness, in Sumeria. There may be some physicians among the Meluhhans in a village in Lagash and also in Dilmun. I will send word immediately."

Thus a search began for Egyptians or Meluhhans throughout the country. The royal physician attended Enkidu every day. Despite his best efforts, the wounds started getting bigger and the greenish pus got thicker. Shamhat was beside herself with worry and fear, dressing the wound and seeing the love of her life deteriorate day by day. He soon lost his appetite and appeared tired and sleepy all the time. He kept to himself in the royal chambers he was given by Gilgamesh. He refused to see even his woman, Shamhat, on occasions.

"I can't let her see me like this. With these horrible wounds on my face, I must look like an ogre to her. Take her away."

Gilgamesh tried to reason with him and when Shamhat insisted that she wanted to look after him and his wounds, he started to get irrational.

"It is because of you I am in this state. I was happy in the forest with my beasts. If you had let me lead my life, I would have been healthy and not facing death now. I would not have gone to fight that demon, Humbaba. It is all your fault."

That accusation hit Shamhat very badly. It wounded her to her heart. It was becoming increasingly painful to hear him rant.

"That is unfair. It is because of me that you have become human and learnt to eat with royalty. It is because of me you have a friend in the great Lugal Gilgamesh. He loves you like a brother. When you die, he will lament for years and he will build a memorial for you. That way you will be immortal in the hearts of Sumerians," she retorted, with tears pouring down her face. She looked dishevelled and suddenly old. No one could see her beauty now. She had aged with worry and sorrow.

Soon, Enkidu relented, got out of his bed and hugged her for a long time. He could feel her sobbing away against his chest. He did not say anything. He just held her like that until she stopped sobbing. Once she stopped crying, he held her by her shoulders and said, "Now, go and get me the best carpenters in Uruk. I had promised my friend Gilgamesh the biggest and best doors for his fort and his palace. I will build the doors if that is the last thing I do."

Shamhat smiled at this and said,

"I will, my darling. You will build the best doors in the world for our Lugal and he will sing your praises forever."

"And get me a mask for my hideous face. I can't show this face to outsiders."

She searched for the best carpenters in all Uruk and sent words to other cities as well. Before long, a dozen of the best of them were standing in front of Enkidu. The royal messengers, by now, had found several physicians living in the Meluhhan village of Urpak in Lagash, who had claimed that they could cure him. Enkidu's room was getting busier every day with carpenters and physicians coming in and going out of it all the time. Enkidu would rather sit with the carpenters, showing them how he wanted the doors to be designed than stay confined in bed. Some of the stuff the Meluhhans had applied on him made him feel strong enough to go to the palace and the gates of the fort to personally supervise the building of the doors. He would go out wearing the mask Shamhat had made for him. He actually looked even more ferocious wearing the black mask and cap. Most people moved away when they saw him coming. That suited him well.

He was very happy with their progress. 'It won't be long before Uruk will have the best cedar wood doors in the entire known world,' he kept thinking to himself. That made him happy. He was beginning to realise that he was not going to live very long and he wanted Gilgamesh and the rest of the world to remember him when he was gone. When the doors were finished, he sent words to Gilgamesh through his woman, Shamhat. Gilgamesh was on his way to Enkidu's chamber when Shamhat met him,

"I have good news for Enkidu. I can't wait to see him." He was beaming from ear to ear. Shamhat said, "Enkidu has some news for you as well, Lugal. But I will let him tell you himself."

Both of them rushed into Enkidu's chamber together. Both Enkidu and Gilgamesh shouted on seeing each other.

"I have great news for you, my friend..."

"I have something to show you, my friend ..."

"My news is more important... I'll tell you first," Gilgamesh said.

"Alright then. You tell me what is so important," Enkidu replied with some annoyance.

"My informers have found a Meluhhan physician who is visiting Ur with his friends. He is said to be one of the best in Meluhha. I am sure he can cure you," Gilgamesh was gushing with enthusiasm.

"Not another physician. I don't want any more physicians. We need a Meluhhan sage. It is too late for physicians to cure me now," Enkidu replied.

"Anyway, come and look at what I have for you." And he literally dragged Gilgamesh all the way to the front of the palace. The main doors had been covered with huge linen sheets. "You can take the sheets off now," he barked orders at the carpenters standing by. The sheets were whisked off to show one of the most magnificent doors Gilgamesh had ever seen. The doors dwarfed everything nearby. The pale wood had been rubbed down to get a glass finish and deep grains of cedar wood shown through the sheer polish. The surface was so shiny that Gilgamesh could see his face on the doors. The panels were embellished with bronze sheets and large brass finials in the middle. As soon as the sheets were pulled off the doors, the fragrance of the wood wafted through the air and Gilgamesh struggled to breathe for a minute. On closer inspection, the sheets were inscribed with hymns for

Shamash and Marduk written in Sumerian. There were three large brass hinges on either side and there was a huge knocker in the shape of a lion's head in the middle of each door. It was the most impressive door that anyone had ever seen. Everyone around gasped in awe and admiration at the majesty of what they were seeing. Gilgamesh could hear mutterings from the crowd.

"This door is only fit for the gods."

"The gods will not be happy that Gilgamesh has this."

"Shamash himself will come and claim it back."

"The gods will send the demon bull to destroy the door or even Gilgamesh."

He swung around on his heels to face the crowd. Suddenly everyone fell silent. They could see fury in his eyes.

"My friend Enkidu has made this door for me and the people of Uruk. He has done it with the blessings of our god, Shamash. No one will touch this."

It was more a command than a word of advice. The crowd nodded their heads and did not dare say anything. Enkidu tugged at his elbow and said,

"This is not all. Come to the gate of Uruk and you will see what I have achieved."

Gilgamesh and his entire retinue were literally dragged through the streets by a half-dead Enkidu to the big gate of the fort. This time the workers had covered the entire gate with bamboo cladding. When they saw Enkidu with Gilgamesh coming into view, they started to pull off the cladding. By the time the retinue reached the gate, the massive cedar doors were there for everyone to see in their majesty. Enkidu had excelled himself in building this. These doors were so big that they could be seen from a long distance. They almost reached the top of the walls. The walls were at least fifty feet high. Each door was made up of several thick wood panels and covered with copper sheets held in with large bronze bolts. Even Gilgamesh gasped with awe this time. The doors were massive and it took twelve people to open and close them. They stood there admiring the handiwork of Enkidu and his carpenters for a long time.

"My friend, this must be the best present anyone has ever given me. No enemy can get through those doors, not even the Gutians," Gilgamesh exclaimed at last and turned and hugged Enkidu. "I will build your statue in the highest point of the city and the whole world will remember for you forever."

Shamhat led Enkidu back to the palace holding his hand and supporting him. The exertion of the entire day was too much for him and he was flagging. He was nearly dragging his feet when they reached the palace. Gilgamesh had to support him during the last few steps he took to go to his chamber.

"I will get this physician of Meluhha and he will cure you. I promise," Gilgamesh said and turned away quickly.

Vasishta's Ashram

We left Kadraveya's ashram just after sunrise and were in good time when we reached the southern slopes of the mountain in the late afternoon. The southern slopes were covered with thick bushes. Tall trees formed a thick canopy. As we reached the top of a rise, we saw smoke rising out of the canopy of trees at a distance.

"That must be the ashram," Shushun said. Our eyes followed the direction towards which his hands were pointing, to the path leading up to the ashram. There was a lot of activity on the path. "There appears to be a royal entourage coming out of the ashram."

We could see a royal chariot with the flag of Bharata waving proudly on it. It was being pulled by two white stallions. The gold canopy glittered in the evening sun and could be seen for miles. There was the usual platoon of bodyguards in front as well as behind.

"That is King Sudas's flag!" I exclaimed. "Sage Vasishta is the royal priest for King Sudas."

"I hope Sage Vasishta is not going to accompany him",

Shushun said, watching the entourage go down the path. "It would be a wasted trip for us, if he goes."

There did not appear to be anyone else behind the royal entourage.

"It does not look like it. I cannot see anyone else behind the royal body guards," Parthava said. "Sage Vasishta has been known to ride his black horse when he is with the king."

We stood there, fascinated by the scene, until they turned a corner further down the slope and disappeared. We were stopped in our tracks just as we were about to set off by a deep yet calm voice.

"Upaashantha."

All of us looked around to see where the voice was coming from. The unmistakable voice of Sage Vasishta continued, "Please take shelter in the forest there, we will come and meet you."

None of us could make out where the voice was coming from. I had heard of our sages' ability to make their voices travel long distances but had never experienced it before. It was rather unnerving to listen to a disembodied voice.

"Yes, we will, Sage Vasishta," I felt rather foolish speaking to no one. Shushun looked at me rather whimsically and said with a smile on his face,

"I am sure he heard you, Upaas. How did he do that?"

"I don't know. Anyway, we better wait here for him."

"Are you sure? It may be a trick of one those forest demons."

"No. That was the voice of Sage Vasishta, I am sure," I replied, beginning to doubt myself.

We could see a long line of horses with the unmistakable black steed of Vasishta in front coming out of the ashram in the distance where the royal retinue was a couple of minutes before. Two wagons were following a group of horse riders. The sun was on our heads by the time Sage Vasishta and his entourage reached us. Parthava was beginning to get restless and I could see even Shushun pacing up and down the clearing in the path.

The sage stopped near me and said,

"Thank you for waiting for us. We have to get off this mountain as quickly as possible. It is not safe anymore. Better get on your horses and follow us."

He turned and went down the road we had just come from, before I could ask him anything. The four of us followed him on our horses. We were riding slowly but we gradually picked up our paces and soon we were galloping away. We had lost the wagons within a short time of our setting off because they naturally could not keep up with us. As if planned in advance, they took the road leading them away from the main path and went downhill to the west. That would take them directly to Kadraveya's ashram. There was no time to think about the wagons now. We had been running at a decent pace for a couple of hours when I first heard it. It was a distant rumble, more like a thunder but continuous. It went on for a while, getting louder all the time. Sage Vasishta had increased the pace even further. The horses were frothing at the nostrils now. Suddenly the earth started heaving up and down and it became increasingly difficult to stay on the horse. I slowed down a little to let Lopa go in front of me. I wanted to be behind her if she fell. But I need not have worried. She was handling her horse like a professional and kept up the pace with everyone. Both Lopa and Shushun had Elamite steeds which were fast and could outrun any of the others.

The road was weaving up and down and sideways as well. Suddenly wide cracks began to appear in the road with rock and trees disappearing into them. Two apprentices from the ashram, who were ahead of us, went down a particularly large crack which appeared in front of them suddenly. It was too late for them to stop. Parthava, who was just behind them, stopped in time and looked down.

"It is deep. I cannot see either the bottom or the riders. They seem to have disappeared," he shouted over the loud rumble.

Sage Vasishta had stopped ahead and shouted back.

"Don't stop. We cannot help them. Keep moving. We don't have far to go now before we get off the mountain."

None of us needed any encouragement. We kept up the pace for the next few hours without stopping. The road started to lurch dangerously now and began to disappear in front of our eyes with a lot of brown dust and falling rocks from above on the left side. The trees and huge rocks to our right were being swallowed by the earth. It soon became apparent that there was nothing to our right and the mountain whose beauty had so overwhelmed us a few days back was collapsing into itself. The rumbles only grew louder and the air was dense with dust.

Suddenly a gaping chasm appeared in front of Lopa and

Shushun. Shushun shouted something in Elamite and leant forward on his horse and I could see Lopa do the same. My heart was in my mouth as the two of them did not stop and jumped across the chasm. Both the horses appeared to float in the air for a minute and landed safely on their hind legs. Expert horsemanship kept Lopa and Shushun still on the saddle. The chasm was getting wider by the second and any minute now we would be swallowed up. I leant forward on to my horse, Shankara's ears, stroked his neck and shouted,

"Come on Shankara, our lives are in your hands. You can do it. Come on. *Jai Jai Mahadev!*" I nudged his flanks with my knees and Shankara did not even hesitate. He picked up more speed and jumped from the edge of the chasm. I could not feel anything and I could not hear anything. Suddenly the world stopped moving and appeared to have gone silent. We appeared to hang in mid-air for a long time and I thought, this is it; I'll not make it.

But Shankara landed with his hind legs just scraping the edge. I could just see Parthava shouting from the corner of my eyes.

"*Jai Har Har Mahadev!*" he said and jumped his horse across.

There was no time to stop, the horses kept pace with flaring nostrils and frothing mouths. The sage did not stop until we reached a spot where the ground seemed still and the rumbling had become distant and low in intensity. We had stopped in a clearing on the banks of a small lake. The lake itself was amazingly quiet with not a ripple in sight. Sage Vasishta had got down from his horse and was at the edge of the lake. I jumped off Shankara and ran towards Lopa who was also running towards me. We both ran into each other's arms and held on tight for a long time. I kissed her and said, "I thought I had lost you there for a minute,"

Tears bubbled out of my eyes.

"I thought I had lost you as well," Lopa said. Tears were rolling down her cheeks and she had started to sob silently. I held her for a long time, trying to reassure her as much as myself that we were both alive.

Shushun and Parthava joined us with smiles as wide as could be. Both of them were quite shaken by the experience, but appeared to be excelling in it.

"This is what I call excitement. For a second, I was quite sure we wouldn't make it." Parthava was still out of breath.

"I am not sure I could take any more excitement in this country," said Shushun who was leading his horse and stroking his neck at the same time to comfort him. All the horses were beat and frothing at the mouth. "We better get them to the water before they collapse."

We walked our horses towards the water's edge; the sage was sitting on a rock, deep in thought as his horse drank from the lake. He looked up as we approached and said,

"Is everyone okay?"

All of us nodded our heads and said, "Yes, sir. We are fine."

"That was very close. I knew this was coming sooner or later. The Nagas had awakened evil forces by their occult practices and the last straw was the human sacrifice. This surely is Lord Indra's punishment on the mountain for harbouring such people. The mountain has lost its peak by the earthquake." He was looking over our heads as he spoke. All of us turned around to see dust settling on the mountain. The jagged peak we had seen a few days before was missing. There was an audible intake of breath.

"We were lucky to have escaped. I feel sorry for all those hermits and their wagons. We surely have lost Pindara," I said, suddenly realising the enormity of the destruction.

"You are quite wrong, Upaas. I sent them down the path to Kadraveya's ashram on purpose. That was the only way they could survive the disaster. The ashram itself is low in the valley and well-protected. Most of them have survived and your Pindara is safe as well. However, it will be months before they get out of there through all those debris." The sage replied to the relief of everyone. "Now, we better freshen ourselves and be on our way. Our ashram is completely destroyed and we will have to look for another suitable place for a new ashram."

Shushun, who was listening to this, coughed politely and cleared his throat before saying,

"I would like to thank the great sage for saving our lives today. I would like to invite the sage on behalf of my father, King Awan, to visit our country and see the great temple built for Lord Varuna in the city of Susa, before settling down again."

The sage looked at him, thought for a while and replied,

"Thank you, Prince Shushun. I would like that. I have heard a lot about the thousand-pillared temple of Varuna in your city. I wanted to see the temple myself. The best plan of action would be to proceed towards Saraswatha and arrange some ships for the journey."

"My ship is at your disposal, oh great sage. I had ordered a second ship to be built at Saraswatha as we had lost our cargo ship on our way to Meluhha," Shushun replied.

"I would not like to impose any further on you, Prince. I will send messages to Saraswatha to get some Harappan ships ready for us. Anyway, we will need more ships to take my apprentices along with me," the sage replied. He was smiling when he said that, but it was more of a command than a request.

"As you wish, Sage Vasishta. That is settled then. We will all go to my city, Susa," Shushun said, delighted. I looked at Lopa enquiringly. She smiled and squeezed my arm before saying,

"I would love to go to Susa and see Elam. But we have to go home to Harappa and ask for our parents' permission before we leave."

"I have some unfinished business as well in Harappa before going back home. Come on Parthava, let's get going."

And turning to the sage, Shushun continued, "We will take your permission to leave, great sage. We will meet in Saraswatha in a couple of weeks time."

And so the journey to Elam was realised long before I had anticipated. I was excited as well as apprehensive about the prospect. All of us were deep in our own thoughts as we galloped off towards Harappa.

We were home within three days and my father was quite surprised at the news of our impending journey to Elam with Sage Vasishta. They had heard of the massive earthquake on

Arbuda and were glad to see all of us safe.

"It would be a great opportunity for you to spend time with one of the greatest *maharishis* of our time. Make use of it and learn as much as you can during the sea voyage."

Both my mother and my sister Nivya were quite upset about my prolonged absence. The next few days were spent preparing for the journey and meeting Master Ashwin and Ma Ashwin. I had never spent more than a few weeks at a stretch over all the years that I had spent training under Master Ashwin. Ma Ashwin was like my mother. She had always treated me as her long lost son. She was full of tears and reluctant to let me go away for such a long time. Master had already given me permission to go to Elam before we set off for Mount Arbuda and he said,

"Elamite physicians have learnt a lot of new things from the Egyptian physicians of the Pharaoh. Learn as much as you can from them and bring back the latest technology."

Exactly two weeks after we left Sage Vasishta, we were at the docks of Saraswatha admiring the ships at the dock. We had sailed down the river Parushni and then the Sarasvathi to reach Saraswatha in a large Harappan boat. Two large ships were being loaded and prepared at the dock. Three more were in the harbour. Shushun's royal ship stood out with golden embellishments and their royal flag billowing at the end of the huge mast. It had huge sails, massive drawn-up oars and the god of thunder looking menacingly over the prow. The second ship was almost equally big, but less ostentatious. It was rather plain and here, the Harappan flag was at the mast with Varuna standing guard at the prow. That was obviously Sage Vasishta's ship. Shushun had acquired yet another ship to take his cargo of wood, gold, lapis lazuli and silver. He had replaced the ship, Ashiana, he had lost on the way to Saraswatha and so now had three ships at his disposal. It would be a convoy of five ships sailing to Susa. I was quite excited, and so was Lopa. We spent a couple of days with her parents in Saraswatha and her father had come down to the dock to wish us goodbye.

"Your friend has a beautiful ship, Upaas."

Sage Vasishta had walked up behind us with his full retinue. He looked resplendent with his hair tied up in a knot and a gold braid around the forehead keeping the hair in place, a round ash mark on the centre of the forehead, a brilliant white dhoti and a shawl thrown over his shoulder. He had piercing jet black eyes which missed very little. Just then we saw Shushun run down the drawbridge of his ship to the dock.

"Welcome to my boat. Felicitations, oh great Sage Vasishta. My captain tells me that we should be leaving soon to catch the tide," he said to the sage and turning to us, he continued, "My men have loaded your belongings in my ship. I want you to take my cabin at the top because there are two of you. It is more roomy and private. That should suit Lopa well."

"That is very kind of you, Shushun. I am really grateful. I am looking forward to seeing your city," Lopa said excitedly. She was visibly thrilled. Shushun took us into the ship and showed us the cabin on the top deck of the ship. He insisted that we use his cabin for the trip and would not hear any objections from either Lopa or myself. It was luxuriously decorated for the use of their royal prince. The walls of the cabin were decorated with pictures of Susa. The thousand-pillared temple of Varuna adorned one of the inner walls of his cabin. There were two windows covered witht tasseled silk curtains which were also encrusted with semi-precious stones. The floor was covered with a Meluhhan woolen rug. His bed was made from solid oak with brass finials in the corners, and bolted to the floor. There was the national crest of sun and eagle with wings fully spread on the wall which was in bold relief and painted in gold.

Luxury was written all over the cabin. His trusty bow and two quivers full of arrows hung on the wall next to the door. His two swords were in scabbard, slung ready for him on the wall at the head of his bed. There were two tall brass lamps on either side of the bed. There was a sideboard on the far side of the cabin fully stocked with fruits and nuts. I was relieved that Lopa could have privacy and comfort at least on the sea voyage.

It was not long before all the ships were loaded and we set sail. The two captains in charge of the ship were on the verge of hysteria because of missing the tide. We could see our captains relax once we were out of the harbour and on the open sea. It was an impressive sight to see five large ships forging ahead with billowing sails marching in a line. The oars were still drawn up as there was sufficient wind for the sails.

It was a bright and sunny day with only the hint of a chill breeze on the top deck. The journey for the first few days was uneventful apart from Parthava being violently sea-sick. Shushun's physician gave him a potion to reduce the sickness. He did not appear to be enjoying the voyage very much.

"When is this going to end? This is my worst nightmare,"

he kept repeating and looking quite green around the gills and sickly. Lopa was the only one who was sympathetic towards him. The rest of the passengers thought it was hilarious to watch him trundling along like a drunkard to the railings every few minutes for throwing up. He hardly touched food which was most unlike Parthava. The food served by the ship's cooks was excellent and had he felt better, he would have spent his entire time in the kitchen.

It was on the eighth day as we were settling down for the night when the lookout on the mast shouted a warning. The day had been quiet until dusk when dark clouds began to appear and it started to rain. The sea swelled and the ship was swaying more than usual. The wind howled and it was difficult to keep the lights burning as the wind kept blowing them out. Lightning and thunder added to the noise of the howling wind and very few of us heard the lookout's warning. For a minute, I thought I must have imagined it until I heard it a second time. This time I went out onto the deck to see what was happening. It was difficult to keep steady while the ship was being thrown around like a toy in a storm. I grabbed on to the rails and walked to the front to get a good look at the main deck to see what was happening. Just then a lightning struck the sea not too far from the ship and lit up the main deck. There were many people gathering at the prow of the ship looking where the lookout on the mast was pointing.

This must be what nightmares must be made of. I could not see any of the other ships. The sea appeared to be in turmoil with huge waves lashing onto the deck and drenching the people on the main deck. The first thing I saw was a long and large spout of fire being blown out against the wind. There was another streak of lightning which lit up the sea around us. A huge, violet creature was breathing fire on one of our ships. Strangely enough, the ship itself was not on fire despite having been literally drowned in a huge flash of fire. It looked like a large sea serpent with a long, meandering tail going as far back as the eye could see. There were sharp spikes on the back of the creature. It was frightening just to look at it from a distance.

"What is that, Upaas?" Lopa had to shout to be audible over the din.

"I have no idea. I have never seen anything like that before in my life," I replied. "Let us go down to the main deck and see what is going on. Maybe Shushun knows what it is."

We hung onto the rails for dear life when we were trying to go down the stairs. Shushun and Parthava were already there. Parthava looked worse than ever.

"This looks like the creature that attacked us on our way to Saraswatha and burnt our cargo ship," Shushun said as we reached him with difficulty. "We lost our sister ship and all of its crew. None of our arrows can harm that creature. I was told that it was some sort of magic."

The stories I had heard from sailors in the past about sea demons and monsters that could destroy a whole ship in a matter of minutes and eat sailors suddenly occurred to me. I thought the only person who would be of any help was Vasishta. But I could not even see his ship in the storm. I wondered if my telepathic powers were advanced enough to be tested in this danger. I had been warned by my master that to try it before one is ready could be dangerous. It cannot be more dangerous than what we were facing now, I decided. But that was the only way. I turned to Shushun and said,

"I am going back into the cabin. I'll see if I can contact the sage through telepathy. Maybe he will be able to help us."

"Are you sure, Upaas? I thought you said you were not ready," Lopa said with concern in her voice.

"Let me try reaching his ship in one of your small boats. I do not want to put Upaas in any danger," Parthava said bravely. I laughed.

"You can barely stand up. Let alone go in a boat to the sage's ship which we cannot even see. No. I'll be fine. This is the best opportunity to test my powers," I said and turned and set off before anyone else could object.

"I am coming with you," Lopa said and she grabbed my arms as we both headed back to the tricky trip up the stairs back into our cabin. Once in the cabin, I shut the door behind me and sat down on the carpet. I closed my eyes and concentrated hard. I could hear the sage's voice before too long.

"How is everyone on your ship, Upaas?"

"We are fine here. We can see a sea monster attacking one of our ships. We cannot make out what the creature is or which ship it is attacking. Shushun tells me that they were attacked by a similar demon on their way to Saraswatha," I replied, still with my eyes closed. I could not see him in spite of trying very hard.

"It is the act of Panis or Matsyans. This magical creature belongs to the underworld. Some occult practices must have unleashed it. I know how to deal with it. It is attacking the cargo ship in front of us. Let me take care of it. Please tell the soldiers not to use their weapons on the creature. The more weapons you use the more powerful it gets."

"I will, great sage. I will pass the message on."

"I will try to get hold of sailors in the other ships to let them know not to fight it," he said and was gone in a moment.

I opened my eyes to see Lopa staring at me intently. She must have been worried. I smiled at her and said,

"I have spoken to Sage Vasishta. He tells me it is a demon created by either the Panis or the Matsyans and he will take care of it. It is important no one fights it because that is how it gains in size and strength. The more you fight it, the bigger it gets."

I could see Lopa staring at me wide-eyed. "Come on. Let us go and tell the others."

Shushun nodded his head and said,

"Now I know why we could not do anything to beat that creature before. None of our weapons or arrows made any difference to the monster. It burnt down our ship in front of our eyes. Why do they do that, Upaas?"

"I am sorry. I have no idea why. We will have to ask the sage when we dock in Dilmun next," I replied. "All we can do now is wait and watch."

As we watched, we could not really see very much apart from brief glimpses during lightning strikes, and there were quite a few of them. The creature seemed to grow in size after every lightning strike. Obviously the soldiers and sailors on the ship that was being attacked were resisting with their futile arrows and the demon was growing in size every time it was hit by an arrow. That meant that the sage had not been successful in reaching them. I could hear people around us shouting at the ship,

"Stop firing. You are making it worse."

They might as well have been shouting at the wind. We could barely hear them and we were standing only a little distance away. There was no way the people on that ship could have heard us over the storms and lightning. Suddenly a bolt of fire came from nowhere and hit the creature and the creature disappeared in a huge ball of smoke. It was as if someone had turned the tap off. The rain, storms, the howling wind and the lightning stopped. There was a deathly silence and the sea was calm as a pond. There was a full moon and millions of stars above brightened the scene. The scene on the ship was one of chaos. The ship that had been attacked was burning brightly and listing badly to one side. We could see men swimming away from the ship in a desperate bid to save themselves from being sucked down by a sinking ship. Shushun immediately ordered the dispatch of two small boats on the ship to help them and the captain was already turning the ship around towards the swimmers. We could see the other three ships doing the same. The ship sank to the bottom within minutes, still burning furiously. There were many survivors and we wouldn't know exactly how many people had drowned till we docked in Dilmun after a few days.

Thus it was a few days later that we reached the port city of Dilmun. Tired and overcrowded ships were emptied onto a welcome dry land. It was extremely hot when we landed at Dilmun. The dock was not as impressive as the one at Saraswatha.

I could not understand the language spoken by most of the people. I was pleasantly surprised, however, to find a number of Aryans with whom I could converse quite well. Lopa, on the other hand, could speak their language quite fluently. As could Shushun. Both Parthava and I were left looking lost when the two of them were conversing with the locals in what I presumed to be the Sumerian language.

It was time to take stock of the situation and count our losses. We had been very lucky. Only a dozen sailors were missing. It was one of Shushun's new cargo ships that had sunk taking a load of timber with it. He did not appear to mind the loss of his cargo as much as he did the loss of his men. Sage Vasishta had not been able to communicate with anyone on that ship. Both Sage Vasishta and Shushun had questioned the survivors in detail while consoling them at the same time.

"The creature was created by Matsyans and it usually comes with a protective shield. The shield is a powerful barrier for those trying to communicate through telepathy. Unfortunately, the soldiers on the ship tried to defend themselves against this creature and used arrows to hurt it. The arrows enraged the creature and made it bigger and more powerful. It is unfortunate that we lost so many lives and the ship," the sage said to Shushun.

"I am not bothered about the ship, oh great sage. You have managed to save so many of my people. I will be eternally grateful for that," Shushun had replied with genuine admiration in his voice.

Shushun had arranged for us to stay in an inn not too far from the harbour. It would take a couple of days to get the ships repaired and restocked before moving on to Susa. There was not much to do or see in Dilmun. It was only sand and sand everywhere, the monotony broken only by a few scraggy palm trees. The harbour was marshy land with scattered one-storey sundried brick buildings forming what was the main part of the town of Dilmun. The roads and sanitation system were similar to that of Harappa. I later came to know that most of the engineers there were from Bharata. The houses were flat-topped with walkways built on the tops of roofs for women to walk around safely. Most of the people in the town worked in the local copper mines in the interior of the island. The town was surrounded by a massive brick wall with a gate leading out into a desert. I visited one of the copper mines outside the town, with Lopa and Parthava. Shushun was too busy with his business. He was trying to sell the timber and spices he had brought from Harappa and Sindhu. Lopa was a brilliant interpreter. I knew we had brought some copper from Dilmun into Bharata. By the time the ships were ready to sail again, I had managed to pick up a few Sumerian words. I was still struggling with the Elamite language because Shushun refused to speak his language in my presence; "It is rude to speak in a language the guest does not understand."

Sage Vasishta blessed the four remaining ships and tied an amulet on the mast of each of the ships.

"This should, hopefully, keep the ships from being attacked by the demonic creatures," he said after reciting a hymn from the Rigveda.

"Thank you, great sage. We should reach the mouth of River Gihon in about a week. The river will take us to Susa and we can sail right up to the temple of Varuna."

Shushun was all misty-eyed. He was looking forlorn and utterly homesick.

It was over a year since he had left home. They had had their ships refitted and restocked with fresh fruit, vegetable, meat as well as some beer and wine. It was bright and sunny and extremely hot when we left the harbour of Dilmun. The temperatures dropped at night and it became very cold. There was a little stove in the corner of our cabin which kept us warm all the time. We stayed close to the sea coast as we sailed westward towards the Gihon delta. On the sixth day, Shushun was so excited that he had difficulty keeping his face straight. He broke into smiles everytime he spoke. That night it was quite late by the time we went to bed. The four of us stood on the main deck looking at the starlit sky, watching the coastline go by and talking about the extraordinary events of the previous few months in Bharata.

As we were going back to our cabin, Lopa said,

"It is getting a bit windy and cold again."

I looked up and saw that thick, black clouds had appeared, blocking all light and it was pitch black all of a sudden. I was glad to get inside the cabin. It was probably just before daylight that I was rudely woken up by being thrown against the bulkhead. I had nearly knocked myself out. The stove had gone out sometime ago. The ship was being thrown about like a toy. Lopa also woke up with a start and immediately clung to the bedpost which was fixed to the floor.

"What is happening? Don't tell me we are being attacked by another demon?" Lopa asked, wide-eyed.

"I will go and have a look outside. You better stay here," I said and struggled out of the door. I could not see anything outside. It was still pitch black and the ship was swaying uncontrollably. The ship was on the top of a huge wave when I was going downstairs. When I reached the deck, the ship went down to the bottom of the trough at some speed. Anything that was not fixed to the floor was thrown out into the sea. The waves were lashing down on the main deck forcefully. Shushun and Parthava were already there along with the captain. The sails had been rolled in the night before; otherwise the ship would have been broken into bits by now.

"Master Shushun, we don't have much control on the ship, sir. The rudder broke a while ago and we are at the mercy of the sea."

It was eerie. There was no rainstorm, no thunder, no lightning. Only howling wind and wild, massive waves. Waves were heaving up, and their white foam, caught by the wind, was being whipped against the ship. The ship was being tossed about in darkness. We could not see any sign of the other three ships. All the lights had gone out just as in our ship. Suddenly there was a loud creaking noise and as we watched, the huge central mast came down, broken in half. Luckily it swayed wildly for a minute, slowly leaned over to one side and disappeared into the frothing sea.

"That is it. We are now completely at the mercy of the sea. There is no way of navigating this ship up the river Gihon without a rudder and a sail," the captain said. Shushun looked at the soldiers who had all gathered around us and said,

"I think all of you should go back inside and stay there. That is the safest place for everyone in this storm. I have been in these storms. They are quite common in these parts. They don't last very long," and turning to Parthava, he said, "That goes for you too, I think."

As everyone started to move back inside, he pulled me aside and said, "I think you should contact Sage Vasishta and see how they are and if he can help. I think we are in trouble. The ship might break if it hits any of the rocks and there is nothing we can do to stop it."

"I will try to contact the sage. He is the only one who can help us," I replied and climbed back up the stairs into my cabin. Lopa was sitting bolt upright on the bed still holding onto the bedpost and asked as soon as I got in,

"What is happening? What was that sound I just heard?"

I explained what had happened and sat down on the floor against the bulkhead closing my eyes to try and contact Sage Vasishta. No good. No matter how hard I tried, nothing happened. I recited some of the hymns taught by Sage Shunahotra as well as Sage Vishwamitra. It didn't help. There was utter silence in the ether. It was difficult to concentrate while trying to keep myself still in the heavily swaying ship. I could not control my mind.

After a couple of hours, I gave up and opened my eyes to see Lopa looking at me with a worried look on her face. By now the heaving of the ship had increased palpably and the noise was approaching a crescendo. I had to shout to be heard. I was now getting really worried. I got back into bed and held Lopa tightly. I could feel her crying softly.

"Are we going to make it, Upaas?"

"Yes. We will. Shushun won't let anything happen to us. Sage Vasishta must be trying to rescue us as we speak. We just have to hold tight and wait."

I was lying through my teeth. I had no idea where Sage Vasishta was or whether he was alive. I had no idea of the state of our ship or if Shushun's captain could sail through this storm safely. We held on to each other and prayed. It was becoming increasingly difficult to keep still as the ship was being tossed around violently now. We had to secure ourselves somehow. I got out of the bed and got the blankets and tied both of us together to the bedstead. The ship was swaying so wildly that often we were nearly vertical and I had to use all my strength to keep us on the bed. There were creaking noises and loud thuds every now and then. I knew the ship was breaking up at the seams.

Suddenly the ship was lifted higher than ever and came down with a loud crash. It must have hit a rock. The entire cabin fell apart and the bedstead broke loose and we were floating on a wildly frothing sea in the open air. We were drenched to the skin by the waves lashing on to us. If we had not been tied to the bedstead we would have been in the water. I did not think we were strong enough to swim against the force of the waves. I noticed that the sun was coming up and we were being pushed inexorably away from the coast. That was not a good sign. We had, somehow, to go towards the coast. I looked desperately around to see if I could do something to change the direction of our movement. There were plenty of wooden planks floating around. If I could only get hold of one of them and use it as an oar, I might just be able to veer us back towards the coast. I turned to Lopa and said,

"I am going to try and get one of those wooden planks to see if I can control where we are going." And before she could answer, I loosened the blanket, rolled off into the sea and swam across to the nearest floating plank. It was easier said than done. The current was strong and it took all my strength to catch hold of one of them and swim back to bed.

"There you are. We can break this into two and we will have perfectly adequate oars," I said, beaming at Lopa. I stuck one end of the plank at the end of the bed and heaved it hard to break it into two long pieces. "Now we have two oars and we should be able to row towards the shore in no time."

I gave one piece to Lopa and started to row on one side of the bed. It was hard work. We kept looking for anyone else who had survived and it was almost impossible to make out anything in that heaving frothy sea. I don't know how long we had been rowing, but the shore remained elusive. I could see Lopa was tired and she was desperately trying to keep her eyes open. We had better rest a while and start rowing again, I thought.

"Lopa, I think we should rest a bit. You come and lie down here and I'll keep a lookout for a while."

Lopa smiled and put her oar down on the bed and slid over to me to lie down on my lap. She was fast asleep within minutes. The sea was beginning to quieten down significantly. It was over twenty four hours since we had had anything to eat or drink. We had been rowing for several hours. My eyes were beginning to close, however hard I tried to keep awake. The sun was setting rapidly and it was going to get chillier.

We better get going again and try to reach the shore before nightfall. I tried to wake Lopa but to no avail. She would not move. I was getting desperate and tried to sprinkle some cold water on to her face. I bent down over the side to get some sea water from the sea. Just then a small wave lifted the bed up and I hit my head against the post and everything went blank.

The Village of Urpak

I thought I could hear voices but could not see anything. They sounded distant at first and then they got closer. Soon I was able to make out what they were saying. I slowly opened my eyes wider and could see a bright blue sky with large herons flying high above me.

"Hey! There are two more here and they are alive. Come quickly!"

They were speaking Sanskrit! I shook my head in disbelief. It was impossible! The previous night seemed vague and distant. I was not even sure of what had happened the night before. Surely we had not drifted back to Bharata?

We could not have drifted hundreds of miles back to Bharata in the storm last night. I suddenly remembered. Lopa, where was my dear Lopa? I looked around desperately. There was a large piece of wood lying on top of me blocking my view. I could not move because of the weight of the wood and I tried to push it out without any success.

"Please stay still. We will move that wood off you. You are safe now."

Two people were trying to lift the piece of wood off me. I could see Lopa stirring just on the other side to my great relief. They tried to help me up. But I shrugged them off and crawled over to where Lopa was lying. She was just opening her eyes and looked at me bleary-eyed. I looked up and down to see if she was hurt in any way. I called out,

"Please lie still, Lopa. Before you move, let me check and make sure you are not hurt."

Lopa fully opened her eyes and smiled at me.

"I am so happy to see you, Upaas. I am fine. You look bruised and battered. How are you?"

"I am fine. Please stay still. Let me look at you."

I did a quick survey to make sure she had not broken any bones and helped her sit up and held her in my arms, kissed her on her lips, cheeks and eyes again and again. I was so glad and relieved to see she was safe. To think I had come close to losing her twice in the last few weeks made me shudder.

"Are you cold, my darling Upaas? You are shivering," Lopa said, holding me tightly as if to spread some of the warmth of her body to me.

"No. I am fine now. That was another close shave. I don't want to lose you."

"This will keep you warm."

One of the men covered the two of us with a blanket.

"You are very kind. Thank you very much for your help," I replied.

"Welcome to Lagash. We have some of your friends as well on this beach."

"We were on our way from Dilmun to Susa when the storm blew us off course back to …"

I stopped suddenly and looked at him and said, "What did you say? Did you say Lagash? We are not back in Bharata?" Lopa was also quite confused. We had assumed that we were back in Bharata because our rescuers were speaking Sanskrit.

"No, you are not in Bharata I am afraid. You are in Lagash," the man replied.

"Our village, Urpak, is just around the corner from here."

"How come you are speaking such good Sanskrit if you are a Sumerian?" I asked incredulously. He smiled and replied,

"I am not a Sumerian. I am Dhivara, a fisherman of Lagash. I am originally from Bharata, like most of the residents of my village. I moved here several years ago and made Lagash my home. You will find many people from Bharata in our village."

"What has happened to our friends? Have you seen anyone else?" I asked anxiously.

"Yes, we have found several people stranded on the beach and they have been taken care of. You will find your friends when we reach the village."

I was not going to ask him about Shushun because I didn't know if Lagash was a friendly neighbour of Sumer. The enmity between Sumerians and Elamites was long-standing with skirmishes occurring all the time. The Elamites had only regained their independence from the Sumerians. Shushun's father, King Awan, had fought a long-drawn battle against them. It was a lucky thing that Shushun could speak flawless Sanskrit and pass as a Meluhhan. A cart with four wheels pulled by a horse came alongside the beach. Dhivara turned to me and said,

"Here comes our transport. I am sure you will feel much better once you have had some food and water in the village."

I had not seen such a cart before. It was made of cedar wood and had solid discwheels and a flat roof made of reeds. I could see the land was pretty flat with a few, low rolling hills and covered in stunted bushes with a few trees scattered here and there. I was impressed with the quality of the road. The ride was not as jarring as I had thought it would be. The village came into view in the distance as the cart climbed over a low rise in the road. It was not big by any standards. The houses were built with sun-dried pale yellow bricks with flat roofs made of mainly reeds. Dhivara took us to a large building at the end of a square in the middle of the village. It appeared to be a large hall with brick-built columns and the only building with a wooden roof. There was also a brick staircase from the central hall, which led to the first floor. The first floor had several rooms. There were a couple of other horse-drawn carriages in the square.

"The chief of our village, Ambhasika, will be very pleased to meet you. He is always talking about his homeland and meeting someone from Bharata will make his day," Dhivara said with a smile. "Come, let us go in and meet your friends and Ambhasika."

There was a loud "Upaas! Lopa! You are alive!" as soon as we walked through the front door. It was Parthava who came running across the hall and hugged me so tightly that I could hardly breathe. "I am so happy to see you and Lopa alive. We thought you would not make it."

He looked rather odd with a short tunic coming to just below the knees and a shawl thrown over his shoulders. The leather sandals made a clicking noise as he ran across the hard-beaten floor.

"We are glad to see you alive too. I wonder how many of us made it," I replied, wriggling out of his bear hug. By then, Shushun had walked across and hugged and kissed Lopa on the cheeks.

"I am really pleased to see the two of you. We had given you up for good. We searched the beach the whole morning till we were picked up by the villagers."

Shushun looked genuinely pleased to see us. I also noticed that he was still speaking a sort of unaccented Sanskrit. "It does not look like many of us made it. The captain and several of the soldiers are still missing. Have you had any luck contacting Sage Vasishta?"

I had completely forgotten the sage in all this excitement. Before I could answer, a portly gentleman waddled across to where we were standing.

"*Namaste* and welcome to Urpak, the only Meluhhan village in the whole of Sumeria." He had a sort of sing-song voice, almost feminine. He was clean-shaven without a hint of hair anywhere on his face or head. His short tunic accentuated his pot belly, which wobbled as he walked across the floor. He was very light footed for his size. He appeared out of breath just crossing the floor of the hall. "I am Ambhasika, leader of this village. I am so happy to see my fellow countrymen. Please feel at home and ask for anything you want. It would be our privilege to serve you."

"*Namaste*, Ambhasika. Thank you for your hospitality. We are deeply grateful for your help," I replied.

"Come, come. I'll take you to your rooms. There is hot water for you to wash and some fresh clothes for you and your dear lady."

He led us up the stairs to a small room which was quite clean and had a reed mattress for a bed. "The washroom is just on the other side of the small door at the end."

It was a relief to get out of the soggy and, by now, quite malodorous clothes and get rid of the salty grime on us. Lopa emerged from the washroom, looking stunning and fresh in a long, white tunic going all the way down to her ankles, tucked in at the waist with a cotton belt bringing out her lovely figure. The split sleeves showed off her beautifully-formed shoulders and her long, black hair dropping on her bare shoulders with water droplets clinging on to stray strands of her hair glistened in the sunlight streaming through the window. My heart beat faster at the sight of her. As we joined the rest of the crowd, I was aware of the admiring glances every male in the hall directed at her.

"We have good news, Upaas. Our sister ship, Ashiana, has docked in at the port of Ur. It is badly damaged, but thankfully no lives have been lost. There is still no news of Sage Vasishta's ship. I have a bad feeling about it," Shushun said with genuine concern in his voice. At least the ship that Shushun had acquired in Saraswatha was safe with its cargo of cedar wood and cotton.

"It is good to hear Ashiana is safe. Let me try to contact Sage Vasishta again and see what happens," I said and went back into the room to concentrate on my telepathic skills in private. I sat down cross-legged on the floor and recited the hymns taught by Sage Shunahotra and hoped for the best.

"We are safe, Upaas. I have been following the progress of your *prana* and know you were safe. We are heading up the River Karun to Susa and we should be there in a few hours. You join us in Susa when you can."

The sage's voice was as clear as if he were in the same room. It startled me at first, but his soothing voice had a reassuring effect.

"I am extremely glad that you are safe, oh great sage. We are in Lagash in Sumeria. We might as well continue our journey into the country and seek out Sage Utnapishtim."

"You do that, but be aware of your surroundings at all times. *Dheergayushman Bhava*. May your quest be successful."

I was not sure what he meant by that. I felt a bit uneasy at first, but soon relaxed when I saw all the eyes fixed on my face once I walked out of the room. I could see them visibly lighten up, seeing my smiling face.

"Sage Vasishta is safe and sound. He is almost near Susa, on the river Karun."

"That is a huge relief for me, Upaas. I was having premonitions about him. It would have weighed very heavily on my conscience if something had happened to him," Shushun said with a deep sigh. Everything was falling into place and getting back to some normalcy. Now we had to decide what we had to do next. But, those last words of the sage still worried me. Ambhasika walked in just as we were congratulating ourselves on the good news.

"Gentlemen, I would like to invite all of you to be our guests tonight in a feast, at the square in front of this building. It has been a long time since we saw anyone from our homeland. It is something that calls for celebration," he said, grinning from ear to ear.

The feast turned out to be just that. The villagers pulled out all stops and went out of their way to make us feel special. There was a huge, roaring fire in the middle of the square and we were all sitting around it. The smell of freshly baked bread mixed with the aroma of the spices of roasted meat was heady. The villagers took turns roasting the lamb on the fire. Freshly-brewed barley beer was flowing freely and Shushun's soldiers appeared to enjoy it immensely. They had a strange way of serving beer. They served it in a large pot with straws for the drinkers. Groups of four or six people had to sit around the pot and sip from the reed straws, out of the wide-mouthed pot.

"Gentlemen, I have something special for you, all the way from Nineveh," Ambhasika said. One of his sons was carrying a large cask and several goblets. Ambhasika gave each of us a silver goblet and his son poured out dark red wine for us.

"Thank you, Ambhasika. I have heard a lot about the famous wines of Nineveh before, but I have never tasted them," Shushun said, accepting the wine. He turned to me, saying, "Wines from Nineveh are said to be the best and made for the gods themselves. We are lucky that Ambhasika has stock."

I, too, thanked him and took a sip. It was sweet and full of the aroma of flowers. "It is very nice, thank you," I said, raising my goblet to Ambhasika.

"You are welcome, gentlemen. I am only too glad to be of service. I am a scribe by profession and this wine was my fees from a nobleman from Uruk. I hope the wine and food will help you recover from your recent trauma," he replied.

It sure did. The wine was heady and the food that followed was delicious. They had modified some traditional recipes from Bharata. Then there were Sumerian dishes, with added spices from Bharata. The evening was going splendidly when the music started. One of the men had started to sing; softly at first and then, he sang louder when the others encouraged him. He was good, but I could not understand the lyrics. It sounded like the language of the Dasyus from the south of Bharata. I turned to Shushun who was swaying his head in tune with the music and asked, "What is he singing about?"

"I hope the hosts don't realise he is singing in Elamite, otherwise we'll all be in trouble. He is singing about his girl he had left in his village a long time ago," Shushun replied, surveying the men and women of the village to see if there was any reaction. There was none. They appeared to be busy, going around serving all of us with more food and wine. I was just nursing a drink slowly in my goblet. Lopa came up to me, put her arms around me and said, staring into my eyes,

"What is the matter, Upaas, you are not drinking?" I told her about what Sage Vasishta had said earlier.

"That is a bit worrying. But, he might have been giving you friendly advice like elders tend to do. I think you are worrying too much. Try and enjoy yourself."

Soon one of the villagers brought out their musical

instruments. A flute joined in along with a lyre and drums. The music was vibrant but soothing. Some of the villagers got up and started to dance around the fire. All of us were dragged in to dance, protesting as we were, by the hosts. Parthava appeared to relish the beer and the dance. It was several hours before the feast ended with all of us content and tired. It made us forget the trauma of the previous few days.

"We will have to start planning our next move. It won't be long before someone realises that not all of us are Meluhhans. I am still not sure how the Sumerians will react to Elamites. My father had sent an emissary to Uruk to meet Emperor Gilgamesh with an offer of friendship. I still don't know the outcome of that," Shushun said, as we walked around the village the next day.

"I am expecting the captain of the ship which landed in Ur to reach us by tomorrow. I will have to find out where we stand with Sumerians before we make our next move. I have sent a messenger to my father last night to find out."

"Why don't we speak to Ambhasika and find out? He appears to be quite reasonable and friendly with us," I replied.

"That is a thought. I had not considered that," Shushun said contemplatively.

"I am sure he is harmless," Lopa said, as an afterthought. "To be safe, nevertheless, Upaas can broach the subject and see his reaction before going any further. Come on, let's go and look for him. I want to see his work."

As usual, she was pragmatic and Shushun's scheme of thought was quite reasonable. Lopa, being a scribe's daughter herself, was curious about Ambhasika's work. It was not difficult to find his house, where he worked. He was very pleased to see us in his house.

"Welcome to my humble abode, friends. It is such an honour to see my countrymen in my house."

As we had expected, the greeting was rather effusive and expansive. He hugged each one of us and ushered us in. It was one of the larger houses of the village, with a central courtyard leading out to different rooms and a staircase going up to the next storey. He took us to a large hall which had several reed mats to sit on. The walls were bare, with just one wooden cupboard and one square window opening out into the street.

"Please take a seat. To what do I owe this honour, my friends?"

"We have to ask you a question. Are Sumerians here friendly with Elamites?" I asked. Ambhasika was quiet for a minute, and then he smiled before answering.

"I know exactly why you are asking this question, my friend. You have nothing to fear here. Shushun and all his Elamite friends are welcome in our village. However, most of the Sumerians are still wary of the Elamite royalty," he said, staring at Shushun.

"Thank you for your honesty, Ambhasika. How did you know who I was?" Shushun asked. Ambhasika sighed deeply, went to the cupboard and fished something out. Giving it to Shushun, he replied,

"I found your royal seal on the beach, not very far from where you were found. You speak Sanskrit without any accent. Your soldiers and sailors are not that good. The entire village knows who you are. There were some people in the village who wanted to hand all of you over to the Sumerian army, but good judgement prevailed in the end."

"Thank you, again, for your help. We are indebted to the entire village. I am waiting for my father to send me word about the peace emissary he had sent to the court of Emperor Gilgamesh," Shushun replied.

"Meanwhile, I wonder if we can ask you to arrange an audience with the king of Lagash, Ur-nanshe. I will extend the olive branch to him, from my father, King Awan."

"I have done a lot of work for King Ur-nanshe. I am sure I can arrange that. It will take a few days to arrange that, however.In the meantime I want you to enjoy our hospitality."

Lopa, who was very quiet throughout the time, whispered into my ear as we came out again into the bright sun. "For a scribe, there were hardly any writing material in the house."

I suddenly felt uneasy again. That feeling of being threatened came back. "Are you sure there were no writing materials?" I asked.

"For someone who claims to do a lot of writing for the king of Lagash, there were no writing materials anywhere. I had a peek into his cupboard when he opened it for Shushun's seal and there was nothing apart from more seals."

"What are you two love birds whispering about?" Shushun joined in.

"I was just saying that for a scribe who professes to be busy, there is hardly any writing material anywhere in his house," Lopa answered.

"Come to think of it, I did not notice any either. It is rather curious, I must admit," Shushun said. "Unless he does his writing in a school, as in the university town of Nippur."

"I think we are being paranoid," Parthava said, with an uneasy laugh. We spent the rest of the day wandering around the village and its surroundings. It turned out to be a rather uninteresting village with just over a hundred houses, mainly inhabited by Meluhhans. They appeared to be a friendly lot. We were often stopped and asked to speak of Bharata. The soil there was dry, sandy and unsuitable for most crops. There were hardly any trees anywhere in the village, apart from a smattering of date palms. Most of the people either worked for the king of Lagash or the temple of Marduk in Lagash. Some of them, living near the edge of the village, were fishermen. As we ventured out on the road leading away from the village, we came across a lonely house in the middle of a copse of date palm trees. We saw a woman drawing water from a small well. By the dress she was wearing, Shushun reckoned she might have been either Sumerian or one of the Zubi mountain-dwellers. She pulled up the big brass pot out of the well and turned around to walk away towards her house when she saw us. She stopped and waved at us. She turned out to be a friendly Akkadian woman who could speak Sanskrit quite well, although heavily accented.

"You must be the Meluhhan sailors saved by the villagers. It is really hot outside. Why don't you come in and have a drink with us?"

"*Namaste*. Thank you, madam. That is most kind," I said with folded hands and Lopa and Shushun repeated the same.

"I am Nisaba, from the country of Aratta in the Zubi mountain," she replied. "Please come inside and I am sure my husband will be most pleased to meet you."

Her husband turned out to be a most interesting character. He was a young, wiry man, wearing a short tunic and leather sandals. Like most Sumerians, he was clean-shaven with a long lock of hair falling over his shoulders. He was bending over, working on some palm leaves, and did not notice us coming in.

"Shu, we have guests. They are the Meluhhan sailors the villagers saved a few days ago."

He immediately dropped the wet palm leaves and stood up, wiping his wet hands on his tunic.

"Wow! I did not expect to see you here. I am Shu-ilishu, a transcriber for the king of Lagash. Welcome to my house. Please have a seat," he pushed the pile of palm leaves he was working with to one side to make some space for us to sit.

"I had run out of palm leaves to write on, and did not notice you coming in."

"That is understandable, Shu-ilishu. We don't really want to disturb your work," I replied.

"Please stay and have a cool drink to quench your thirst. The palm leaves can wait for a while. We don't often have visitors in our house," He said, his eyes darting between his wife and us. That is when I noticed that he had jet black eyes with a mischievous twinkle in it. He can be trusted, I thought. Nisaba brought us each a mud goblet filled with a cool sweet drink. "It is made from fresh dates grown in our little farm. Very healthy and nourishing."

"Thank you for your hospitality," Lopa replied. "I notice you are using honey to stabilise your palm leaves."

Shu's eyes brightened up. "You know about the palm leaves. You must be a scribe. It is a privilege to meet a scribe from Meluhha."

Lopa smiled and said, "I am not, but my father is a scribe. I have done a little bit of writing myself, but not much."

He showed some of his work for the king. He could translate several languages including Gutian, Avestan, and Sanskrit as well as Egyptian languages into Sumerian. It turned out he was not very welcome in the city of Lagash as he had married the Akkadian Nisaba from the mountain country of Arratta. The Meluhhans of the village accepted them with some reservations and they lived outside the village. It was getting dark when we left Shu-ilishu's house. His parting shot stuck with all of us as we walked quietly back to the village. As he was waving good bye, he had said, "Beware of anyone who is overly friendly with you."

That was the second warning in two days, I thought. "There is something not right here. We better be careful," I said, while wishing Shushun and Parthava a restful night.

It was a restless night spent tossing and turning in the bed. It was a long time before I finally fell asleep. I dreamt of Harappa. My sister, Nivya, was chiding me for staying out late again and my mother was asking me finish the evening prayers quickly to join father for supper. She had made my favourite sweet dish with barley and honey. I heard someone pull up their horse outside the door just as I tucked into my sleep. It neighed loudly.

I was suddenly awake. Was that a dream? Or was there really some one outside? I knew there were no horses in the village. I was not sure if I had heard a horse or if it was part of my dream. I listened quietly for a while and did not hear anything. Just as I was dropping off to sleep, I heard it again. This time it was unmistakable. It was definitely a horse in front of the house we were sleeping in. I jumped off the bed quietly and went to the little square window on the wall.

I could count ten horse riders in the dim moonlight. They were dressed like soldiers, in short tunics and leather vests. They had long, flowing hair which glinted like gold in the starry light. They appeared to be armed to the teeth. I could make out the long bows as well as the short spears in their hands. They did not seem to be doing anything. They were just sitting on their horses and appeared to be waiting for something or someone.

I turned around and was startled to see Lopa standing behind me, trying to get a good look at them with me.

"What does it mean, Upaas?" she whispered.

"I don't know. Whatever it is, it does not look good. I think I should wake Parthava and Shushun."

Before I could finish the sentence, we heard a gentle tap on the door. I looked desperately around the room for some kind of a weapon or an escape route. There was nothing, not even a stick to defend ourselves with and there was only one door. The window opened to a twenty-foot jump in front of the group of soldiers.

"Upaas. It is me, Parthava. Open the door," I was very glad to hear his whisper. Both Parthava and Shushun rushed inside as I opened the door, nearly knocking me over.

"We are in trouble. It looks like the building is surrounded and they don't look friendly to me," Parthava whispered. "We don't have any weapons either."

"If only we could reach our soldiers, we might stand a chance. They are billeted at the other end of the village," Shushun said. "We have to come up with a plan to get out of this somehow."

There were loud footsteps coming up the stairs to the room and there were voices in a language I could not understand. I looked questioningly at Shushun.

"I think it is Gutian. I can make out some of it but not well. What about you, Lopa?"

"No. I have not come across Gutian before," she replied.

There was a loud knock on the door and someone was shouting commands that we could not understand. I said in Sanskrit,

"Who is it? What do you want? We don't understand your language."

There was more shouting and banging on the door. This went on for a while. Someone started to kick the door down. But the thick cedar wood door held fast. Only the brass hinges and bolts seemed to give way. Some rapid commands were shouted by whoever was in charge and there were rapid footsteps of a couple of them running away from the door. It was quiet for a while and the man on the other side started to shout again in Gutian. This time Shushun said, in Sumerian, "You better have a good reason to disturb the guests of King Ur-nanshe of Lagash at this time of the night. His soldiers are on their way as we speak."

Everything became very quiet at that. Shushun whispered to us, "It was a gamble I took because the soldier's dress is something I have never seen. It is, probably, not Sumerian. And I was right. Their captain is now trying to decide if I am bluffing. It also means that they can understand Sumerian."

There were some shuffling noises outside the door and rapid footsteps moving away. It was quiet again. We were not sure if they had left some guards outside the door or not. Parthava, who was looking out of the window said,

"There is something happening. Two of the soldiers have galloped off. There is someone shouting commands at the others."

"Do you think we should open the door and check if any guards are left outside?" Parthava asked.

"They must have left someone. We cannot risk opening the door. We will wait and see what happens. Our chances are better once we are in the open or if we can drag this on till daylight. I would be very surprised if the whole village is in on this," Shushun replied.

We were not left in peace for very long. The soldiers who had galloped off on their horses had returned. There was a lot of noise outside the door. Then there were some running steps followed by a loud thud on the door which shook the walls.

"It is a battering ram!" Shushun said. "The hinges won't hold this for very long. Friends, we'll have to think of a way of escaping once we are out in the open. There is not much we can do here to stop them getting us. I don't know who is behind this.

It is quite obvious they are not the Sumerian soldiers. Someone in the village has betrayed us."

"I think it is the leader of the village who recognised you as the prince of Elam. He has sold you to the Gutians," Parthava said.

"You are probably right. We had heard that some of the Gutians who came down from the north of the country were building a rebel alliance against Emperor Gilgamesh."

I held Lopa closely and must admit that I was petrified. I did not know how these Gutians treated their prisoners. Shushun must have read my mind. He said,

"Gutians are reputed for having huge respect for women. As long as we are careful, they will leave Lopa alone."

That was small consolation for me. My mind was working overtime to look for ways out of this situation and get Lopa back to safety.

"Please don't worry about me, Upaas darling. I can look after myself. You know the great Nahusha has trained me in defending myself," Lopa said , trying to smile at me.

It was not long before the hinges on the door gave in and the soldiers rushed in. Six of them had their bows and arrows at the ready, pointing at us. It was all over within minutes. There was nothing we could do and we knew the resistance was futile and would result in unnecessary loss of lives. There was a lot of shouting and gesticulating from the soldiers. We could not understand anything they were saying, even Shushun. By their actions, it was quite obvious that they wanted Shushun. For a bunch of renegade soldiers who were fighting a guerrilla war, they were quite well-behaved. We were bunched into a covered cart drawn by two horses and driving down the only road in the village in no time.

It was still dark but I could make out the strong men with long, golden hair mixed in places with brown, unkempt facial hair, guttural accents and piercing, blue eyes always searching everywhere. All of them were quite tall and fair-skinned. They were fairer than even the Avestans of the far west and even Nisaba from Aratta who had the reputation of being fair. Their movements were crude and their actions were rough. They appeared to be averse to human contact. After we surrendered, they kept a distance from us.

Bhrigu's children

Ishvant lit the last lamp and the Magus said the hymns to appease the gods. It was exactly one year to the day since his younger brother was killed by the soldiers of King Vishtaspa. He had been doing his honest duty as a righteous soldier. His act of kindness towards a poor boy cost him his life. There was a huge reaction within the city once the King's army left the city. Ishvant did not have time to perform the last rites because he was going with the army. It was left to the wife and small children to do the rites with the Magus. Ishvant had never forgotten that and it still rankled him. He had never forgiven King Vishtaspa for his decision. When he came back from the disastrous battle, nothing but misery faced him. He had held his little nephew, who had been named after him, in his arms, and cried for a long time. The family wanted him to give up the leadership of the council.

"It is only a titular post. You don't have any power — the king controls everything from Mundigak. He is an Avestan and does not care about us. You should get out of that council," his wife was quite adamant.

"That would be a defeatist attitude. Our state has got into this difficulty under my rule. It would be unfair to leave it now, in its hour of need," Ishvant had replied.

"And who will come to your help in your hour of need? The king summarily executed your brother without as much as a by your leave. He is not going to help you," his wife continued. "Sistani soldiers were at the front line and fought bravely. Nobody recognized that. We are Bhrigus and no inferior to the Avestans."

She always had this notion that Bhrigus were not really Avestans.

"Master, that finishes the ceremony. Your brother will be at peace in heaven." The voice of Hutana, the Magus, brought Ishvant out of his reverie. He thanked the Magus and paid his dues. He sat there, staring into nowhere after the Magus had left, reminiscing about his brother. The two of them had grown up together and were very close. He thought of the days they had spent hunting together as young boys and he remembered their trips to Mundigak. Those had been happy times. Both had joined the army together and had risen up the ranks very quickly. When Ishvant was appointed the leader of the Council of Elders, it was his brother who celebrated most. He had grown in stature in the Sistani army and had been made a captain. He was touted to be the next leader of the council when he was killed. Tears started to roll down the cheeks of Ishvant.

"Your brother is happy in heaven. He died doing what he loved best, fighting for the weak. You should not cry for him," his wife said.

"No, these are not tears of sadness. They are tears of

remembrance. I am sad that he is not here anymore, but proud of what he did," Ishvant replied. "Anyway, I am late for the meeting of the council. I am not looking forward to it today. It is the open meeting."

He was beginning to dread these open meetings. Inititating open meetings against the advice of all other elders had been one his proudest decisions. Once a month, the Council of Elders meeting was thrown open to all citizens of Sistan. The 'open day', as it was popularly called,was gradually accepted by everyone in the council. On that day, anyone could come into the council and air their grievances or make requests.

People started grumbling when Sistani soldiers were forced into a war with the Meluhhans and it increased when the captain was executed by the king's soldiers. The meetings had become a battleground since the return of the defeated army. The city of Haozdar had lost a lot of its sons and they were unhappy at the loss of their kith and kin in a war which had nothing to do with them. They had no quarrel with the Meluhhans. They had lived happily with their neighbours for hundreds of years. A lot of them had married into Meluhhan families and lived across the border in several Meluhhan cities.

Even the elders regretted the number of deaths during the battle with the Meluhhans at Harappa. There was talk of secession from Ariana and becoming an independent state.

Ishvant was deep in thought as he made his way to the Council Hall.

"You are deep in thought."

It was his senior Magus, Hutana.

"There is a lot to think about. We might be forced to take a decision today. I am not looking forward to that," Ishvant replied.

"I am sure you will do the right thing. The gods always favour people who do right," the Magus replied.

"I have not seen much in the way of help over the last few years from any of the gods," Ishvant said as he entered the council chambers. It was packed to the brim. All of the elders were already present and there was no space on the floor of the chambers with people jostling each other for more space. There was silence as soon as Ishvant climbed up to the platform at the top end of the chamber. He went to the front of the platform and raised his hands.

"Citizens of Sistan, I welcome you into your Council. We are going through troubled times and we need to work together to face them successfully."

There was a chorus of 'Hear, hear!' and 'Hail to Ishvant!' from the crowd on the floor. All the elders looked at each other rather gravely, unsure of what was happening. They had never seen Ishvant go onstage and speak like a politician before. "If we hold fast and strong, we can show ourselves for what we truly are — a race of proud warriors."

A lot of people started to talk all together at once. Again, Ishvant raised his hands up in the air as if to silence them and said, "I am sure all of you want to say a lot of things. We will be able to understand each other if we can speak one at a time."

"We should decide our future ourselves. It is time we got

rid of this foreign domination. We are Bhrigus. Why should someone else control us?" said the man who was doing most of the talking.

Ever since the Sistani army had returned after the defeat at Harappa, utterly broken in spirit and body, the theme of the open council meetings had been the same. There was unrest among the people and some of them were not afraid of showing it. "Bhrigus are descendants of the greatest Magus that ever lived, the great Sage Bhrigu. We don't want to destroy our culture and ancestry. We are powerful enough to stand on our own. We don't want to fight for the king of Ariana."

Such words would have automatically meant treason and a death sentence just over a year ago. Now, this had become a common theme. Ishvant's spies had brought information from other states of Ariana and the stories sounded very similar. There was a wave of discontent spreading through the country of Ariana. The Druhyus of Gedrosia were most vociferous and there were rumours from other regions as well. Ariana was falling apart. Ishvant, however, was rather apprehensive of this approach.

"My friends, I understand your concern. Believe me, I have lost as much as you here in the war with theMeluhhans. But we have to think of the future. Are we strong enough to break free of Ariana? Do we have the resources to look after our people? Can we protect ourselves from any foreign invasion? We may give way to sentiment and break loose, but are we sure we will stand up and stand strong, or might we just stumble?"

The hall was silent for a while. Then it broke into a mêlée

of protestations from all corners of the floor. Ishvant raised his hands again to calm them down.

"We are not going to achieve anything by arguing among ourselves. Please, one at a time. Let me listen to some reason."

"We are strong enough to defend our state. I would rather fight and die for my own people than for some strangers," the vociferous man continued. "The king and his men have accused us for causing the problems the country of Ariana faces. Everyone knows that it is not true. Some people have angered the gods. It is not us."

Ishvant looked at the other elders sitting at the table, in a sense of exasperation more than anything else. Hutana, the Magus who was sitting next to him, whispered in Ishvant's ear,

"This is something we should discuss amongst ourselves. We should discuss this behind closed doors. We have to see if this can be possible."

Ishvant thought for a moment while the people on the floor continued shouting. Then he stood up again to speak. There was quiet again to listen to him,

"My friends, I hear what you are saying. I will discuss this with the elders and see where we stand in our resources. We will have a decision waiting for you by the time we meet next in a month's time."

That appeared to calm the people down. The meeting concluded with most of the people going home partly appeased. But he knew this was temporary and they would be baying for his blood next month if he did not produce the goods. Ishvant and all the elders stood quietly as the throng gradually receded and the hall was again empty. The guard also left, closing the doors behind him. The hall appeared eerily quiet after that brouhaha.

Ishvant looked at Vispa, his second in command and also the oldest in the Council of Elders, and said,

"Master Vispa, you are the most experienced of us all here. You have been through good times and tough times before. What is your take on the situation?"

Vispa was considered extremely wise, and not just because of his old age. He had been through many wars, he had visited many countries and he could speak several languages, including Sanskrit. He was one of the very few Bhrigus who knew so many languages.

"Master Ishvant, you are too kind. Yes, I have been through some tough times before, but never one as bad as this. I have served under the King Famah, when Sistan was an independent state. I can only tell you how it was under his rule. That would be the closest comparison."

He had everyone's attention then. Vispa must have been very young when Famah was ruling Sistan. Ishvant had not even been thought of when King Famah had ruled Sistan. "Our army was smaller and we did not have the sort of equipment we have now and the chariots and big Elamite horses were not available. But, we were very friendly with the Meluhhans. There was no threat from any outsiders."

"Do you think we can go it alone without the support of the king?"

"We do not have any quarrel with the Meluhhans. The Magus who caused the trouble has been apprehended and is behind bars in Mundigak hopefully. The Meluhhans have promised us a supply of *haoma* for our *yasht*. There is no reason to be subservient to the king anymore. We are paying our taxes. No help has arrived from Mundigak so far."

There were choruses of 'Right, right!' from everyone at the table. The discussion went on late into the night. Almost everyone wanted to be independent. There were one or two dissensions and a lot of concerns were expressed.

A tired Ishvant was walking back to his house alone that night. A figure detached itself from behind the shadows of a doorway and started to walk with him. For a moment, Ishvant was scared. He regretted not carrying his regular short sword with him. He stopped and turned to the man,

"Is there anything I can do for you, my friend?"

"I am sorry to accost you in this way, Master Ishvant. I am Budii, a Magus from the village of Harhar in the south," he replied and as soon as he started to speak, Ishvant recognized him as the man who had been doing most of the talking at the meeting. "I did not want to speak in front of everyone. I have a friend in Lagash who can help us with an alliance with King Ur-nanshe. Developing links with the Sumerians can only help us. It will be to our advantage. If we have them as our friends, foreign powers will think twice before attacking us."

"What you say makes sense, Budii," Ishvant replied. "However, why should King Ur-nanshe help us?"

"I only need to meet the king for a shortwhile. I can charm him into accepting our offer of friendship."

The visions of Magus Maitreya and the debacle at Harappa came back to haunt Ishvant.

"I am sorry, I have had enough of the interventions by Magi to last me a lifetime. I don't want anything to do with your spells and magic."

"I can understand your aversion towards Magi. But not all Magi are like Maitreya. We do good work for our community and our spells do work. Anyway, what do you have to lose? I will be doing all the work and taking all the risks. All I need is the seal of approval from your office."

"And what do you want in return?" Ishvant retorted.

"Nothing. Absolutely nothing. Not all Magi are greedy. When we are sworn in as Magi, we have to swear allegiance to our people and our God. We should not expect any returns."

His answer took Ishvant by surprise. But the Magus appeared genuine and his offer was definitely worth considering.

"Okay. I'll have to speak to the Council. Then I'll let you know."

"Thank you, Master Ishvant. I will wait for your answer. I am staying at the inn and you can send for me when you have a decision."

And he disappeared as quietly as he had come.

Ishvant thought about the Magus's proposal for a long time. He was not even sure if he should place it in front of the Sistan council. The debacle caused by the last Magus had left a bad taste in everyone's mouths. But Ishvant made up his mind overnight. When the sun rose, Ishvant had decided to put the proposal in front of the Council and let them decide if it was worth trying. He called for a Council meeting that afternoon to discuss the offer.

"This is an outrageous proposition. First we talk of secession and now we are talking of inviting yet another disaster. Have we not had our fair share of disasters from the use of magic before?"

It was the elderly chief of army who reacted first to Ishvant's proposal.

"Please hear me out first. This is not as outrageous a proposal as you think. What Magus Maitreya did was treacherous and illegal, but we are not doing anything against any state or individual. We are just developing friendship with a powerful king. I cannot see any harm in that. If this Magus fails, all we stand to lose is the expense of his trip to Lagash."

The discussion went on for a long time and, finally, the Council reluctantly agreed to fund Budii's trip to Lagash with a letter of friendship to the King Ur-nanshe. A letter offering friendship was prepared by the scribe of the Council and the seal of both the Leader of the Council and Commander Vispa were visible on the letter. Later that day, Ishvant sent for Budii and gave him the sealed letter.

"The letter is already sealed! How do I know what is written inside?" Budii was not entirely happy.

"You don't. It is a confidential letter written by the leader of the Sistani Council to the King of Lagash. There is no need for you to know the contents of the letter. Rest assured that there is nothing in it to harm you in anyway. Here are the deeds for fresh horses on the way and supplies for your journey. When are you leaving?"

"Thank you, Master Ishvant. I do trust you, but I wish I had laid my eyes on the letter once. It would have made my job easier. Magi do not have any attachments as you know. I can leave tonight as soon as I get all the supplies," Budii replied.

"I thank you for your offer and may God Mithra be with you on your journey."

Budii went straight to the Council store with the deeds and stocked up on the provisions for his journey along with a horse and a donkey. It was quite late that night when he managed to get the donkey loaded with all the supplies and set off from Haozdar. As he passed through the massive gates of Haozdar, he looked back at the huge mud fort of the city he had been born in and had grown up in till he had become a Magus and moved away south to Harhar. He loved the city and his country of Sistan and would do anything for his people. He painted a fine picture as he rode out of town on his tall, black horse with a fully-loaded donkey trailing behind. For a young man in his thirties, he looked wise with a long beard and a broad forehead and dark brown eyes. He was tall and wiry and carried himself like a statesman. He was extremely intelligent; he had faced no difficulty while training to be a Magus. He had travelled to Elam and Media to learn ancient magic from the priests of Media and had spent some time in the ziggurat of Varuna in Susa learning from their priests. He would cross the Zubi mountains through

Aratta in about a week where he would catch up with old friends. He had met Shu-ilishu while in Aratta and had become very close friends with him. Budii would speak of the downtrodden Sistanis and how he would devote his life to help his people. Shu had fallen in love with a fellow student, Nisaba from Aratta. The three of them had spent a lot of time with the Magi of Aratta. While Budii was learning magic spells, Shu was concentrating on languages and writing. Shu had gone back to Lagash to work for the king when Budii returned to Sistan after two years of learning.

The next stop would be the city of Susa where he would meet his old masters in the temple of Varuna and brush up on his spells before finally crossing over into Sumeria. He had never been to Sumeria and his knowledge of the language was rudimentary. He knew that his friend Shu lived in a village in Lagash. He had sent a message to Shu about his trip and had received an ecstatic reply. It would be just like old times, his friend had written to him, with the three friends reminiscing about their days in Aratta. Finding Shu's village had been a bit of a struggle, until he had come across a Meluhhan traveller who had taken him there.

As Budii entered the Shu's farm, he saw four strangers leaving his friend's house. He thought he recognised one of the strangers as Prince Shushun of Susa. What would a prince of the powerful Elam empire be doing in his friend's house? He wondered.

He knocked on the door. Nisaba, eyes wide open with excitement, unlocked the door and hugged him. She was literally jumping with joy at the sight of the long-lost friend.

"Welcome home, friend. It has been a long time since we saw

you," she was bursting with happiness. "Shu, see who is here. Come quickly."

She grabbed hold of Budii's hands and dragged him inside. He had hardly had a chance to greet her properly. Shu came and hugged Budii with a great deal of affection. They all hugged each other and laughed and cried. None of them could hide their feelings of elation. Nisaba was bubbling all over. There were questions thrown at each other and they wanted to know everything about Budii, his life, his job and his ambitions. The three friends spent the next few hours catching up on how life was treating them while Nisaba ran around, serving them barley bread, roasted goat meat, date jam and cold beer. They finally sat at the edge of the pond under the shade of palm trees watching the sun set, talking about old times. Budii told Shu about his work and his idea of meeting the King of Lagash and the struggle of his people in Sistan. Budii was heartbroken to hear about how Shu was treated because of his marriage to Nisaba and how he lived under a threat most of the time. They were so engrossed in each other's stories that they did not realise that it had become very dark.

They were rudely woken out of their reverie by the sound of several hooves bearing down on them. Shu said,

"Quickly now, hide behind these trees. Let's see who it is first."

The three of them hid behind the trees and saw the riders come hurtling down the road at top speed. There were about fifteen fully-armed men riding powerful, tall, black horses. The armed riders were not interested in them as they rushed past the farm.

"Gutians!" Shu exclaimed, "That does not look good. They are Gutian renegades. I wonder what they are up to so far south in the country. I know they have been raiding outposts in the north around Sippar and Kish. But this must be the furthest south that they have ventured. They had only gone to Shuruppak so far.They must be after Shushun and his friends."

"Prince Shushun from Susa? I thought I recognised him as he was going out of the farm," Budii replied. "What is he doing here?"

"He is obviously travelling incognito. I did not recognise him as the prince. These Gutians must be after him. He would make for a valuable hostage."

Budii thought for a while and said, "I think we should help them out. If we can help him, Sistan will gain a powerful ally."

"I was thinking of helping them anyway because Gutians are not welcome in Sumeria," Shu-ilishu replied. "But, we are only three people against trained men. I can send for help from the Sumerian army, but that will take time."

"You forget, Shu. I am a trained Magus. I may not be able to fight them with arms, but I can keep them occupied for a long time. I have brought my bag of tricks for just such an occasion," Budii said, with a wry smile.

Shu-ilishu slapped him on his back gently and called for his servant. He said something rapidly to the servant in a language Budii could not understand. The servant rode out on a tall, Elamite horse towards the direction the soldiers had gone.

"That is Busae, a Median from Ecbatana. I saved him from being sold to slavery when he lost a gambling bet in the city and he has been working with me ever since. He was a royal messenger in Media, and if anyone can reach the army camp in time, he can," Shu said.

"That is good. I can keep them occupied for a few hours. I need a place where we can attack them at close quarters without being seen," Budii replied.

"The soldiers will have to use the road going towards the coast if they want to escape from the Sumerian army. I know a place where we can ambush them with your bag of tricks. Let me get some bows and arrows as well, just in case. You probably don't remember, but Nisaba is a brilliant archer."

Shu busied himself, collecting three bows and two quivers full of arrows. Large rolls of thick hemp hung on his shoulders. Nisaba brought three horses around. Budii took out his 'bag of tricks' and checked it to make sure he had the special powders and potions he had spent some time preparing. He had never had a chance to try them out in real life. He just hoped they would work. He asked Nisaba to get several pieces of cotton cloth, which he dunked in the pond to get them wet. They set off south across the farm, going behind the village to avoid being seen by anyone.

Shu knew where he was going. But it was not easy for him to find things out in the rather dim moonlight across the dry, sandy ground interspersed with date palm trees and thick, thorny bushes. The land was pretty flat with not much cover for an ambush anywhere. They soon reached the spot Shu-ilishu was looking for. The road here appeared to curve around a high mound covered in thick bushes. There was a clump of palm trees on the other side of the road. There was no sign of any traffic at this time of the night and they had the place to themselves. Shu tied the thick hemp rope around one of the trees on the other side of the road and trailed it across the road to where they were hiding among the thick bushes on the mound. Both of them spread loose soil over the rope to hide it from sight. Not that anyone could see even if they had left it as it was because there was hardly any light. Shu looped the rope twice around the only palm tree on this side of the road and tried pulling it tight. The rope sprang out of the soil to about the height of their hips. Once they were satisfied with the height and the tension of the hemp, they covered the rope again with loose soil. Budii picked out a few tiny mud pots from his bag, gave some to Shu and said,

"When you see my signal, you start throwing these pots at the front of the horses. Nisaba, where are you going to be?"

"I will take up position behind that thick bush over the edge of the mound. I have to have good visibility of the road without being seen myself, and the ground is flat for me to stand," Nisaba replied.

"What will be your signal?" Shu asked Budii.

Budii smiled and said, "You will know when you see it. If it does not work, there is nothing much we can do anyway." He took out some small, cotton satchels and, handing them over to Shu, continued speaking, "Once you see a fire starting, I want you to throw these satchels at the fire. I hope your aim is good enough for that."

"Don't worry about my aim. I'll make sure these satchels hit the fire all right," Shu said with a weak smile. All three of them were nervous. They had never done anything like this before in their lives. It was exciting as an adventure, but it could be dangerous if it went wrong.

"And, last of all," Budii continued, handing the two of them wet, cotton towels, "tie these around your faces and make sure your noses and mouth are well-covered, like mine." He showed them how to do it by tying a cloth around his own face. It covered the entire face quite well, and only the eyes were exposed.

"I don't think it matters if we are recognized. We don't need a mask," Shu-ilishu remarked.

"It is not a disguise. The chemicals in those pots and satchels can be dangerous and I am hoping they will affect only the Gutians. We have to make sure your friends cover their faces as soon as we free them," Budii replied. "Now, we had better take our places and wait."

The three friends must have sat there for a long time because Budii had nearly dozed off when the sound of the hooves startled him out of his stupor. Budii ran across to the other side of the road and pulled hard at the rope, tying it around the only rock on that side of the road. He tied the wet cloth around his face and crouched behind the rock, holding on to one of the small mud pots from his bag. It was not long before the riders came hurtling around the corner and the horses stumbled as they tripped over the taut rope across the road. Four of the riders went down in a heap and the horses landed on their knees. The wagon was just behind them and the driver tried to pull up the running bullocks sharp without much luck. They stamped over two of the riders before coming to a halt. Budii threw his mud pot against the wall of the wagon as the rest of the riders behind the wagon pulled up behind. There was a blinding flash as the pot hit the wagon and broke into pieces. That was the signal for Shu to start throwing the little satchels. One of the wheels of the wagon caught fire and thick, yellow smoke was billowing out of it.

There was utter confusion among the Gutians. They had no idea what had hit them. The horses were neighing loudly in panic and started to rear, throwing more of their men down. There was a twang in the air followed by a thud as the first of Nisaba's arrows hit the wagon. But the next one appeared to find its target as one of the soldiers cried out in pain.

I was holding on to Lopa inside the wagon, wondering how to get out of the situation when the attack started and the wagon shuddered to a halt throwing all of us against the front of the wagon. As we struggled to get up from the floor of the wagon, I heard the first of the loud bangs. Soon I could see fire through the slits between the cedar logs of the wagon walls and I smelt something vaguely familiar.

"Sulphur!!" I shouted. "Cover your faces quickly!" I started to rip pieces of cloth from my tunic and wrapped it around Lopa's face, covering her mouth and nose. I could see Parthava and Shushun do the same. I could see smoke rising out of the side of the wagon through the slit and it was joined by a crackling sound.

"The wagon is on fire!" Parthava shouted the obvious. I could see bright yellow flames licking the sides of the wagon near the front and it was spreading fast. The situation was grim and if we did not get out of the wagon soon, chances were we would be burnt alive. There was no fire inside the wagon yet. I kicked at the wooden plank which appeared to be burning on the outside. There was loud crack. Both Parthava and Shushun joined me and the wood gave way very quickly. It was dry as cinder, having been exposed to the hot sun over the weeks, and the fire had weakened it considerably. Our relief was short-lived as the fire now had access to the insides of the wagon and the wagon was full of thick black smoke almost instantly. All of us were coughing uncontrollably, despite having covered our faces with pieces of linen.

We had to get out of the wagon soon. We renewed kicking all sides of the wagon with increased zest and one side came down very quickly. All four of us jumped out of the wagon and ran across to a clump of trees on the side of the road. The Gutian soldiers were in disarray and too busy trying to save themselves from the attack to be bothered by our escape. As I scampered to the cover of the tree, I was pulled down by a strong pair of hands and a muffled voice said,

"Get down and stay down if you don't want to be killed."

I was shocked to see Shu-ilishu's wife. She was straddling a palm tree, wearing a belted tunic and a shoulder strap with a quiver-full of arrows. She did not turn around as we scrambled to the safety of cover, provided by the mound and the clump of bushes. She continued firing arrows at a rapid pace at the group of Gutian raiders who had taken refuge behind the burning wagon. The fire and smoke made visibility extremely poor. We could just make out shadows in the dim light of the fire. I was not sure whether she would be at all successful trying to fire arrows at shadows. The quiver was now almost empty.

"Thank you, Nisaba. We are extremely grateful for your help," I said.

"Don't be too hasty with your gratitude. At the rate we are going, I am going to run out of arrows soon and God help us all then. We are vastly outnumbered and they have many more weapons than us. Shu is across there, throwing the little pots with powders given by Budii," she said without turning around.

"Is there anything we can do to help?" I repeated.

I could feel Lopa huddling next to me. I put my arm around her and hugged her tight as Shushun and Parthava scrambled behind trying desperately to take cover from the onslaught of incessant arrows. "How did you know we were being kidnapped?"

Nisaba stopped firing and sat down facing us. "We saw the Gutians ride past our farm last night into the village and our friend Budii recognised Shushun as the prince of Susa." I could see Shushun's eyebrows rise at this. "Gutians have had their eyes on our cities for a while. It was not too difficult to put two and two together. Ambhasika has sold you to the Gutians."

"Who is Budii?" Shushun asked.

"He is a dear friend of ours from Sistan. He is an Avestan Magus. All that fire and smoke is thanks to his magic potions and powders," Nisaba said, with a wry smile.

"I hope our Busae gets to the army camp to get some help in time. Otherwise we are sunk."

When she saw the questions in our faces, she continued, "Busae used to be a royal messenger in Nippur. We think he is the only person who can go to Lagash and come back in one night."

Before she could complete the sentence, we felt the thundering hooves of horses in the distance. The eastern sky was lightning up with the pre-dawn sun colouring the sky reddish orange. I was quite uneasy at the thought of being helped by an Avestan Magus. I hoped he would not turn out to be like Matriya, who had nearly destroyed Bharata sometime back. Shushun must have read my mind, for he turned around and said,

"Not all Magi are villains and not all Avestans are bad."

"I am sure, but you can understand my concern after what we have been through in Harappa."

"Here comes the cavalry. Thank God for Busae," Nisaba sat down with a sigh of relief. "That looks like a platoon of Sumerian soldiers on the horizon. They will be here any minute now."

We could see a cloud of dust rising in the distance against the faint light of dawn. The Gutians must have heard it too. The firing slowed down and eventually stopped as the Sumerian soldiers came into view. The Gutians must be weighing the situation. I wondered what they would do. Would they stay and fight or make a run for it? I did not have to wait very long. As we watched, the Gutian raiders crept back onto their horses and rode off, in a tearing hurry, towards the coast.

"That explains how they managed to get here without being noticed. They must have landed at the coast south east of here. It is pretty deserted there."

As we watched, what had initially appeared to be a small

group in the distance grew bigger and some of the soldiers broke away from the group and went after the Gutians. Budii and Shu came out of their hiding places and joined us. By the time the introductions were over, the Sumerian soldiers had reached us.

"That is the Sumerian Royal Standard in front," Shushun said to no one in particular. He did not look particularly concerned, but I could see his eyes were on Nisaba's bow and quiver. He edged closer to Nisaba when the leader of the group came forward. He was wearing a deep violet silk tunic with a leather belt, a deep red, broad linen cap with a gold braid on top. There was a leather scabbard at the waist with a gold-handled sword, a bow slung over the shoulders and a leather quiver full of arrows at the back. He was quite muscular, flat-nosed and carried himself straight on the back of his tall white stallion. Their leather sandals were strapped to their legs all the way up to the knees. Both Shu-ilishu and Nisaba dropped to their knees and bowed their heads at him saying,

"Greetings to Lugal Ur-Nanshe."

And Shu continued, "Our grateful thanks for saving us from the Gutians."

The leader raised his right hand, with his palms outstretched in the universal sign of protection, and said,

"Rise, my friend Shu-ilishu. It is my duty to keep our country and our friends safe." He smiled at all of us and continued, "Welcome to our country, my dear friends. I hope you have not been distressed too much by the treacherous Gutians. My particular welcome to Prince Shushun of Susa. I only found out about the prince from the messenger yesterday. When Busae came to the camp with the bad news, I had to come personally. It is the least I can do. I would be grateful, if one of you can introduce me to the prince."

Shushun stepped forward and said,

"I am Prince Shushun, son of King Awan of Elam. Thank you, mighty Lugal, for saving us. I hope you have received my father's seal as an offer of friendship with the Lugal of Lagash."

The Lugal came down from the horse, and coming forward, embraced Shushun and kissed him on both the cheeks. That was the traditional Sumerian method of greeting someone special.

"I am grateful to God Marduk that no harm has befallen you, my friend. I am in receipt of your great father's seal indeed. It is a privilege to me and my country to befriend the empire of Elam." Looking at us, he continued, "I extend my welcome to all your friends and you are our guests in Lagash. Please ask for anything you desire. Your wish is my command."

"Thank you, Lugal Ur-Nanshe. My friend, Upaas, is an eminent physician from Meluhha and he would like to visit your medical centres and meet some of your expert physicians to gain knowledge of the kind of medicine you use," Shushun replied, looking intently at the Lugal for his response. He continued, "We are also looking for the great Sage Utna-Pishtim. Can you please advise us about where we are likely to find him? Any help you provide would be appreciated."

"I'm afraid the Sage is a difficult person to trace. You will have to go through the mysterious waters of Apsu. There are more Magi in the cities of Ur and Shuruppak who may be of help. I will arrange for you to be introduced to the chief magi and the royal physicians. Let us go to Lagash and rest in the palace for a few days before you resume your travels." He turned around and barked a few orders at the captain of the platoon. There was a flurry of activity among the soldiers. Shu-ilishu, who had been quiet all this while, now spoke.

"I will request the Lugal to allow me to take our guests to my farm. They can freshen up and partake of some small refreshments before they travel to Lagash."

And so it was that we were on our way back to Shu's farm once again, this time escorted by a platoon of Sumerian soldiers. The Lugal insisted that Prince Shushun have a royal escort for the rest of the journey. We all agreed that having a company of soldiers during the rest of our time in Sumeria might hamper our purposes and we would somehow have to convince the Lugal to let us continue our journey on our own.

The city of Lagash proved to be a typical Sumerian city with one of the branches of Hidekal river dividing the city into two parts. A bridge across the Hidekal led to a busy marketplace. It was lively, what with local traders competing with those from Elaam, Meluhha as well as from other states within the country. The river was as busy as the main street. Numerous boats took passengers back and forth, up and down the river and there were a few busy docks along the way. The city was dominated by a huge ziggurat built for the city's deity, Enlil. The Lugal's palace was towards the north eastern part of the city and was an imposing building on its own.

As guests of the Lugal, we were treated with deference where ever we went. Ur-Nanshe had arranged for me to meet the royal physicians at the court. I liked the elderly chief physician who endeavoured to show me around his domain, which was filled with hundreds of jars of potions and powders, roots and leaves as well as berries and fruits he used to prepare medicines. He had a particular interest in making medicines out of dried fish and seaweed. He was obviously very proud of Sumerian medicine, but showed a keen and polite interest in our medical practice as well.

The captain of Shushun's ship had joined us and it turned out that we had not lost everything. The ship's cargo was virtually intact, to everyone's surprise. Shushun left instructions with the captain to dispose of the goods in the markets of Ur and meet us in the city after that.

It took all of Shushun's diplomatic skills to convince Ur-Nanshe to let us go on our way without a retinue of soldiers. It was nearly a week later when we said goodbye to the Lugal and thanked him for his generosity. He had provided us with new wagons, horses and supplies for our onward journey. There was a surprise inside the wagon in the form of a virtual arsenal with a number of bows, quivers, arrows, swords, spears and maces loaded into one of the carts. The royal carpenters had built a false compartment in the floor of the wagon to hide the arsenal in. Ur-Nanshe gave us seals as introduction to the inn-keeper in Ur and Shuruppak because Shushun wanted to remain anonymous for a while still. He also gave us seals as introduction to priests in Ur and Shuruppak to help in our search for Utna-pishtim.

We made our way towards the city of Ur with a sad heart.

Also, we were not sure about how we would be treated in those parts. We were apprehensive about going deeper into Sumeria. Shu-ilishu insisted on accompanying us as did the friendly Budii.

"We have wanted to visit places like Ur and Shuruppak for a while. Anyway, as you head up north, all of you will be quite lost if I am not around to translate all the languages you will hear people speak."

I had learnt to respect Budii, after being initially cautious of the fact that he was a Magus. Now he was a part of our troupe. He turned out to be most unlike any other Magus I had come across before. He would chat with us like any other commoner and he got on well with everyone. So it was that there were seven horse-riders (including me) and two wagons traveling to Ur. We saw the huge river Buranuna for the first time as we came closer to the city of Ur. We crossed the river well south of the city where it was possible to be ferried across without being taken down along the fast-flowing stream. It was so wide here that I could not see the western bank. We loaded the horses and the wagons onto the ferry with some trepidation. It took us nearly the whole morning to cross the river and get back onto the road to Ur.

Ur

The city walls of Ur appeared huge in the distance as we approached the eastern gates. We were stopped by the guards at the gate but the check was perfunctory and Shushun's command over the Sumerian language helped. The gates opened into a large road lined with numerous shops selling all sorts of goods from grains to oils to semi-precious gems. Despite the early hour of the day, there were many people on the street. We had to negotiate our way between several carts carrying produce and horse-riders along the street to the inn. Many people on either side of the road seemed to be waiting for something or somebody. We did not have to wait much longer. There was low-pitched music accompanied by a slow-beating drum and the crowd was excited. We pulled over on a bylane and got off our horses to take a look. A large platoon of soldiers dressed in full regalia mounted on black horses marched in front of us trying to keep the crowds in order.

The Queen Puabi was majestic even in death. She was wearing a purple velvet tunic covered in carnelian beads and gold threads. She had a head dress made of gold leaves, ribbons and strands of lapis lazuli and carnelian. The wealth of the city of Ur was on display at the death ceremony. Her attendants, who were walking on either side of her, were wearing similar, but slightly less ostentatious clothes. The Lugal of Ur was sitting upright on his white stallion in the front of the cortege along with a retinue of his bodyguards. I had never seen such mourning before. I could not decide if they were mourning or celebrating and the whole affair startled both Lopa and me.

"The Queen Puabi was the consort of the Lugal of Ur and she was much loved by the citizens. She died yesterday and this is the funeral march."

Shu turned to us from talking to someone in the crowd and said, "The city is full of people from all over the state. I hope the innkeeper has room for us."

The crowd started to wail, with tears pouring down their cheeks, as the cortege came into view. The women were beating their chests and the men were hailing the queen. It was their way of saying goodbye to a much loved monarch. We followed the cortege on foot to the northeastern corner of the city toward the royal necropolis. The gates into the necropolis were two huge columns inscribed with names of the gods of Ur and carvings of animals. We soon reached the place where the queen would be buried. It was a large brick building with walls sloping inwards. The ceiling was flat. There were two wooden columns by the side of the huge door inscribed again with names of gods. Once we passed through the door into an antechamber, it led down a flight of stairs to a large chamber below.

It was a gaily-dressed crowd that assembled in the mat-lined pit for the royal obsequies, a blaze of colour with the crimson coats, the silver and gold; clearly these people were not wretched slaves killed as oxen might be killed, but persons of honour, wearing their robes of office, and coming, one was hoping, voluntarily, to a rite which would in their belief be but a passing from one world to another, from the service of God on earth to that of the same God in another plane.

Twelve attendants were lined up on either side of the chamber. There was a cart full of personal items and delicacies from the queen's chamber. There was a large copper cauldron on a fire at the corner. Two men were stirring something inside the cauldron. The smoke and steam rising out of the vessel smelt sweet and intoxicating. There were five soldiers of the royal body guards standing to attention at the head of the wooden platform where the queen was laid. A large wooden chest at the side of the platform displayed all the royal regalia of the monarch.

The royal priests started chanting an incantation once the body was laid out on the platform. The ceremony lasted a few hours during which the Lugal made several gestures towards the queen and the gods above. The music intensified when the low-pitched wind pipe was joined by several lyres and three huge drums. The attendants working on the cauldron stopped stirring and poured out a small jug full of the liquid from the cauldron to everyone in the chamber except the priest and the Lugal. The attendant would give a jug to each lady, watch her drink and help her curl up and lie down. This was repeated with everyone in the ensemble, until the whole ensemble appeared to fall asleep as we watched. Each of them had curled up on one side and gone to sleep. The royal priest was the last one to drink from the jug and lay down. We were all ushered out and the door was sealed shut. Only the musicians were still up playing at the end. We could hear the faint music being played inside for a while longer and it soon started to lose the thread and finally stopped completely. The crowd had become completely silent and gently started to walk backwards towards the gates of the necropolis.

"Don't turn around. Keep walking backwards," Shu-ilishu hissed at me as I tried to turn around. It was quite strange to see thousands of people walking backwards in absolute silence. After the intense and rather disturbing music for the whole day, the silence was deafening. We did not turn around until we were through the gates of the necropolis and sighed a deep sigh of relief once we were outside.

"That was a draining experience. I would not want to go through that again too soon," Parthava spoke for all of us. We walked back to where we had left our horses and wagons that morning. It was getting dark by the time we reached the inn. The door was opened by a tall, wizened old man.

"Can I help you?"

"Yes. I am Shu-ilishu from Lagash. I believe you have a room for me and our friends here." His eyes opened wide at the sound of the name and he immediately ushered us in. As we walked through the door into a darkened hallway, another door opened at the far end and a gruff, female voice said,

"Who is it? Tell them we don't have any room here."

"Will you shut up, woman? Don't interfere with business," the old man literally screamed at her and, turning back to us, continued, "Please don't mind the old witch. She is not very friendly today. Please come in. Of course we have room for the guests of the Lugal of Lagash."

"Our horses and wagons are outside," Shushun started in his best Sumerian only to be cut short by the innkeeper with,

"Don't worry about your horses and wagons, sir. They shall be taken good care of. Please come with me and I'll show you your rooms."

We walked through a maze of corridors and climbed at least two flights of stairs before coming to a corridor with several doors on either side.

"Please pick the rooms you want. The entire floor belongs to you. The bathrooms are at the end of the corridor."

And turning to Shu-ilishu,he asked, "May I ask how long you intend to stay with us?"

"We don't know at the moment. We will let you know," Shu said with a completely non-committal face. As the innkeeper withdrew, Parthava turned to us and whispered,

"I am not sure I like this place. There is something odd going on here."

"Parthava, you have a suspicious mind. All inns are the same and all innkeepers are always cagey," I replied.

"All the same, I will go and get some of the weapons from the wagon for us. You stay here and make yourselves comfortable."

We let the two girls decide which rooms they wanted and the rest was left for the other three. Our room was comfortable, with a large wooden bed and a window facing the narrow street outside. I could see Parthava fussing about the wagon from the window and smiled.

"What are you smiling at, Upaas?" Lopa asked.

"I don't know what we would do without our friend Parthava. He has such a suspicious mind and he is usually right. But I think he may be wrong this time. He has been such a boon to us, and me particularly. I would not have got you back from Sistan without his help."

"Yes, darling Upaas. I would have lost you forever without him. God has sent him to us."

We went down to the large hall downstairs where the old innkeeper and his grumpy wife served us samples of typical Sumerian fare with the beer made famous by the erstwhile Queen Puabi. During dinner, we planned the next day.

"We will have to go and see the high priest of Nanna in the Ziggurat," Shushun commented. "Ur-Nanshe thinks he might have some information on Ziusudra's whereabouts."

"I am not sure we would be able to see him for a few days now. The funeral schedule will keep him busy for the next few days," Shu-ilishu replied. "Royal funerals last about five days."

"We might as well spend some time visiting the physicians and seeing the great city," I said. Shushun came with me and Lopa to visit the royal physician while the others wandered around the city. He was pleased to see us and quite enthusiastic about his work.

"Visitors from the great country of Meluhha are a rare sight. To be visited by an eminent physician from the great city of Harappa is an honour indeed," he enthused. I blushed visibly and replied,

"You are embarrassing me, sir. I am no expert. It is you, on the other hand, who is blessed with wisdom and experience."

"You are being too modest, Master Upaashantha. Meluhhan, especially Harappan, physicians are known throughout the world for their expertise in modern medicine. I think we have much to learn from you."

He continued, "Please tell me about the great city of Harappa first."

Lopa and I tried to describe Harappa and its surroundings. We spent the next couple of hours discussing medicine. As the day went on, I learnt that he had been fortunate enough to have physicians from Egypt, Media as well as Aratta working with him for a number of years. His grasp of medicine was wide and far-reaching. I could easily compare him with my own master Ashwin. He took me around a room at the back of where he practiced his surgery. The room was full of earthen jars and pots containing seeds, powders, dried leaves and fruits. My interest was caught by a couple of jars containing some strange-looking eggs, and another one had bones. He saw me looking at them and smiled,

"I know what you are thinking. The eggs are allowed to dry out before we make powders from them. Ostrich eggs are particularly useful in treating several diseases. The bones are from desert snakes which are used in treating fragile bones."

His assistants brought us some food while we were still talking. I had lost track of time. Shushun appeared to be fascinated by the vast array of medicines on display. Lopa was taking a lot of interest especially in the cosmetic creams on some other shelves. It was quite late in the evening when we returned to the inn. The others had just returned from their wanderings of the city as well. They had been around the dock of river Buranuna. The massive city walls went down to the river's edge in places.

"You should see the number of ships at the dock," Parthava gushed, looking at Shushun. "There are ships from everywhere, Egypt, Dilmun, Bharata and even some countries I did not even know existed till today. We met many merchants from Harappa."

My ears perked up at the sound of Harappa. I turned around and grabbed Parthava and asked him,

"Did you really meet someone from Harappa? Who was he? What was his name? How is everyone in Harappa?"

"Really, Upaas! Slow down. Not so many questions all at once," Parthava was slightly taken aback at my passion. "Yes. There were many merchants from Harappa as well as from Sindhu and Saraswatha in the port. They were all selling precious stones, cotton, wood and spices. Plenty of spices. I tell you, the smell of spices took me back home."

There were tears in my eyes at the thought of home. I wondered how Nivya, my sister, was. And how my mother was carrying on, without any of her sons at home. I could see father coming back home and reminding us of the regular chanting of the *gayathri mantra* in the evening. Lopa could see I was immersed in Harappa and completely lost. I was brought back to earth by Shu-Ilishu.

"We have found out that the royal physician will be able to see us in two days." He had been busy talking to people he knew from before and had made some inquiries and contacts. We spent the next couple of days wandering around the city and even climbed on top of the massive city walls thanks to a friendly captain of the guards. On the third day, we went to the ziggurat to see the physician. He was a dour, portly and elderly gentleman with very little sense of humor. He invited us into his chamber at the top floor of the ziggurat. He sat on the only chair in the room and looked up at the ceiling, saying very little. It was rather uncomfortable to say the least. Shushun cleared his throat a couple of times to see if he would say anything. When he would not budge, he started with,

"Thank you for seeing us, great priest. We have some questions to ask you and we need your help."

"The Lugal of Lagash has asked me to help you. But I have very little time, really. Tell me quickly what you want and I'll see if I can help you," he replied without taking his eyes off Shushun.

"I thank you for that. We have come all the way from Harappa in Meluhha seeking the great Sage Ziusudra." There was the first sign of life on his face at the mention of the sage's name. He raised his right eyebrow ever so slightly and said,

"Why do you seek the great sage?"

"We have some questions to ask him," Shushun continued.

"What kind of questions?"

"I would rather not say. It is a personal issue for me and, to some extent, for my friend Upaashantha from Harappa."

His eyes clouded over and he did not say anything for a minute. Then he bent his head down for the first time since we got into the room and said with a deep sigh,

"I don't know exactly where he is. Even when he was ruling Shuruppak, it was quite difficult to meet him. And ever since he has ceased to be monarch, he has almost disappeared. Some people have gone looking for him and never returned. He lives in the middle of the mysterious waters of the Apsu, guarded night and day by fierce creatures. You will have to ask the chief priest of the temple of Enki in Shuruppak. The Apsu is somewhere in Shuruppak. That is all I know."

And that was that. It was a dismissal as far as we were concerned as he kept his head down and stared at the seal Shushun had given him a few minutes ago. We waited for a few minutes before letting ourselves out and climbed down the steps of the ziggurat. We wandered down to the river Buranuna's banks. Parthava started to throw stones into the river.

"Now what do we do? Do we go to Shuruppak? We have to journey north for a few weeks if we have to go there and the Gutians have been active on these northern roads. We can get there quicker on a boat but we will need a large river boat. Shushun's ship won't be able to go past Ur all the way up to Shuruppak."

It was Shu-ilishu who broke the silence. The reaction of the priest had disappointed all of us. "And even if we do reach Shuruppak, we still have to tackle the Apsu and the mysterious creatures guarding the sage."

"I don't know why all of you look so dejected. We know a lot more today about the sage's whereabouts than we did yesterday. The priest has narrowed down our options to the city of Shuruppak. I know it is not without danger. But since when did we start balking at the mention of danger?" Shushun sounded positively enthusiastic. "We have come all this way and survived the worst the ocean could throw at us. All of us are skilled in fighting and we have the magic of Budii with us. I have seen his work in Lagash and I am sure it will come in handy again in the Apsu. From what I hear, these creatures have to be magical."

"I think Shushun is right. We know a lot more about the sage now than we ever did and there is a good chance that we will be able to find him. That's more than what most people have done."

"I agree with Upaas. I don't think we should give up now after all we have gone through to come this far," Lopa replied. Budii, who had been quiet all along, suddenly spoke up.

"I agree with Shushun too. The creatures sound magical. I know how to deal with such creatures. We have more than our fair share of magical creatures in Ariana."

The discussion went on for a while before finally returning back to the inn. As we were walking up the main street towards the inn, a little boy came running up the street and nearly crashed into us. Parthava grabbed onto his tunic and said,

"Hold your horses. Watch where you are going, young man."

The little boy started to wriggle and mumbled something in a language I could not understand. The only thing I could make out was a heavily accented "Upaashantha!"

He obviously did not understand what Parthava was saying

in Sanskrit and was getting increasingly agitated until Shu-ilishu decided to intervene and calm him down. It was the innkeeper's son who had been sent out to look for me. It was difficult to understand him as he was speaking very fast in his language. Shu-ilishu said something to the little boy in the same language. That appeared to calm him down and he started to speak more slowly. I figured out that he was speaking Akkadian when he slowed down, but could not understand what he was saying. Shu-ilishu turned around to speak to us.

"It appears that there are some visitors in the inn for us. They are soldiers from Uruk asking to see Master Upaashantha. The innkeeper wants to know if he should get rid of them."

"I don't see any reason to. Bharata does not have any quarrel with the city of Uruk. In fact, they are one of our biggest trading partners. Even Shushun has had a good reception from Ur-Nanshe," I said.

"I think so too. Let's go and see what they want," Shushun said, and turning to Parthava, said, "We best be on our guard though."

"Just what I was going to say. Give me a head start of a few minutes before you reach the inn," Parthava said and shot off in the direction of the inn at a fast clip. Shu-ilishu took the cue and started to ask the little boy questions about his town, friends and the inn stalling for time. As we turned a corner of the road onto the narrow street where the inn was, we saw half a dozen soldiers standing by their horses, waiting, presumably for us. They were smartly-dressed in greyblue knee length tunics with leather belts and shoulder straps embellished with copper buttons and strips. Each one of them was wearing a scabbard at the hip with a long sword. The horses were tall, brown stallions with leather saddles carrying full quivers and bows. As we passed them into the inn, they bowed their heads in acknowledgement and said nothing. There were two of them sitting in the hall talking to the innkeeper. The innkeeper turned to us as we entered and said,

"Ah, Master Upaashantha. These two gentleman have been sent by Emperor Gilgamesh to see you."

Both of them stood up and walked towards us, with their right arms raised and their palms outstretched in the manner of the typical Sumerian greeting and said,

"Hail Master Upaashantha."

The taller of the two men continued, "I am Me-ulang, captain of the royal guards. We bring greetings from our great emperor Gilgamesh." And he handed me a clay tablet. "This tablet has his seal. The emperor's message is on the tablet."

The clay tablet had writings in Sumerian which I could not read. I turned to the captain and said, "These are my friends and I would like my friend Shu-Ilishu to read the tablet to me because I cannot read Sumerian." I went on to introduce everyone to the captain. The other soldier kept quiet throughout the conversation. I gave the cylinder to Shu-ilishu who read it out. "The bearer of this seal is my captain Me-ulang. My greetings to the great Meluhhan physician Upaashantha and the crown prince of the empire of Elam, Shushun."

There was a sharp intake of breath from all of us at that. We did not expect the news of us to have reached Uruk so quickly.

Shu-ilishu went on to explain that the captain had brought some confidential information and he needed the 'help of master physician Upaashantha of Meluhha.'

"Master Upaashantha, the emperor wants you to come to Uruk urgently. His close friend, Enkidu is seriously ill. None of the royal physicians have been able to help him. The emperor needs your help to save his friend. He has been told that only Egyptian physicians or Meluhhan sages can save him. We are here to escort you and your friends to Uruk where the emperor awaits you."

This was something we had not anticipated. A request from the emperor of Sumeria himself! Well, it was more an order than a request, really, coming from the emperor Gilgamesh. He carried with him a reputation as formidable as anyone including the great pharaohs of Egypt. One did not take any request from him lightly. The captain did not appear to have any more information about the emperor's friend or his illness.

"I am honored to be summoned by the great emperor Gilgamesh. It would be my privilege to help in any way I can," I replied, "I must, however, tell you that I am not a sage. I am a mere physician. My knowledge of medicine is not the best in the world and not as good as my mentor, Master Ashwin. I also don't have all the equipment and medicines I might require with me."

"The emperor has been told that his friend Enkidu can only be saved by a physician from Meluhha. You have been recommended by the ministers of the emperor as well as the royal priest," The captain said and, looking at Shushun, continued, "Prince Shushun is also known to have extensive knowledge of Egyptian medicine. Between the two of you, you can save the emperor's friend. We will provide you with whatever you require. The city of Uruk has a very large pharmacy and anything that is not in the pharmacy, we will get in the forests and hills around us."

We were taken aback by his detailed knowledge of us. I wondered what else the emperor knew about us, particularly me. I looked at Shushun who was looking very thoughtful indeed, but did not appear to be especially concerned.

"I will certainly do my best to save your emperor's friend. We will need some time to pack our things."

Upstairs, Parthava turned around and said,

"I am a little worried about travelling to Ur with these soldiers. There have been rumours of Gutians attacking Sumerian soldiers around Ur."

"I would not be concerned, my friend. These soldiers look professional enough and I feel more confident travelling in their company. Anyway, we have to pass Ur to reach Shuruppak. We have more chances of arriving at our destination if we have these soldiers to protect us. If we do help the emperor, he would be obliged to help us to get to Shuruppak and maybe, even find Ziusudra," Shushun replied.

"I agree with Shushun, Parthava. The Gutians would not dare attack a large Sumerian company of soldiers. They normally attack only small outposts and small platoons of soldiers. They claim this to be their land and want to rule Sumeria. There is no chance of that happening while Gilgamesh is their ruler," Shu-ilishu replied.

"I think I better let Sage Vasishta know where we are heading before we leave. He may be returning to Bharata by now," I said.

It did not take long to pack our things and leave the city of Ur the following morning. I stayed back in the room to contact the sage before setting off. He was anxious when I told him we would be going deeper into the country.

"Beware of strange places and strange beings!" was his parting shot. We insisted on taking the wagon given to us by Ur-Nanshe with us. It had all the weapons we had been presented with, not to count Budii's magic potions and powders hidden under the floor. The captain had brought with him one of the royal carriages sumptuously furnished with silk, wool and gold. We managed to get the two ladies to agree to travel in the royal carriage. We set off towards the docks as the sun was rising in the east, towards our right. The guards stood to attention when they saw the royal carriage coming towards them and cleared the road of traffic. The company of soldiers was riding in front and the captain was behind the wagons alon gwith his deputy. Parthava had insisted on riding a horse. So it was left to Shu-ilishu to drive the wagon behind the royal carriage being driven by two fully armed soldiers. There was a large royal boat at the dock waiting for us. We watched as the soldiers helped the sailors load the boat with our boxes and horses and we were sailing up north by the time the sun was high in the sky. The captain had arranged for men to get the wagons up to Shuruppak with a small retinue of soldiers as protection against Gutian attack. We would meet the wagons once we finished our work in Uruk. I looked back at the city walls as the boat pulled away from the jetty. They were massive, with great bastions every hundred yards and guard towers every few yards. It was enough to put fear into any enemy. They looked impregnable.

"Those walls have not been breached in living memory."

It was the captain, Me-ulang, who had walked up to me unnoticed. It startled me for a bit.

"I cannot imagine how anyone can get past that wall. They are so high. So massive. A monkey couldn't climb that wall," I replied.

"Monkey?" He looked at me questioningly. I had forgotten that monkeys didn't exist in Sumeria.

We reached the city of Larsa as the sun was going down on the second day. The captain had decided to break the journey in the small city of Larsa for the night, before travelling the last leg of the journey on the river. It was a much smaller city than either Ur or Uruk on the banks of the river. But the dock was big enough to handle the large, royal boats. We stayed in the royal guest house within the city for the night. I was quite impressed the way the boat was cleaned up and ready to sail by first light next morning. The captain was on the boat and pacing up and down as we climbed aboard.

"We have to set sail as soon as possible. I have had messages from the emperor that the condition of Enkidu had deteriorated."

He was looking worried indeed. He knew the result of being late. If Enkidu dies before we get to Uruk it will be his head for the chop. I am sure his soldiers knew of the consequences as well and we could sense the urgency in whatever they did. Unfortunately, we were sailing against the current on the river and were entirely dependant on the oarsmen most of the time. The captain of the boat insisted he had the best oarsmen of all Sumeria and promised to get us into Uruk before nightfall that day.

The scenery of the country was outstanding. It was mostly brown soil interspersed with clumps of palm trees and several small hills on the way. The captain kept the boat hugging the east coast of the river most of the time. In some stretches, the river was so wide that we could not see the west bank. On a couple of occasions, he took the boat to the middle of the river to avoid rocky banks when both the east and west coasts disappeared from sight.

As we sailed further north, we had to go through deep gorges lined by towering, reddish-brown stone cliffs. They were high enough to block the sunlight from reaching us. It was much cooler in the shade of the cliffs. The cliff face was home to thousands of birds and some of these flew down to the boat hoping for some tasty morsels.

"This is the place for most Gutian ambushes. We have to be doubly careful until we pass these gorges." It was the captain who had been busy positioning his best marksmen with bows loaded with arrows at all the vantage points on the boat. Luckily for us, the journey passed off without any such attacks and I was beginning to think that all this talk of Gutian attacks must be an exaggeration. Most of us had dozed off during the afternoon heat on the boat. All of us, that is, except the soldiers and sailors who kept an anxious watch all the time. All their sleep had disappeared at the mention of an ambush.

"The only Gutian action we have seen was on land and in

Lagash. I have not seen any Gutians since then," Parthava voiced what all of us were thinking. Captain Me-ulang smiled and replied,

"Two merchant ships from Dilmun were attacked on this very spot a few days ago. Survivors had to swim to the shore to save themselves. We found the debris of the ship scattered all over the east coast of the river for several miles."

That seemed to quieten Parthava for a while. In fact, it set the rest of us thinking as well. The captain of the boat was as good as his promise. There were several hair-raising moments on the way when he had to negotiate between some tiny rock islands in the middle of the river with fast-flowing eddies. I am not sure whether it was luck or expert boatmanship, but he narrowly missed smashing our boat to smithereens on more than one occasion and we reached the impressive docks of the city of Uruk as the sun was setting.

Uruk and the Plight of Enkidu

If I had been impressed by the walls of Ur, this was something else. These cities were obviously intensely afraid of being attacked by ferocious enemies to build such huge walls and bastions. The walls were not only imposing. One could sense that violence and power were in a delicate balance in this place. Most ferocious villains would think twice before attacking a city of this stature. The dock was huge. Several sea-going ships already docked. There was a brick jetty stretching almost to the middle of the river to stem its flow. There were huge limestone steps leading up to a rock platform teeming with activity. My heart skipped a beat when I saw two very large ships from Bharata docked beyond the jetty. I hoped we would meet some of my countrymen and they might have some news of Harappa. I could see some activity on one of the ships with people moving about carrying boxes and sacks. The ships were gaily painted yellow and ochre mixed with blue stripes in the middle and a saffron flag flying on the central mast. There was the usual image of Varuna, the God of oceans at the prow in front of both ships.

As soon as the soldiers on the dock saw the royal ensign on our boats, they set down a few rowing boats into the river to help dock the huge boat safely and quickly. The dock and the path were cleared for us. The captain did not waste any time in lowering the gangplank to the dock for us to climb out. I could see sweat pouring down the side of his face despite the chill in the air. He was flustered, to say the least, and could not get off the boat fast enough. I could see the relief on his face when he found out that Enkidu was still alive. His face visually relaxed at the news and his eyebrows started to move again when there was commotion on the dock.

"Where is he? Is the boat here yet?"

All of us turned around to see a burly Gilgamesh rushing down the dock while his bodyguards were pushing everyone else out of the way of the emperor. He was all I had imagined him to be. He was stocky and extremely well-built and toned muscles were bulging out of his tunic. As he bulldozed his way down the dock with big strides, his head dress bobbed up and down. Long golden-brown tresses almost reached his shoulders. His long, silk robe, held fast at the neck by a golden tassel, was flying behind him as he rushed down the embankment. His footsteps sounded like thunder on the wooden platform of the dock. They were only made louder by the wooden soles with brass tacks underneath. It was a sight to behold with awe and fear.

The people on the dock knelt down with bowed heads as soon as they realized who was on the dock. The captain was flustered again at the sight of the emperor himself at the dock and started to sweat profusely.

"Make way for the emperor of Sumeria. On your knees,

soldiers," he shouted to the soldiers who were already petrified at the sight of their angry emperor dashing down the dock. He rushed forward to greet the emperor. "Greetings, O great emperor Gilgamesh. I bring you the great Meluhhan physician Upaashantha and the crown prince of Elam, Prince Shushun."

"Good, it is about time. We have no time to lose. You will have to hurry."

I stepped forward and greeted the emperor with folded hands with my head bowed slightly. I did not take my eyes off him. This was the way Harappans greeted each other. "*Namaste*, great emperor Gilgamesh. I bring greetings from the city of Harappa, the land of Bharata, and our great sages."

"Greetings, Master Upaashantha. Welcome to my country. I have heard a lot about you and your skill as a physician. I hope you will be able to save my dear friend, Enkidu," Gilgamesh replied in heavily-accented Sanskrit. Turning to Shushun, he said in Sumerian, "You must be the crown prince Shushun from Elam. My greetings to you and the great emperor Awan of Elam. I have been told that you have knowledge of Egyptian medicine."

"I bring greetings to you from my father, King Awan. I do have some knowledge of Egyptian medicine. I spent some time in Abju some time ago. But I cannot call myself a physician. I do not know enough of medicine to do that," Shushun replied, in perfect Sumerian.

There was no time for royal niceties and introduction to others. Time was of the utmost importance and we were rushed past the gawking spectators down the main street all the way to the palace where Enkidu lay dying. I had insisted on carrying my medical supplies with me and had sent messages earlier on for some roots and seeds that I did not have with myself. I was not sure how much of the stuff I had asked for would be there when I reached the palace. Sage Vasishta had promised to contact Master Ashwin for help. I had tried my best at contacting him myself through telepathy with no success. I still had not perfected the art of telepathy over vast distances. I hoped Master Ashwin would contact me soon.

The visible stress on the captain's face was making me more apprehensive than I already was. I did not even notice the impressive wooden doors of the city walls that Enkidu was supposed to have built for the emperor Gilgamesh. I did notice the canals constructed on either side of the main street. There was water everywhere. It was almost like the city was built on the banks of a network of canals. It kept the city pleasantly cool and as the sun was setting rapidly, it was getting chilly.

We were taken straight to the room where Enkidu was being nursed by Shamhat. I did not know what to expect because no one had told me exactly what was wrong with him. What I saw inside the room shook me for a minute. It took me back to the time when we had treated all those patients with chemical burns Magus Matriya had caused in the valley outside Harappa. We had lost men there due to chemical poisoning.

The figure lying on a low wooden bed was covered in blankets to his neck. The mask had been removed from his face. The face looked disfigured, from the little I could see. On closer inspection, it turned out that the chemical burns on the face was actually greenish, purulent liquid oozing out of wounds. Part of the nose had been eaten away from whatever was causing the disease and both eyebrows were missing. What must have once been a luxuriant beard now looked like a used brush with bits missing in the middle. His breathing was laborious and weak and he looked like he was on his last legs. My heart sank at his sight and I turned to look at Shushun. He was looking intently at the figure on the bed. The girl who was leaning forward to feed the figure on the bed stood up as we entered the room and smiled weakly at us. She must have been a stunning beauty once upon a time. Shadows of that radiant beauty were still discernible under all the lines in her face.

"Thank you, Master Upaashantha, for coming to save the love of my life."

She spoke in Akkadian, which I could barely understand. "I will be your servant for life if you can save my love."

Tears rolled down her beautiful cheeks. Lopa, who was just behind me, went forward and held her gently while consoling her.

"Take heart, my sister. My husband and his friend Prince Shushun will do their best to save your man." Shamhat started to sob uncontrollably and Lopa took her outside to console her. I turned to the emperor and asked,

"Can he speak any Sanskrit? I am not very good at either Akkadian or Sumerian. I need to know what happened to him and when."

Gilgamesh took a deep breath and started to speak. "Unfortunately, my friend Enkidu does not know either Akkadian or Sumerian and he definitely does not know Sanskrit. I'll have to tell you what happened. I was there when it happened." It took him some time to tell us all about a trip he had taken with his friend to a cedar forest, where they had fought with a deadly demon called Humbaba, who had hurt Enkidu during the fight and had cursed him at the end of the battle. There was deathly silence when he finished his narrative.

"We will need to examine him properly. What treatment has he had so far?" I asked.

"We have been using honey poultice and ginger paste on the wounds," a voice from the back of the room said in perfect Sanskrit. I turned around to see who it was. An elderly gentleman stepped forward and continued. "I am Upakrama, a Meluhhan physician from Lagash. I am one of the group of physicians looking after Master Enkidu recently. Before we came in, the royal physicians had applied palm leaf poultice with some paste underneath on the wounds."

"*Namaste*, Master Upakrama. I am indeed glad to meet you," I said with folded hands. "What is your opinion of his wounds and the disease?"

"You must forgive us, Master Upaashantha. But we have never seen anything like this before. He does not appear to be responding to anything we have done so far. His condition worsens day by day," Upakrama replied. By now, three other physicians had joined him in the room. "And he has high fever every night."

Shushun, who had been quiet all this time, now asked Upakrama, "Has he been eating and drinking well? How has his bowel movement been?"

All of the physicians looked at one another and looked blank. One of the younger ones started to say something when he was interrupted by the royal physician standing in one corner of the room. "I think he is being fed by his woman, Shamhat, regularly. We don't know about his bowel habits. His nurse might be able to tell you, though." I could detect a tone of resentment in his voice. He belonged to the old school who did not think mundane things such as food and bowel habits could be a part of the process of diagnosis. Our Master Ashwin always insisted that a person's food and bowel habits tell a physician more about the disease than any other form of examination.

"Then, why don't you get the nurse here, please?" Shushun said with some irritation.

"I am here, Prince Shushun," a faint voice said from the back of the room.

"Come forward, nurse. Don't be afraid," Gilgamesh said, raising his right hand up in the air. A little nurse stepped forward towards the patient slowly, and, glancing at the glaring royal physician, made a slight movement with her head, to show she was ready to speak. The royal physician had not uttered a word since we had come in. "Tell the prince and Master Physician Upaashantha what you know."

She kept her head down, occasionally glancing at the royal physician with some apprehension and said, "Master Enkidu has not been … eating at all … for the last few days. He has been taking … sips of the water and liquid gruel Shamhat prepares everyday for him". She stopped and looked at Shushun for some help. I could see Shushun smiling at her encouragingly. She continued again with some hesitation."He has not ... opened his bowel for the last three days and ... he passes a little urine, very dark in colour".

The words came slowly in broken sentences and she kept her head down all the while, except when she was glancing at the royal physician. She was obviously petrified of speaking in front of him and the emperor. The royal physician was getting more and more irate at being ignored almost completely.

"Don't be afraid, nurse. What you have told me is of immense importance and will help us treat your master." And turning to Gilgamesh, Shushun continued, "Now, we want some privacy to examine your friend. I would like everyone to please leave the room, apart from the nurse and ourselves."

"So be it. I will leave guards outside the door if you need anything. They will make sure nobody disturbs you."

Gilgamesh said this in one breath and walked out of the room. Every one walked out except the royal physician and the Meluhhan physicians. I was not sure how to tell these people to leave as well, when Parthava ushered them out saying, "And that means you as well. Master Upaashantha will send for you if you are needed." He gently pushed them out of the door, closing it behind him. I bent down at Enkidu and lifted his eyelids to see two sunken eyes almost dry and lifeless. That did not look good, I thought. His systems are shutting down. We were probably too late to be of any help to this man, I thought.

I turned to the nurse and said, in the best Sumerian that I could manage, "Can you undress him, please? You might need some help because we also need to get all the dressings removed for us to examine the wounds."

The nurse smiled and left the room without saying anything. I hoped that she had gone to get some help. Four nurses came into the room within minutes after she had gone off. They must have been waiting just outside the door, I thought. They were quite efficient with Enkidu. The clothes and the dressings were removed smoothly. Their actions were so smooth that Enkidu only moaned a couple of times when they were rolling him over for us to look at his back. His whole body appeared to have been covered in infected chemical burns. I could not understand that.

"The emperor said he had been scratched. Didn't he?" I asked Shushun, just to be sure.

"Yes, he did," Shushun replied, with a pensive look on his face. He was deep in thought.

"But these look like chemical burns. I don't understand."

"I have seen this once before. Someone I don't remember had been scratched by some swamp animal," Shushun said, after a minute or so of thinking. "The scratches were superficial, more like abrasions to start with but they soon turned septic with pus pouring out just like this."

"Anyway, we'll have to get all the wounds cleaned thoroughly and get rid of all the purulent material and whatever dressing they have been applying so far before starting our treatment."

Shushun spoke rapidly to the nurse, who nodded her head and started to clean all the wounds with fresh water. It took the four of them the better part of an hour to get everything cleaned up. In the meantime, we picked up some honey and dried seaweed powder from our bags and prepared a large amount of paste. I asked the guard at the door to get me some of the fresh *neem* leaves I had asked for earlier. Both of us worked hard with the nurses to dress all the wounds with the paste we had prepared and covered them with *neem* leaves. Parthava prepared some splints to stop him moving his arms unnecessarily. We bandaged his hands so he could not scratch his dressings off. I asked Lopa to prepare some *soma* juice from the extracts we carried with us. We watched as Shamhat managed to make Enkidu drink some of the *soma* juice. It must have been close to midnight when we finally decided to wait and see how he would respond and walked out of the room.

"I want one of you to keep constant vigil over him day and night. Feed him half a glass of *soma rasa* every hour with one glass of water. You must take turns throughout the night. Come and call us if there is any change in his condition," I said to the nurse as we walked out of the room. She smiled weakly again and appeared grateful. It must have been the first time she was being spoken to by a physician with some respect as a professional. "We will try not to disturb you, sir. Please get some rest."

It was quite surprising to hear her speaking quite fluently and without a stammer. I smiled and replied,

"Please don't hesitate to ask us if you are worried about anything. You have done an excellent job today."

That made all the nurses beam from ear to ear. They were shattered physically, but felt extremely happy at being appreciated. We bid them goodnight and followed the guard outside the room to our quarters to freshen up. It was not long before there was a knock on our door. It was the emperor himself, with half a dozen attendants carrying all sorts of delicious-looking items of food — fruits, freshly-baked bread, cooked meat, wine and spring water to drink.

"I hope I did not disturb you folks. Here is something to keep your strength up. I have just come back from Enkidu's chamber. He is already looking better. I am sure you will be able to cure him. I will be eternally grateful to you if he does recover."

Parthava had heard the noise and came out to investigate. Our group got together for a midnight feast in the garden of the palace. That is when I discovered Shu-ilishu and his wife were such wonderful singers. As we sat there drinking wine, Nisaba started humming a tune, only to be joined by Shu-ilishu turning it into a fabulous, musical evening. It was soulful and uplifting at the same time. It was quite late by the time we went to bed, tired but at the same time happy that we had achieved something.

I woke up the next morning thinking that there was something wrong. The nurses had not come to wake us up even once during the night. I hoped they were not too scared to call us and Enkidu had deteriorated through the night. I ran all the way to Enkidu's chamber and just as I was about to enter, the nurse opened the door and came out looking quite refreshed despite having spent all night tending to the patient. She smiled widely at the sight of me and said,

"Good morning, Master Upaashantha. I hope you slept well."

"Yes, yes. I am well. Good morning to you too," I was in too much of a rush for pleasantries. "Tell me first, how is the patient?"

She smiled even more widely before replying, "He is much better, thanks to you, sir. He actually ate some breakfast this morning for the first time and he is talking as well."

I could not control myself any longer and burst into the chamber. I was shocked to see the transformation in the patient. He was actually sitting up and drinking from the jug held by one of the junior nurses. He smiled when he saw me and said something which was barely audible. I could not understand him.

"He says thank you, sir." The nurse had followed me into the room and was now standing next to me.

"That is good. Please tell him that he is welcome. I hope he continues to recover like this. The next few days are going to be crucial. We have to be extra-vigilant." And turning to the nurse, I said, "I shall be back with my friend soon. Please continue the regime till then. You will need more nurses to help you, perhaps."

When I got back to our quarters, Lopa was already getting ready. After the morning routine and prayers, we went back to Enkidu's chamber to see the emperor waiting for us there. He was beaming from ear to ear and rushed to embrace Shushun and me when he saw us coming.

"My friend, Master Physician Upaashantha,you and your friend are magicians! You have brought my friend back from the jaws of death." And turning to Lopa, he said, "You have married the best physician in the world, madam. You are extremely lucky."

"Thank you, Your Highness. But we are not out of the woods yet. The poison has not left his body completely. The next few days are going to be crucial," I said, feeling rather embarrassed at all the adulation.

"It does not matter. I have not seen my Enkidu like this for a long time. At this rate, he might even be ready for hunting trips in a week. You do your magic and not even Goddess Ishtar can stop you."

I looked at Shushun, wary and in need of some tactful support. The emperor was getting carried away by the improvement the *soma rasa* had brought about. We still had to purge Enkidu's system of the poison which was killing him from within. Shushun intervened.

"You are extremely gracious, Emperor Gilgamesh. We have a long way to go before the poison is removed from your friend's body. We will do our best to help him purge the poison."

Gilgamesh suddenly stopped and looked at Shushun with a quizzical expression on his face.

"Do you mean to say he might still die?"

"Yes, Your Highness. If we are not able to purge his body of the poison which has been destroying it, we will not be able to save him," Shushun said, quietly and seriously. Gilgamesh was considerably chastened. He looked at me and said,

"No matter. I have faith in both of you. You do your best and I will make sure that the Goddess Ishtar does not take my Enkidu away from me." He quickly turned and walked out of the chamber without looking back.

I breathed a sigh of relief. "That was close. I hope we can manufacture the miracle the emperor expects us to work out of thin air. He loves his friend dearly."

"I find it extremely odd, however. This Enkidu is a coarse man of the jungle. There is nothing remotely noble about him," Parthava said. "How can the emperor have such feelings for him?"

"The two have been together now for a while. It is possible they have forged a strong bond of companionship. They have faced death and extreme danger together. Enkidu has saved him from a certain death at least once," Shushun was thinking aloud. "No wonder they have developed a lifelong bond. I am sure Enkidu would have reacted the same way about Gilgamesh."

Enkidu improved over the next couple of days. We still could not understand what he was saying, but he was talking a lot. Or should we say moaning a lot. He literally wailed most of the time he was awake. Finally, Shamhat had to translate what he was saying.

He was unhappy that he was ill and that he was dying. He blamed the whole thing on Shamhat. He blamed her for bringing him into the city and getting him involved with Gilgamesh. "I was happy in the jungle. I was happy till I met you."

Shamhat tried her best to explain that he had become 'civilised' only after he came to the city and the emperor would build a statue of Enkidu after he died. That would make him immortal. He would smile and quieten for a little while, only to start wailing again. We figured that the *soma* juice and Shamhat's ministrations were cheering him up for a little while, but it was by no means permanent.

On the fourth day problems started. He stopped eating again and refused point blank to drink anything. We had to force feed him. His urine stank and started to dwindle. He would ramble on inaudibly for sometime and then he would fall into a stupor. He was becoming more and more irrational during his waking hours. Shamhat was getting desperate and the emperor was spending more time in Enkidu's room. We had to force Gilgamesh out of the chamber at least once daily to attend to the dressings which in fact were healing, to everyone's surprise. The royal physician used to come everyday to look at Enkidu. Muttering something derisive under his breath, he would leave the room almost as soon as he entered. I was getting increasingly worried. We had been with Enkidu now for over a week and after the first spurt of improvement, nothing seemed to be working. There appeared to be a downward trend. I had been trying to contact Master Ashwin through telepathy since the first day without much luck. He finally did connect with me on the third night. He agreed with my method of treatment. That relieved me a little. Unfortunately, there seemed to be nothing for us to do but pray.

"What about Budii?" Lopa suddenly said on the eighth day when Enkidu was showing signs of further deterioration.

"What do you mean? Try his magic potion and powders?" I asked.

"Well, you have tried modern medicine and it does not seem to be working anymore. Why not try some Avestan magic?"

"I was going to say the same thing," Shushun said.

"I am not so sure," Budii said, thoughtfully. "I have never seen anything like this before. The chemical burns that magic spells cause normally yield to the treatment he is under. It is not as if we can reverse the spell, because it was not magic which has caused his wounds."

"You are right. Besides, I am not sure how the emperor or his royal priests would react if we start using Avestan magic in their country," I said.

The condition of Enkidu deteriorated over the next few days. The wounds were healing quite well, but he was rapidly going downhill. He had his lucid moments, and during these times he would speak to Shamhat and Gilgamesh. On the twelfth day, he was particularly lucid and spoke at length to both Shamhat and Gilgamesh. He told them the story of his life. How he had been raised by the forest animals and how he had lived in harmony with both the animals and plants of the forest. He still regretted coming into the city, despite making friends with Gilgamesh and Shamhat who adored him. His greatest lament was that he was going to die a common death. He was dying of a disease. He was not dying the heroic death he deserved. He knew he was going to die that day. He begged Gilgamesh not to leave his side that day.

There was nothing we could do. He had stopped drinking the *soma rasa* and the medicines Shushun had got the pharmacy to prepare. He asked for some meat and plenty of wine.

"I am going to die a happy man. I am going to die with a beautiful woman in my arms and a powerful friend by my side," he declared. Gilgamesh ordered the royal kitchen to prepare the best cuts and wine for him. Shamhat laid down next to him and caressed him, soothing his painful body. Quite surprisingly for someone who had never shown any hankering after music, Enkidu wanted music to be played in the chamber. The palace musicians came and sat down in the already crowded chamber and started playing the kind of music he preferred. They started slowly, with a low-pitched wind instrument joined by a drum beating at a rhythm of heartbeat followed by a string instrument. The music was so soulful that it brought tears into everyone's eyes. It was all too painful to watch. Lopa and Nisaba broke down and started to cry silently. I could see Shamhat smiling. She looked absolutely ravishing that night. She had taken special care to make herself beautiful for him. She was wearing his favourite clothes and looked like a young bride on her wedding night. As the music reached a crescendo and the drum started to beat slower, Enkidu opened his eyes and looked around at everyone and smiled as if to say that he was happy and closed his eyes. His chest stopped moving at that instant and I knew he was gone.

The music continued, Shamhat held onto her lover and Gilgamesh sat next to the bed holding Enkidu's hands for a long time. It is a picture that will stay in my mind and heart for the rest of my life, I thought. Here was a picture of friendship and love at its best. A man from the jungle, coarse, uneducated and uncultured for all intents and purposes, in the arms of one of the most beautiful women in the world and holding the hands of one of the most powerful men of the world and in the background, a most soulful music to bring tears out of one's heart.

After what appeared to be an eternity, Shushun tapped on Gilgamesh's shoulder. He turned around to look at Shushun.

There were tears in his eyes rolling down on his cheeks. The most powerful man in the world reduced to tears!

"I know. He is no more in this world. Goddess Ishtar has taken him to her abode. It is not fair. He belonged here, in this world, with me. How am I going to live without him next to me?"

He went on for a while, extolling the virtues of his friend Enkidu and how unfair it was that the gods had taken him away from him because he fought and defeated the demon Humbaba. Shushun tried to console him as best as he could.

"Just think of him being in a better place than this world."

"How can it be a better place than this? Gods don't have the right to have a better place all to themselves. I am going to show them. I am going to build my friend such a tomb in here that he won't want to leave. I will build him a tomb under the river so that the gods cannot take him even if they want to."

Tears rolled down his cheeks and his words came out amidst sobs and I was having difficulty following his Sumerian. All this time, Shamhat was holding onto a dead Enkidu, softly sobbing away. It took all of us to separate both of them from Enkidu and get his body prepared for the last rites. The royal priests were extremely efficient with this part of the work. The preparation was smooth and unobtrusive at the same time.

The emperor Gilgamesh fell apart at the seams. It was often difficult to reason with him. And at other times, it seemed he knew exactly what he was doing. He ordered the most elaborate funeral for his friend, one fit for a king with full royal honors. The funeral was as extravagant as that of Queen Puabi in Ur we had witnessed not too long ago. He wanted the small river, Ulaja, which was a tributary of Buranuna flowing down from Shuruppak, to be dammed up. The idea was to build a massive tomb under the river bed and let the river flow on top of it so that the gods could not reach his friend. He also ordered sculptors to build a statue of Enkidu, covered in leaves and bird feathers, as he would have lived in the forest. But when he spoke of building a temple to Enkidu, the royal priests put their feet down.

Gradually he cut himself off from public engagements, apart from supervising the construction of Enkidu's statue. He spent his time cut off from people in the palace in the company of temple prostitutes, inebriated with wine and beer. Whenever he turned up at the construction site of the memorial, he looked disheveled, unshaven and scraggy. He always appeared to have a jug of wine in his hand and his speech was slurred and he looked bleary-eyed all the time. Alcohol numbed him completely. We tried to get an audience at the palace with no luck. Shushun decided the best place to try and catch him was near the construction site one day.

He could barely stand up when we saw him. His speech was slurred and he looked bleary eyed and smelled of beer. His robe was soaked at places and covered in mud and grass where he had been rolling around. I could not believe this was the most powerful man on earth. Even under that alcoholic stupor, he recognized us and came towards where we were standing. Walked is an overstatement, he rolled over towards us was more like it. Even though his speech was slow and broken, we were taken aback by what he said.

"What is the point of all this? I am the most powerful emperor of the known world. Even the pharaohs bow down to me. And the pharaohs are living gods, or so they say! I represent divinity, they say. But I could not save my friend from death. I have to find a way to beat death. Why should it be an exclusive right of the gods?" He lamented to us as we watched the building of the platform on which Enkidu's idol would stand. His speech took us by surprise and none of us knew what to say. Then something I had not expected happened, the emperor started to sing. It was more like wailing than singing, and Shu-ilishu had to translate the words for me to understand what he was singing. This is how the song went:

"Hear me, Oh elders of Uruk, hear me, oh men.

I mourn for Enkidu, my friend,

I shriek in anguish like a mourner.

You, axe at my side, so trusty at my hand...

You, sword at my waist, shield in front of me,

You, my festal garment, a sash over my loins...

An evil demon appeared and took him away from me.

My friend, the swift mule, fleet wild ass of the mountain, panther of the wilderness,

Enkidu, my friend, the wild ass of the mountain, panther of the wilderness.

After we joined together and went up into the mountain,

Fought the Bull of Heaven and killed it,

And overwhelmed Humbaba, who lived in the cedar forest,

Now what is this sleep which has seized you?

You have turned back and do not hear me!"

The wailing went on for a long time. Shu-ilishu stopped translating as the words became increasingly garbled. Gilgamesh started to pull at his robes and tunic harder and harder as the wailing progressed, until by the end his clothes were in shreds. Tears rolled down his cheeks and his words became more unintelligible. He was sobbing his heart out and rolling about on the floor. All of us were standing there stunned into silence by this overt and rather excessive (I thought) display of grief.

"He is describing some kind of statue of Enkidu he has ordered to be built. Something about his chest being made of lapis lazuli, body made of precious stones like ruby, carnelian, agate, emerald and his skin to be made of gold," Shu-ilishu said. "He is going to put up this statue on a pedestal and make the citizens of Uruk worship him."

Shsuhun finally plucked up enough courage to say,

"We have heard that the eminent Sage Ziusudra in Shuruppak is immortal. We could ask him how he did it."

"You mean Utnapishtim? He was the ruler of Shuruppak before he became immortal and a sage," Gilgamesh replied. "But, no one knows where to find him."

"We do know that he lives in the middle of the Apsu in Shurppak. I believe the priest of the ziggurat of Enlil knows where the Apsu is," Shushun continued.

"Then that is where we will go," said Gilgamesh. And turning to all of us, he continued, "My friends, you have helped me during my last days with Enkidu. I want you to come with me to find Sage Utnapishtim and help me find the answer to immortality."

This was working out to be better than I thought. We were planning to ask for his help to find Ziusudra and the situation had turned on its own head. The emperor was asking for our help to find him. Our chances of finding this elusive sage suddenly looked great and almost assured.

"We would be honoured to help you find the sage, Your Highness," I said with alacrity.

Ziggurat of Enlil

A nd so it was that a few days later, we found ourselves in the royal boat once again. We were heading up north towards Shuruppak in search of the elusive Sage Ziusudra, or Utnapishtim as Gilgamesh called him. The boat was even more luxurious than the one we had used to travel there from Ur. It was not quite as big, but had several cabins for the emperor and his guests on the top deck. Gilgamesh appeared to have transformed. He looked almost normal, which was quite a change from his disheveled state the day before. He was already on the boat, waiting for us, and greeted us as we climbed aboard. The boat set off north towards Shuruppak at a gentle pace and we were again surrounded by the beautiful scenery of the river valley. There were reddish mountains and lush trees all around us and bushes giving a surreal appearance. The contrast of red sandstone cliffs bordered by deep dark green trees and bushes gradually thinning out into the pale yellow desert in the distance was breathtaking. We were still going against the current and it meant a lot of hard work for the oarsmen. The river meandered and took in several tributaries. As we went further north, the river narrowed in places with fast eddies when it passed through deep gorges of red sandstone. It was as if the river had gouged a path for itself through a crimson rock down to the sea, collecting little streams on the way. It was not long before we entered the river Ulaja which would take us to Shuruppak.

Gilgamesh appeared much calmer today and spent most of his time on the open deck speaking to us, asking us questions about our country and the city of Harappa. I was quite impressed by his knowledge of our culture. He appeared to have a fairly substantial knowledge of our scriptures, particularly the Rigveda. His command of Sanskrit, albeit heavily accented, was more than adequate. Once we were well on our way, he started to tell us about Sage Ziusudra. He explained that Utnapishtim meant 'one who found life' - it was a name which had been given to the sage after he had been blessed with immortality by God Enlil. He was the Lugal Atrahasis of Shuruppak until then. Once he attained immortality, his name was changed to Utnapishtim and he left the city for the forest in the middle of the Apsu. He also told us the story of Shuruppak. How it was once considered the center of the known universe and about King Shuruppak, who built the city and controlled all the cities in Sumeria for a long time.

"Ziusudra is similar to your *Maharshi*s in Meluhha. He is the direct descendant of the seven sages of Apsu who helped Enki create the world after the great deluge. He is widely travelled and has met several of your sages on his travels in Meluhha. If I am not mistaken, he has even been to Harappa. He always travelled incognito and is known to have the power of traveling long distances in an instant. He has had divine powers granted to him by none other than the Sun God Marduk. He knows answers to all questions. I hope he can help me."

He was looking wistfully into the distance, at a mountain where the glint of the sunrays made it look as if it was on fire. It was interesting that the Sumerians had seven sages similar to our Saptharshis in Bharata. Gilgamesh sighed deeply when he finished and turned around.

"I am sure Sage Ziusudra will be able to answer your questions," I replied.

"Now, tell me why you want to meet him."

I took him through the events of the previous few months, the story of the Magus Matreya and the Avestan attack and the futility of war. I could see he was interested in the events and said at the end,

"As I see it, war is justified for a king. It is the duty of a king to expand his country and provide for his citizens. As for the Magus and his spy, I cannot explain the greed of some men."

The rest of the journey went on without any mishap or excitement, unlike our trip to Uruk and we reached the docks of Shuruppak three days later. It was much smaller than either Ur or Uruk and seemed to have seen better days. The dock platform was crumbling in places and needed repairs in more than one place. Word that the emperor was coming to Shuruppak had obviously reached the city. There was a welcoming party at the dock which included the Lugal Upar-Tutu. We were given a grand welcome and taken to the palace of the lugal in the royal chariots, four-wheeled contraptions made of cedar wood and each pulled by four horses. The dock led into a wide main street which rose steeply but gradually to end in the grand palace gates. A huge square in front of the palace was lined by massive brick-built columns on either side. The columns were engraved with drawings of animals like lions, foxes and snakes as well as sheep and cats. The main street was lined with square builthouses, mainly made of sun-dried bricks which were pale yellow in colour. The wooden doors were gaily painted in bright, if somewhat garish colours. It was like being in a child's dream. Even the people wandering around the street were dressed colourfully. Most of the houses had at least one, if not more courtyards enclosed in a perimeter wall.

We could see the palace from the dock because it was on top of a hill in the city and it was probably the highest point of the city. Just to the left of the palace was the famous ziggurat of Enlil. It was an imposing structure occupying a vast expanse. It was built with red bricks, contrasting with the houses of the city. It was built on four levels. The first level was of the maximum height, measuring at least ten yards in height. A long staircase starting well away from the main building led to the top level. The climb was long, but the incline was gradual. There were staircases on the sides to go up to the second and third levels. The temple of Enlil was at the top level. The temple at the top glowed in the sunlight due to the precious and semiprecious stones in the wall. The walls of all the four levels sloped gently inwards to the top. The spire at the top of the temple reached out to heaven.

It was late afternoon by the time we reached the city and we could see plenty of activity on the streets as well as on the steps leading up to the temple. The high street ran diagonally across the main street and was full of shops selling all sorts of things: grapes, dates, foodgrains and jugs and vessels. It was a bustling city with a busy population.

"Welcome to our ancient city of Shuruppak, Your Highness. This is indeed an honour for the city." The Lugal was a rather thin, elderly man with graying hair and a clean-shaven face. He bowed his head to the emperor and nodded to us. "And welcome to the emperor's guests as well."

"Thank you, Lugal Upar-Tutu. We have come seeking the wise Sage Utnapishtim. I hope you will be able to help us find him."

At the sound of the name, several heads turned around and there was a sharp intake of breath from the royal priest who had also come to welcome the royal party. He was a well fed gentleman with a large belly which flopped every time he took a deep breath and every time he coughed. And he coughed almost incessantly. He gulped and said,

"You ... you want to see Sage Utnapishtim? Why? It is impossible. He is in the middle of the great Apsu. The way to Apsu is guarded by demons and ferocious scorpion men."

"We know it will not be easy, priest. I believe you know the way and you will lead us to him." It was not so much of a request as a command from Gilgamesh. All of us were looking curiously at this exchange which was getting rather comical. I could see the royal priest sweating profusely and his face went pale.

"Me? Come with you? I am not sure... I can't... you see..."

"What is the matter, royal priest? We have been told that you are the only one who knows the way to Apsu," Gilgamesh continued glaring at the man.

"I am sorry. But I can't... you see, my knees... my eyesight...," He rambled on and kept mumbling under his breath until Gilgamesh lost his temper and shouted at him,

"You will show us the way to the Apsu and you will take us to Sage Utnapishtim. Or else we will have your head cut off."

The royal priest immediately fell to his knees and touched Gilgamesh's feet.

"Please don't do that, Your Highness. Not my head. I will get killed if I go to Apsu. I have six young children to look after," he started to sob uncontrollably now.

"Have some nerve, man. You are the royal priest of Shuruppak." Gilgamesh turned to the Lugal and said, "See that this cretin prepares himself and takes us to the Apsu."

The Lugal was a virtuous man and did not bat an eyelid when he replied to Gilgamesh,

"Your Highness, I don't think the royal priest will be able to help you. I have a suspicion that he does not really know the way to the Apsu and I am sure he won't know how to get inside the Apsu to the sage's abode. We must seek the help of his predecessor, who still lives in the ziggurat. I will take you to see him tomorrow." And turning to us, he continued, "He is very old but extremely knowledgeable. I am sure he will be able to tell you how to get to the wise sage."

That appeared to calm the emperor down somewhat. We breathed a sigh of relief as well. I was beginning to think that this was a wasted trip if the only man who was supposed to know the way refused to help and I was not too keen on seeing another beheading. The last one I had seen in the forests of Saraswatha several years ago still gave me nightmares.

"Get out of my sight. I don't want to see your ugly face again."

And Gilgamesh kicked the kneeling royal priest with a force that threw the fat man quite a few yards away. "Take him away and you better find someone better to be the royal priest of the temple. God Enlil will not be happy with such a spineless man to worship the God of storm."

The royal priest was unceremoniously rushed out of the angry emperor's presence, still whimpering under his breath.

"If it pleases Your Highness, we will take you into the palace where you can rest for tonight and we will go tomorrow to see the old man at the ziggurat," the lugal said.

"Thank you, Lugal. I hope this old man of yours is better than that wimp," Gilgamesh replied with undisguised scorn and stomped off towards the palace followed by the Lugal. We looked at each other, unsure what to do next.

"We might as well follow them," Parthava said and went after them. The crowd that had gathered on the jetty and the dock held their heads down most of the time and continued to do so. None of them dared lift their heads up for the fear of losing them altogether! We were shown our quarters within the palace and we promptly went to town to have a look at the sights of Shuruppak.

It was yet another Sumerian town with its shops, inns and beer houses. Parthava wanted to taste the local cuisine and the famed wine of Shuruppak. We walked into the nearest tavern that he could find. The landlord lifted his head as we walked in through the door and smiled as he walked across to us. It was a big room with several tables spread around. Most of the tables were occupied by men and women already drinking from silver jugs. Waitresses were pouring wine from an amphora. Some were sipping beer in large, earthenware jugs, constantly being refilled by eager waitresses carrying large pots on their waists. There was a hive of activity which suddenly stopped for a moment to look at us as we entered the room, before they went back to their drinks. All of them stared at us for a while, making us feel rather uncomfortable. Just as we were wondering if we had a mistake and whether it would be wiser to get out of the tavern, a door at the back opened and a large muscular chap walked in, his hands held out in a welcoming gesture and a forced grin on his scarred face.

"Welcome, friends. I am Anzud Sud, the landlord of this tavern. Have a seat and ignore the local ignoramus. They are harmless, though. And I'll serve you the best beer in the world." He pointed to a table with benches on four sides of it. He spoke Akkadian with an accent I could not quite place.

"Thank you, landlord. We were actually looking for your famous wine, if you have any," Shushun said.

"I certainly do. You will not find better wine anywhere in Sumeria," he said, smiling broadly and wiping invisible dust off the table with a piece of linen. "I will be with you in a minute," he said and disappeared behind the door at the back of the big room.

"I cannot place his accent. I don't think he is Sumerian," I said.

"I am very impressed, Upaas. Your Akkadian has improved a lot. Well done. You recognized the accent," Shu-Ilishu said with a smile. "You are right. He is not Sumerian or Akkadian. He is a Gutian."

"A Gutian? Working in Sumeria?" Parthava was concerned.

"There have been Gutians working not only in Sumeria but also in Elam," Shushun replied. "Most of them are law-abiding and harmless people".

Something caught my eye just then. The landlord appeared to have stopped just behind the door and was watching us from the shadows. He was talking to someone we could not see behind the door. There were lots of gesticulations and grunts, but we could not hear anything. The others had their backs to the door and could not see any of this apart from Lopa who was sitting next to me. She looked at me and gave me a nudge.

"I am not sure if everything here is as they seem," I said with my head bent down.

"What do you mean?" Parthava said. looking around the hall. "It all seems pretty innocuous to me."

"Don't look now. But, the landlord has been standing behind the door in the shadows and watching us for a while."

"That is strange. Why would he do that?" Shushun asked.

"It is definitely odd. We better be careful now," Shu-ilishu replied.

"You men are all the same. Seeing demons in every dark corner," Lopa said, with a smile.

"All the same, there is no harm in being careful," I replied. "Something else you might notice. The room has become very quiet."

The tavern which had been bustling with energy only

moments before, was suddenly quiet. There was a scraping noise of a chair being pushed back followed by a couple more. We could see some of them moving towards the side of the room which was in darkness. There was one table at the far end of the room which had half a dozen men drinking beer in large jugs and had their weapons on the table in open view. They did not look like any soldiers I had seen. They stopped their drinking, put the jugs down on the table and stood up slowly with a purposeful movement. It did not look good. By now, I was quite certain that the landlord was up to no good. I wished we had picked up the weapons from our wagon before coming here. It was too late now. The others had noticed it as well.

"I think we should move towards the door slowly and hope for the best," Parthava said. "I will cover your backs and catch up with you."

I was just going to protest along with everyone else at the table at this gallant gesture of Parthava, when the door flung open behind us and Me-ulang, the captain of the guards who had picked us up from Ur, walked in with some of his soldiers, still armed to the teeth. The four of them stood at the door taking stock of the situation and obviously realised what was happening. He looked at us getting ready to leave and the six armed men movied towards us purposefully. He smiled at me and drew his sword out of the scabbard. His men did the same.

"No one is going to do anything silly now. We don't want any trouble. I have a company of soldiers surrounding this building as we speak." The captain said quietly, but everyone could hear him. "So, I would not even think about escaping."

We were taken aback, as much as the rest of the drinkers in the tavern. The six armed men sat back on their benches and the landlord crept back into the room again with a beaming smile and outstretched hands.

"Welcome, captain. There is not going to be any trouble. We were just going to take care of your guests."

"You can stop it right there, landlord. I have heard about you and your tavern. If you care for your life, don't make any sudden moves. I have two expert marksmen pointing their arrows at your heart. In such a small room as this, it is unlikely they will miss." And he turned to us. "My apologies, Master Upaashantha and Prince Shushun. I should have warned you of certain places in Shuruppak which are not very friendly. I have an escort waiting outside for you who will take you back to the palace."

The two men had their bows loaded and ready standing just to the side of the captain. Their hands were steady and eyes unblinking. Nobody doubted their strength of purpose or intentions.

"Thank you, captain. We are again grateful to you for your timely help," I replied.

"You are welcome. We were on our way to the Kengi when we heard that you were seen going into this tavern. This is not a safe place for you," and turning to the landlord, he continued, "As for you, the landlord, my commander and the general of the army of Shuruppak have a few questions to ask you."

As we walked back out into the sunshine, I turned to Shu-ilishu and asked,

"Where is Kengi?"

"Oh. It is the garrison town just outside of Shuruppak which is shared by the armies of all the city states. One can find the armies of most cities billeted there at any time. Anyone can ask for help from Kengi when they are in trouble".

"Interesting. I had not heard of that before," Shushun said. "But why here? What is special about Shuruppak?"

"I am not too sure. I suspect it is geographical. Historically, the threat has always been from the north and the Gutians from the Zubi mountains in the east and, I suppose, Shuruppak lends itself as a central point," Shu-ilishu replied, looking rather doubtful.

"That is definitely an interesting concept," Shushun continued. "I must have a look at this Kengi if it is possible. There may be a lesson for us Elamites to learn here."

"We can ask Gilgamesh tomorrow," Shu-ilishu replied. "I think we better be getting back to the palace before we get into anymore trouble."

Our sojourn into the city was thus short-lived, much to the disappointment of Parthava who was looking forward to the local cuisine. But it was not a total washout as we were well fed and watered in the palace that night. As we bid each other good night, Gilgamesh entered the dining room of the palace and said,

"I heard what happened in the city today. I must apologise for not letting you have an escort to go into the town." He looked serious as he said that. "Gutians have been rather active in these parts and they play dirty. They resort to tactics such as kidnapping and murder to get their own and you are ripe candidates for a kidnap. But they are good workers and a lot of landlords use them in their farms around Shuruppak."

"We must apologise to you too, Your Highness," Shushun was quick with his response. "We should have taken your permission before venturing out into the unknown."

"No matter. It was fortuitous that the captain of the guards had just reached the city with your wagon," Gilgamesh replied. "We will be going to the ziggurat of Enlil tomorrow to meet the old priest. I don't want to waste any more time to find out about the Apsu."

We were indeed looking forward to meeting this old man who had actually met Sage Ziusudra and knew the way into the famed Apsu. All of us were ready early next morning, eager to start the journey. We had decided to go to the Kengi and pick up our weapons before we went to the ziggurat.

The sun was just peeping out from behind the tip of the temple spire as we approached the ziggurat the next morning. As the sun rose overhead, it bathed the entire ziggurat with an orange glow which made the red building look as if it was on fire. There were a few thin, wispy layers of cloud on the eastern horizon. This made the ziggurat look like a burning falcon about to spread its wings and take flight. The long staircase to the top looked like the beak of the falcon and the entire scene was surreal. All of us were taking in this amazing scene, and climbed up the long staircase in silence. It took us a good half an hour to reach the top and we were nicely warmed up by the time we reached the temple at the top.

It was not very high compared to the ziggurats of Uruk or Ur, but it still had breathtaking views of the city and beyond, from the top. The city was slightly smaller than Lagash, surrounded by the ever-present city walls and the four gates. There was the main street, climbing from the river, and a high street intersecting each other in the middle. The roads were not straight and even, like what we see in Bharata and often narrowed quite a bit in places. The small streets were in a haphazard fashion and even narrower, barely allowing a horse rider, let alone a cart. The houses were square sundried mud-brick structures, built and packed together, mostly single storey with some two storeyed houses. The quarter nearest to the palace was obviously more affluent with large houses, with some of them going up to three floors. The largest building was a multi-storeyed building which straddled the high street and was very close to the affluent part of the city. It was massive, even bigger than the palace. It appeared to be the centre of a lot of human activity. A number of people went in and out of it carrying bags over their shoulders. I turned to the Lugal Upar-Tutu, who had accompanied us and asked him what it was. He smiled and replied,

"That, Master Upaashantha, is our pride and joy. It is the school for scribes. It is the biggest such school in Sumeria and everyone comes to Shuruppak to learn how to read and write. We have produced some famous scribes. The most famous one is King Shuruppak himselfwho wrote down the 'Instructions.'" He said with a huge amount of pride.

"King Shuruppak? Who…?" But before I could complete the question, a quiet voice from behind me said,

"He was the wise king of antiquity who made this city what it is now and it is named after him. Also, he was the greatest scribe of all."

I turned around to see an ancient man, frail, bald, with a gray beard that almost touched his chest. He was leaning on a gnarled staff in his right hand. His face was wrinkled and difficult to make out the features, but his eyes were sharp and there was the glow of knowledge in it. He had crept up silently on us as we were facing the city and admiring the views. Even Gilgamesh was taken aback at the suddenness. It was the Lugal who recovered first and said with folded hands,

"Greetings, oh wise Sage Ishme. I have brought some visitors to see you."

"So I see, Lugal Upar-Tutu," he replied, with a twinkle in his eyes. Old he might be but his eyes were sharp and missed nothing. What he said next took all of us by surprise, "Welcome to my humble abode, Emperor Gilagmesh, crown Prince Shuhun of Elam and the physician from Meluhha. And welcome to you, Master Shu-ilishu, the translator from Lagash. I am also honoured to have the ladies, Lopa and Nisaba here. I am sure Magus Budii will be of immense help in your journey through the Apsu. And I am not ignoring Master Parthava, the brave soldier, either. Welcome to all of you."

After that long speech, everything was deathly quiet for a while because none of us knew what to say to the old sage.

"I am amazed at your powers, great Sage Ishme. You already know why we are here. I do hope you will be able to help us." It was Gilagmesh who broke the silence.

"Please come inside, out of the sun, and we will discuss your problems and see if this old man can be of any use to the most powerful man in the world." He said this, turned around and walked slowly back into the temple with the wooden staff making a loud clicking sound on the stone floor. We followed him into the temple. I could not help noticing that the walls on either side of the corridor had quite extensive writing on them mixed with animal motifs. Lions, mainly with some sheep and snakes in between. It was written in a language I could not read. I stopped at the end of the corridor just before the door, trying to figure out if I could read it.

"That is the text of the 'Instructions of Shuruppak'," The old sage said behind me, from across the other side of the door.

"What are the instructions for?" I asked.

"They are the messages of King Shuruppak to his son Ziusudra," said the wise man and he came back into the corridor. "Here, let me read some of these out to you.

'In those days, in those far, remote days, in those nights, in those far, remote nights, in those years, in those far, remote years, at that time the wise one who knew how to speak in elaborate words lived in the land.

'My son, let me give you instructions,

May you pay attention to them!

Do not neglect my instructions!

Do not place a field on a road, it is disastrous.

Do not buy an ass.

Do not build a house in a field.

Do not buy a prostitute, it is horrible.'"

He moved further down the corridor and said, "Some of these are as good as the laws of the land. Here are some more – *'You should not make a well in your field, people will cause damage to it for you. You should not place your house next to a public square, there is always a crowd.'* And there are some wise words to help one lead a good life – *'You should not vouch for someone; that man will have hold on you; and you yourself, you should not let somebody vouch for you; that man will despise you.'* It goes on and if you follow his instructions, you will lead a long and fruitful life."

"Thank you, great sage. I am really impressed by the wisdom in those words. I would very much like to read the entire text someday. They are very similar to the laws laid down by our own *Swayambhuva* Manu at the dawn of time," I replied, following him back in through the door. He turned and smiled at me before saying,

"You will, my son, if you come back from the Apsu. The ancient Manu's laws from Meluhha have been repeated by several cultures and will be repeated again and again all over the world, mark my words."

The others were waiting rather impatiently in the temple for the old sage to finish and get back to the job in hand—to show them the way to and inside Apsu. Gilgamesh was getting rather impatient.

"We will certainly return after meeting Sage Ziusudra. Now, let us not waste any more time. Please tell us the way."

"I will certainly impart the way to Apsu in your minds if you pay attention to my instructions," Sage Ishme said as he turned and walked towards a tiny door at the back recess in the wall. "Please follow me inside and be careful you don't hit your head against the door."

We could not see anything inside once the door was opened, and it was pitch black inside. The door was really small and narrow. I am not very big and even I had to bend down and squeeze through it. Once inside, I had to wait a couple of minutes to get used to the darkness before I could see anything. It was quite a large, windowless room and the sage was standing at the far end, facing us. There was a huge, open cauldron in front of him.

"Please close the door behind you once all of you are inside," the sage instructed. Parthava, who was the last one, came in and closed the door. "And lock it, please. Now you will need to watch me closely and do exactly as I say. No questions asked".

Parthava locked the door so no one from outside could get in or even hear us. It was so dark that we could barely see one another. It was quite chilly inside, despite the rising temperature outside the room. The old sage walked to the corner of the room, bent down to pick something up from the floor and walked back to the cauldron. He had a cloth pouch in his hand from which he took out some powder and threw it into the cauldron. There was a swoosh, and the cauldron burst into bright orange flames. It took us all by surprise. Even Budii, who was used to such things, gasped. The old man walked to the other corner and signaled to Parthava. He pointed to a brass lever on the wall and whispered something to him. Parthava reached up and pulled the lever down. As the lever came down, I could hear loud metal clicking and clanging noises at a distance somewhere inside followed by a hissing noise and felt a draft of wind blowing against my cheeks. There was a faint smell of camphor mixed with the smell of belladonna. By now, the flame in the cauldron had become a roaring fire, but still there was not much light in the room and no smoke. We started to feel cold, despite the roaring fire right in front of us. The entire atmosphere was really rather strange.

The old sage raised his arms to the ceiling and started slowly chanting in a language that sounded like chaste Sumerian. I could barely understand him. The ceiling started reverberating with the sound of a low, clear whistle. The whistling sound transformed into a low-pitched horn which rose to a crescendo before diminishing into a rhythm kept up by a kettle drum. The combination of the rhythmic chanting, the drums and the horn was actually very soothing and I was trying to keep myself awake. Sage Ishme stopped chanting and opened his eyes.

"Please come, one at a time, and drink the juice which will give you the strength and the knowledge to go into the Apsu and come back".

As each of us slowly walked up to him, he dipped a brass jug into the burning cauldron and brought out some kind of smoking liquid. I could not see what was in the jug because it was covered in thick, heavy smoke which stayed put at the mouth of the cauldron. It did not rise, it kept flowing out the jug, more like thick soup spilling over onto the table. It was tasteless and it must have disappeared in my mouth because I could barely feel the liquid going down my throat. As I came back to my place in the room, I started to feel light-headed, and soon he resumed his chanting and, by now, the sound had increased in intensity and the rhythm had changed to a faster beat. The beat seemed to keep up with my heartbeat or was it my imagination? I swear I could hear a whole group of sages chanting, not just one old sage. The last thing I remember was that the room had given way to a large clearing in a forest. Many sages were swirling around the burning cauldron and, at that moment, everything went black.

The Apsu

The lake looked more beautiful than ever and Lopa looked absolutely gorgeous. Was she becoming more beautiful everyday? Was that possible? We were sitting beside the lake in our favourite place. The place where I brought Lopa the first time. I was sitting with my back against the *amra* tree and Lopa had her head on my lap. We had left Harappa that afternoon on our horses, me on my favourite Shankara and Lopa on her Elamite steed. My mother had cooked a delicious dinner and I could still taste the sweet honey on my tongue.

I don't remember how long we had been sitting there throwing stones into the lake and eating the *amra* fruit that I had dropped with my slingshot. Lopa had been talking for a long time about her family, her brothers and sisters and her mother. She missed her sister most. The lake was placid, with not a ripple on the water. The lotus blossoms were in full bloom, and they were showing off the bright pink, yellow and spotless white petals. The mesmerizing scent of the flowers wafted across to where we were sitting because of the gentle breeze. The sun was going slowly down on the horizon and now it looked like a large, orange ball sitting on the still waters of the lake. I could see the Pariyatra mountains in the distance with the snow caps getting bigger with the onset of winter. It was so peaceful and lovely that I did not want the moment to end. I wished I could freeze time at that moment, with the love of my life on my lap and this wondrous bounty of nature around me.

I looked down into the deep, dark eyes of my love and bent down to kiss her soft lips when someone tapped on my shoulder. I turned around, startled, as I had thought we were alone. But there was no one. A disembodied voice said,

"Wake up, Upaashantha. You have work to do. You have been shown the way to Apsu and how to get through it." It was Sage Vasishta's voice speaking to me. "You have a long way to go. You have the responsibility of taking the emperor Gilgamesh and Shushun to their destiny of meeting Sage Ziusudra."

I could not understand. What Gilgamesh? What Ziusudra? Someone was shaking me rather violently by the shoulder.

"Upaas. Wake up. It is time to go now." It was Shushun leaning over me and trying his best to wake me up. I had come down to reality with a thud. It had been a beautiful dream while it lasted. I was annoyed with Shushun for breaking my dream. I stood up, wiping my eyes, to see the rest of them getting ready and getting on their horses, even Lopa. All of them were dressed for a journey and loaded with weapons. Emperor Gilgamesh was wearing his leather tunic anda short cape and leather sandals held together with straps. He had a leather cap on his head and was carrying a short bow and a quiver full of arrows slung on the side of his horse. There were a couple of long spears and a mace as well on the side of his horse.

Shushun and Parthava were dressed like Sumerian soldiers, in short linen tunics, short capes and leather belts. Both of them carried their bows and Parthava had a short, curved knife at the waist and a short blade stuck to the straps on his left calf. Shushun carried a sword in the scabbard at the waist. Even Lopa was armed to the teeth. Lopa, again, was a sight for sore eyes. Even in a soldier's attire, she looked gorgeous and a goddess of love, I thought. She was draped in white clothes, tightly wrapped around the legs and the top held together by a leather belt. I looked down at myself. I could not remember changing into these soldier's clothes. A short tunic made of cream brown linen with a leather belt around my waist and a short sword in the scabbard. I had my trusty bow on my shoulder and when I stood up finally, I saw my horse tethered to the tree with a long spear and two quivers full of arrows strapped to its sides.

"But, where are Shu-ilishu and Nisaba?" I asked, not seeing them anywhere.

"We thought you might be able to tell us," Shushun replied. I racked my brain to understand what had happened. Sage Ishme's voice said, 'They are civilians and there is no reason for them to risk their lives.' I tried to explain to the rest of the group that they decided to return to Lagash and their farm.

Only Budii looked really different. He was wearing a long robe and a headdress of nondescript colour. He was carrying his old satchel over his shoulder and there were two other bags on the horse, no doubt containing his magical pots and potions. He was obviously disappointed that his friends had left without saying goodbye.

Everyone was looking at me expectantly. They obviously were expecting something from me. As I climbed the horse, my toe hit something on the saddle and a sharp pain seared through me. Suddenly, everything came back to me. The visit to the old sage in the ziggurat, the smoke-filled room, the chanting and the haunting music coming from a distance. The last thing I remembered was drinking the smoky liquid the old sage had given me. That is when it came to me, the images of paths, forests, the twin mountain peaks, the waterfall, the lions and the water.

"For some reason, the sage has given you full instructions of the path we have to take." It was the emperor speaking. "You will have to take us to the Apsu."

"Of course. I remember now," I said, coming out of a reverie. "We better start as there is a long way to go to Mount Mashu. Come on, Parthava, I'll race you to the top of that hill."

As we reached the top of the hill at a trot, I stopped and looked back to see my group. They were not too far behind. As my eyes scanned the hillside, the city of Shuruppak came into view. I could see the spire at the top of the ziggurat shining in the light of the rising sun. I could see the top of the large scribe school building as well as smoke rising out of some of the larger houses. The palace top, with its bastions in the corners still in the shadows looked somewhat forbidding. The huge grain silos dotted the western borders of the city just inside the walls. The huge city wall obscured the rest of the city and the guards were busy pacing up and down on top of the walls.

The citizens would be stirring in their houses and getting ready for the day. Women would have been up at the crack of dawn to get breakfast ready for their men. Men would be getting the fire in the bathroom stocked up for hot water. I was impressed by the cleanliness of the Sumerians. They cared for cleanliness as much as we, the Harappans, did. They bathed at least once a day and washed their feet before entering any house or temple. We were not too far north of the city and I could see the river meandering past the city walls on the west. I traced the river north, as it curved around a high place and disappeared. That was where we were headed, I thought. And then we were to follow the river before going west again.

By now all of them had caught up with me and I turned back towards the path at the high place near the river. The path was wide enough for two carts to pass at a time. The ride was quite easy and smooth and we made good time. We had reached the valley (the one with red stone cliffs on either side of the fast-flowing river) by nightfall. I knew we would have to leave the path soon and head towards the cedar forest once we left the valley. The valley with steep rocky cliffs and jagged edges at the top, made a perfect place to rest for the night. No one apart from a monkey or a bird could get down those cliffs. There were no paths to climb down even for a mountain goat. This was Gutian country and well-known for ambushes.

The valley floor was lush with huge trees and bushes on either side of the river. In some places, the vegetation was so dense that we could not see the river. We were in a clearing surrounded by large red boulders and away from the path. I thought this would be a perfect place to rest for the night. Shushun and Parthava agreed.

"I think we should rest here, Your Highness, for the night, before going into the cedar forest," Shushun said.

"You are right. If we post a sentry on that rock over there, we should be well-protected from any ambush," Gilgamesh replied.

The sun was going down and there was a chill in the air. Parthava had a roaring fire going by now. The horses had been tethered to a tree at the edge of the clearing and they were peacefully chewing on the leafy branches of the tree.

"We will take turns to keep watch. I will take the first watch and wake Upaas up at midnight," volunteered Parthava.

A combination of physical exhaustion along with the residual effects of the potion that old sage of the ziggurat had given us, mixed with a stomach full of excellent meal cooked by Parthava and Lopa with roast meat had put us in deep slumber. A deep growl woke me up. I woke up thinking that I must have been dreaming. The fire was still burning, obviously stroked up by Parthava. I could see him sitting on top of the large rock in the distance looking towards the path away from the face of the cliff. Just as I was about to close my eyes, I heard the growl again. This time it was unmistakable. It was coming from the direction of the cliffs. I sat up bolt upright, reaching for my bow. Parthava must have heard it at the same time as me. He jumped down from the rock and came running towards the camp. He was crouching as he ran towards the cliffs and stopped when he saw me getting up.

"Lions. A pride of lions by the sound of the growls," he said.

"We better wake the others."

"You do that. I'll go and scout the area." And Parthava ran off towards the cliff. I managed to wake the rest of them as quietly as I could. We grabbed our weapons and moved towards the cliffs. The growls had stopped completely by now. The horses were becoming restless and started to neigh loudly.

"Are you sure you heard lions?" Gilgamesh asked, having listened intently for the growls and not hearing anything.

"I am certain. Parthava has gone ahead, scouting," I said. Parthava was back before I could finish the sentence.

"There are at least five of them that I can see. They are finishing off an onager not far from here," he said. "That will not fill their stomach and they will be looking for more prey."

We started discussing what to do. Should we try to escape or face the lions?

"I have never run away from danger before and I am not going to start now," Gilgamesh stated. "We should increase the watch to two people and the rest should get some sleep. I would be quite happy to stay up and take the watch." "No, Your Highness. I will keep Parthava company and we will wake you up if there is any sign of danger," I said.

All of them went back to their places. I could see Gilagamesh still had his hands on his sword as he lay down. Parthava went to the horses to calm them down. I added a few more sticks onto the fire. I had heard somewhere that lions were scared of fire. It was best to keep a large fire burning to scare the lions off. We sat down again on the rock, ready to stay awake throughout the night.

It was just after midnight as the moon was right at the top when the attack took place. We were chatting away about Harappa, our adventures of the previous year, the war and the Magus when suddenly Parthava shushed me. The rustling sound was so faint that I was surprised Parthava heard it. The first thing I saw were their eyes peering through the darkness amongst the bushes. It looked like they were just sitting there, waiting. They were staring at the sleeping figures with unblinking eyes.

"There are two of them," I whispered.

"Three," Parthava said, getting his bow ready and reaching for his quiver. "Then there are two in the bushes at the edge and one behind the rock to our right. I'll take the one on the right and you take the other one. We better wake Shushun."

He took a small stone and threw it at the sleeping figure of Shushun who woke up with a start and immediately grabbed his bow, staring in our direction. Both of us had our hands to our mouth, signaling him to be quiet. As soon as he looked at us still lying down, I pointed my finger at the bushes and raised three fingers. He was sharp, despite having woken up from deep sleep, and caught on to what was happening. He grabbed his bow and the quiver which was lying next to him. I thought it was best that we take the initiative before the lions decided to attack. Lions have an inordinate amount of patience and could have sat there stalking us the entire night if necessary. It was best that we took advantage as we could see them and they were stationary, making an easier target. I signaled Shushun to aim at the lion near the rock behind the bushes. I loaded my bow as did the other two and fired the first arrow at the lion on the right.

Thinking back, I am not sure that it was a wise decision. All hell broke loose as soon as our arrows hit their targets. We were literally rampaged by a horde of lions. There were many more of them. Our assumption of three lions was completely wrong. The snarling onslaught woke up the entire camp and there were arrows flying in all directions. We were now virtually face to face with the lions and I saw one of the lions had Gilgamesh pinned to the ground. The next thing I saw was Parthava flying onto the back of the lion with,

"*Jai! Har har Mahadev! Shambho Mahadev!*"

He pulled out an axe from his waist and buried it in the neck of the lion just as it was going to hit the emperor with his paw. I was too busy trying to stop one of them charging at me. I was loading the bow as fast as I could and it still kept hurtling towards me. Finally, I picked up the spear and braced myself as the lion lunged at me. I squeezed my eyes shut waiting for the fatal blow. I was flattened by the heavy lion, but the expected attack did not come. It must have weighed a ton and I had difficulty pushing the lion off me. As I stood up with my hand on the sword at my waist, in case another of the lions attacked me, Budii decided to take part. There was a loud bang and a huge orange flame sprang out of the fire in the middle of the camp. It looked like the whole world had caught fire. I was completely blinded by the bright light.

It took me a while to realize what had happened. Budii had thrown one of his satchels into the fire. That was what had caused the huge explosion and flames. It had frightened not only us, but also the lions. They had run off into the darkness. I could see Gilgamesh struggling to push off the lion which was lying on top of him. I ran across to give him a hand. He had sunk his sword to the hilt into the chest of the animal. We had managed to get out of the scrape virtually unscathed, apart from some minor scrapes and bruises.

"This place, obviously, is not safe for us to stay any longer," Shushun was the first to recover. "We better move to an open space where we can see all around."

That meant moving out of the valley and into the dry prairie land further west.

"I agree with Prince Shushun," Gilgamesh replied. "Let's move out into the open land."

I was holding Lopa in my arms, more as a security blanket for myself than anything else. She looked into my eyes and smiled.

"What are you thinking about, love?"

"Nothing. I have made a mistake by bringing you in here. The whole trip looks dangerous to me," I said, distinctly worried and I was sure she would pick that up from my voice. "I would be worse than the emperor was when Enkidu died if anything were to happen to you. I would not be able to live without you."

She just smiled and held me even tighter before replying,

"Upaas, dear, don't forget that I am a trained warrior and I would not miss this trip and the chance of meeting one of the greatest sages of our times for anything."

Before I could protest, Lopa kissed me on my lips and hurried off. Parthava brought the horses and everyone was getting ready to move out. Shushun and Gilgamesh had doused the fire by now. We travelled north first before turning west. We left the valley for the open prairie. We started to climb and, before long, we came to a spot which looked like a high plateau. We could see all around for miles even under the dull light of a waning moon and stars. Some time was still left for the sun to rise, so we decided to get some sleep. Shushun and Budii kept watch.

I saw the eastern horizon light up. First, it was streaks of dark magenta outlining the little mists of cloud floating very low, almost near the horizon. I could just see the dark shadows of birds high up in the sky as large groups of them flew overhead. As I watched, the entire eastern horizon was swathed in bright dark reddish orange and the small crescent of the sun peeping over the thin line of trees in the distance. The sun changed colours quickly to dark red and then to bright yellow before hitting me in the eye with its brilliant luminescence that I had to avert my eyes.

As I moved my head to the north to avoid being stung by the bright light, I saw them. It was a cluster of mountains in the distance, each higher than the other. The pale yellow sandy prairie changed gradually to green highrise carpets merging ever so gently into the thick green carpet on the hills. Small rolling low hills covered in green carpet gave way to higher, pinkish gray stony mountains. One of them stood out against all, reaching up to the sky. It was tall and somehow foreboding, with its southern face shining in the early morning sun and the rest still in darkness. It was Mount Mashu in the middle of Apsu. The twin peaks of Mount Mashu have been called the guardians of the night and day, and the sun and the moon. The jagged peaks were slightly uneven, one being higher than the other. Both the peaks were snow-capped and looked as if they ruled the surrounding terrain. The sunrays bounced off the snow caps; the snow caps shone like jewels. The Apsu was still hidden amidst the little hills and the dense forest that covered the hills. That was my first view of the mountains we were heading towards. It looked like an awful long way from where we were. I better get everyone going soon, if we were to make it before sunset, I thought.

"It is an awesome sight. Isn't it?" I was taken a little aback by the voice of Lopa who had sneaked up on me. "You were lost in your own there. I can see why now. It is beautiful and at the same time scary to look at. Is that where we are going?"

I smiled, seeing my Lopa nice and fresh even that early in the morning. I took her in my arms and kissed her and she responded. Still holding her in my arms, I said,

"Yes. That is where Gilgamesh, Budii, Shushun and I are going. You are going to stay with Parthava at the edge of the cedar forest."

"No, Upaas. I am not going to let you go in there without me." She looked beautiful even when she was petulant.

"I am afraid those were the instructions of the sage from Shuruppak. He has given amulets only to the four of us to go into the Apsu."

"Well, I am not very happy with that."

I tried to explain why it was important for me to accompany Gilgamesh on this trip. I was the only one who knew the way inside the Apsu to Ziusudra's place. She finally agreed, rather reluctantly, to let me go.

"What are you two lovebirds up to?" Shushun's dulcet tones interrupted us.

"I was just coming to wake everyone up," I replied, and pointing to Mount Mashu, said, "We have to reach the base of that mountain before nightfall."

"What mountain? Is it far?" It was Parthava climbing up to where we were standing. Soon, all the group had woken up and I explained the route to Mount Mashu. Parthava busied himself with getting the horses ready and we were on our way again. The journey was quiet for a while. Everyone was thinking of what lay ahead, full of apprehension and anticipation. The path up the low-lying hills was a gradual climb and not too taxing for our experienced horses and we reached the base of the Mount Mashu just as darkness fell. The prairie gave way to shrubby land and then to low trees before the tall trees appeared. As we crossed the last of the row of hills, we realized we would have to cross a thick jungle. The base of the mountain was covered in tall trees. The mountain looked enormous and even more foreboding close up than before. It was immersed in darkness, except the two highest peaks which caught the last rays of the setting sun. The rays were hitting the peaks at a low angle and picked up the colours of the desert in the west. The dark red light made the twin peaks glow in the dark background.

"Stop right there if you value your life." The voice was booming and menacing. We could not see anyone in the darkness. There was nothing but trees and bushes. All of us pulled up short and Gilgamesh took his sword out. He raised it above his head and shouted, equally loudly,

"Who dare stop me, Gilgamesh, the emperor of all known kingdoms and ruler of the world?"

All of a sudden, things began happening all at once. All the trees came alive and we were surrounded by hordes of very fierce looking men and women armed to the teeth with strange-looking weapons—oddly shaped swords, maces, axes and chains. All of them were burly and well-built, even the women, and covered in thick, black hair.

"The dreaded scorpion men!" Shushun hissed under his breath. That is when I noticed the scorpion claws around their necks, along their belts and across their chests as well as claw-shaped earrings. That was a bit of luck, I thought. I was to look for the scorpion men to find the gate into the mountain path. The sage had told me what to do to get their help. I jumped off my horse and went forward towards the leader of the group, my palms outstretched.

"Oh, great Scorpion King, I bring you the Emperor Gilgamesh, descendant of Utnapishtim, two thirds divine and one third human. He seeks audience with Sage Utnapishtim."

"And who might you be? No human who goes into the mountain comes out alive."

"I am Upaashantha of Meluhha and I come with the blessings of the Seven Sages. Here is the amulet of the Seven Sages to protect me through the mountain and the Apsu."

I took the amulet from my neck and gave it to the leader of the scorpion men. By now, several of the scorpion men had surrounded me and were poking me with their sharp weapons. I could feel searing pain and see thin streaks of bloods where the points had dug in. I was trying my best to control the pain. The sage had told me not to show fear or pain to these people. The leader took the amulet in his hand and just passed his fingers over the amulet without looking at it. He passed it to the woman standing next to him, who appeared to examine the amulet in a bit more detail. He kept staring at me throughout. I held his gaze, unblinking. It helped me forget the pain to some extent. The woman said something to the leader and he raised his hands and shouted something loudly in a language I could not understand. Suddenly all the men moved back and disappeared as quickly and as quietly as they had appeared. He turned to me and said,

"Do you intend to take all the humans with you?"

"Yes. All of us have our own amulets to protect us." I could see Lopa looking at me quizzically. "That is if you will let me take everyone".

"That is enough now. Open the gates immediately!" Gilgamesh had lost his patience. "If you don't comply, you will have to face the consequences."

What was he saying? There were hundreds of them, probably more. We were six in number. They had weapons that looked dangerous. He cannot be naïve enough to enrage this barbarian army, I thought. I wondered if he had some plan up his sleeve that I did not know of. To my surprise, the scorpion king replied in a subdued tone, with his head bowed.

"My apologies to the emperor who is more god than human. But I will get that gate opened for you presently." Turning to the forest, he shouted something in his own language. The forest again appeared to come alive and the scorpion men emerged, running forward, and knelt in front of Gilgamesh. The scorpion king shouted some commands. The group of scorpion men withdrew immediately, walking backwards with heads bowed down until they reached the cluster of rocks at the base of the mountain. They started to clear the overgrown bushes in front of the rocks while one of them moved aside and pushed one of the small rocks sideways. There was loud clanging and the huge rock started to glide sideways with a grinding noise. It rolled over completely, revealing an opening into a dark cave. As the rock moved away, puffs of dust and smoke blew out of the cave. There was a pungent smell from within. The scorpion men slowly withdrew and disappeared again into the forest. The scorpion king turned to Gilgamesh and said,

"I must warn you, emperor, who is more god than human. This tunnel can kill humans. No human comes out of this alive. It opens only at night and closes as the first sunray hits the Mount Mashu. Nothing can survive it. You have to reach the end of the tunnel before sunrise."

"Be that as it may, the more time we spend talking to you, the less time we will have to cross the tunnel. Now, get out of our way," he said, and turning to me, he continued. "Now Upaashantha, are you sure you have protective amulets for all?"

I could see Lopa looking at me, as did Shushun.

"Yes, Your Highness. The sage has given me additional amulets for just such an event. No one can be sure of the scorpion men. Our first plan was that I accompany you and Shushun to the Apsu. But I do not want to leave anyone at the mercy of these scorpion men."

I took out the additional amulets I had in my satchel

and handed them to Lopa, Budii and Parthava. There were protestations by all the three and they shouted almost in chorus,

" So you were just going to leave us behind on a whim!"

"I am sorry, but we do not seem to have too many chances of getting out of this alive. I did not want to risk everyone's lives." I could see Lopa was still angry at being lied to in the morning. But it would have to wait till later. If we came out of this alive, I would explain everything to her. We unloaded the horses, carried as many things as we could carry and moved towards the door of the cave.

"Wait. You need some light to enter the tunnel." It was the scorpion king. Each one of us was given flaming torches to light up the dark insides of the cave. As we entered the cave, light from the torches showed a huge cavern with no end in sight at the back. Our eyes got used to the dim light soon and we could make out that the walls of the cave were covered in thick vines. The floor was water-logged and we sloshed our way forward. The torches were flickering around wildly. There was a gentle breeze blowing. I was leading the others, and I could still hear the grave voice of the sage in my mind. The sage had said, "Just keep moving ahead and don't look back once you are inside the tunnel, whatever happens. Just keep the wind on your face, don't turn back at any point."

As we gingerly stepped forward in utter darkness, the torches began to waver and just as I was wondering if they might go out altogether, the rock behind us started to close with a grinding noise. Now was the time for anyone wanting to back out and make a run for it. And I waited to see if anyone would run, but no one did. As the rock came to a grinding halt, the torches stopped flickering and became steady. There was no going back now. The whole place became darker and we could just about see each other in the little light that the torches gave out. Not really enough to light our way forward. I would just have to follow my instincts and the old sage's instructions to the letter. There was some mention of pools and a couple of chasms on the way. There was no way of seeing any of those in this light, I thought. God Indra would have to help. I closed my eyes and uttered the hymns taught to me by the wise sages Vishwamitra and Vasishta under my breath.

"Don't waver, Upaashantha. Trust your instinct and God Indra will take you to your destination," the disembodied voice of Sage Vasishta came to my rescue. I turned to everyone and said,

"We have to hurry if we want to make it to the end of the tunnel. I want everyone to follow my steps exactly. The path inside the tunnel has several obstacles. There are deep wells, pools of acidic waters and deep chasms in the path. One wrong step could be your last one."

I stepped forward slowly at first, and as my eyes got adjusted to the pitch dark insides of the cave, I started to see things more clearly. I could make out the walls covered in dark vines; the water dripping from the ceiling had produced stalactites and stalagmites of different shapes, and some with extremely sharp ends. One could get easily spiked by one of those. The ground became a bit more solid as we progressed and I became more sure of our footing. I became increasingly confident as the night wore on and I thought we were making good progress when the first accident happened. I was about to turn to speak to Parthava who was just behind me when my foot could not find anything solid and I started to slip, slowly at first, and then rapidly. I was slipping down a chasm with no visible bottom. I thought I'd had it when a rope came swirling from above and hit me on my chest as it looped around me. I was pulled up sharply and I thought it must have scraped most of the skin from my face. I was soon being pulled up by the strong hands of Parthava, assisted by Gilgamesh.

"And you were going to leave me behind?" was the first thing Parthava could say to me. I was so winded that I could not speak for a minute. "I had to come to keep an eye on you and save you from yourself."

That was not the first time Parthava had saved my life. He had become a guardian angel for Lopa and me now. I thanked Gilgamesh as well for saving my life and saw Lopa looking at me with disapproval before giving me a hug and a kiss.

"Now, I think you should be more careful."

That was typical of what I had come to expect from Lopa. No recriminations and no cross examination. Just support and encouragement. She knew as well as everyone else in the group that we had to take chances if we were to make it to the end of the tunnel. I got up, scrubbed the mess off my clothes and said,

"I think that proves that the sage was telling the truth. We have to hurry now as we have wasted some time in this effort." And as I turned to step forward, Shushun put his hand on my shoulders to stop me and said,

"Wait. This can happen to you or anyone else in the group. We better link ourselves together with rope quickly to be on the safe side."

"I agree. We should do that to stop losing any more time," Gilgamesh agreed and Parthava got busy linking everyone with a long line of rope leaving a few feet between each of us. Thus, the chain of six set off again and I picked up speed again to make up for lost time. There were a couple of more mishaps. Gilgamesh slipped once and Parthava got his rope all caught up in a stalactite.

We had been on the move now for several hours. There was no way of knowing how long we had been going in the tunnel. The darkness made space and time immeasurable. I just hoped that we would reach the end of the tunnel before the sun rays hit the mountainside.

The torches were dying down and the breeze on my face was getting stronger. But I still could not see any end for the tunnel. Did the sage say there would be a door at the end of the tunnel? It did not matter how much I racked my brain—nothing came to my mind. The tunnel started to get narrower and the walls started to close in on us. We could feel the walls with our hands and soon the rough walls started to scrape our sides. Is the tunnel closing in on us? Had the sun rays hit Mount Mashu? Have we failed in our quest ? Soon we had to go sideways to keep going forward.

"Upaas, are you sure you are going in the right direction? This does not look like it is taking us anywhere," Gilgamesh looked worried. Being the biggest of all of us, he was having the most difficulty going through the crevice the tunnel had turned into.

I was sure of the direction as the breeze was still directly on my face as the sage had told me and I had not turned anywhere as far as I could remember. The images that had been instilled into my brain by the sage did not have any pictures of the tunnel. Everything was just black and empty. I said loudly,

"Yes, Your Highness. We are going in the right direction. I am sure we are not far off from the end of the tunnel." I sounded confident and even cocky, more to convince myself than anything else. Suddenly the breeze got brisker and the wind was biting cold on my face. The crevice opened up and became wider and soon we were practically running on flat ground. The torches were nearly out, but we could see the walls. The space in front of us was distinctly brighter than behind us. That is when I saw a dim slit of light at the end of a long corridor. The tunnel ceiling was high up and the space had become cavernous and our footsteps were echoing in the huge space. We ran towards the slit of light we could see in the distance. There were steps cut into the wall of the cavern near the end of the tunnel. We were still attached to one another as we climbed the steps towards the opening high up. The last few steps were steep and very slippery, covered in moss and our progress was slow. My heart was pounding as the light from the opening was getting brighter.

My heart was in my mouth, I was breathing heavily and sweating profusely as I grabbed the edge of the opening and climbed out into the open. I found myself on a steep ledge on the eastern side of the mountain. I did not wait to look around but got myself busy hauling Parthava out. He was just behind me. The two of us literally pulled everyone out of the opening. The last to come out was Shushun. None of us spoke as we lay there on the short grass on the steep, eastern slope of the mountain, watching the eastern horizon over the desert lands. The horizon was bathed in orange glow and the sky lit up enough for us to see the rolling dunes of sand in the distance. We were engrossed in looking at the sunrise when we felt the earth underneath us move. The opening was closing in just as the first rays of the sun hit the taller of the two peaks of Mount Mashu. It was silent and eerie to see the whole side of the mountain appear to move ever so slowly to close the hole in its side.

We started to scramble down the side of the mountain when I noticed the lagoon at the bottom of the mountain. It must be the Apsu. The Apsu we had come so far for. The lake was vast and I could barely see the farside shoreline of the lake. The waters were a clear and deep blue, reflecting the mountain like a mirror. I was fascinated to see not a ripple on the surface. There was an island in the middle with a dense cedar forest with tall tamarisk trees reaching the skies. The reflection of the trees in the water made a pattern at the edge of the lake. As we reached the bottom, we had to look for the tavern of Siduri, the veiled woman. The land at the bottom of the mountain was heavenly, full of trees bowing down with flower and fruit. I could see Lopa brightening up at the sight of thousands of trees and bushes filled with fragrant flowers. It looked like the plants had emeralds and lapis lazuli growing out of their branches. The sunlight bathed the trees in gold and silver. Parthava went straight to the nearest fruit tree and plucked some juicy apples and pears. All of us were hungry because we had eaten a day back. Once we had filled ourselves with succulent apples, pears and apricots, Gilgamesh started speaking.

"Where to next, Upaashantha?" Gilgamesh was getting impatient. The journey had been longer than he had thought.

"We have to find the tavern of Siduri, the veiled woman. She can tell us the next stage of the journey."

"Come on, then. We are wasting our time here."

"I saw what looked like a building as we were coming down," Shushun replied and pointed towards the north side of the Mount Mashu. "It was in that direction."

It did not take us long to find the tavern. As we started to move northwards, a mouth-watering aroma of roast lamb dragged us toward the tavern ever closer. I could see a figure at the window of the tavern as we neared the place. The figure turned, saw us and ran across to shut the gate and the door and locked both of them. Gilgamesh was furious. He shouted,

"Tavern keeper, what have you seen that made you bolt your door, gate and lock? If you do not let me in, I will break your door, and smash the lock." He was literally seething with anger. He had not come all this way only to be kept out by a tavern keeper. "I am Gilgamesh, emperor of all known worlds, more god than human, destroyer of Humbaba of the cedar forest."

"If you are Gilgamesh, the destroyer of Humbaba and more god than human, why are your cheeks so emaciated, why do you look so haggard and why do you look so desolate? Why do I see so much sadness inside you, why do you look unkempt as if you have been roaming the wilderness?"

"Why should I not look haggard, emaciated and sad? Have I not lost my dear friend with whom I went to destroy Humbaba?

I mourned six days and seven nights for my dear friend who turned into clay."

The tavern keeper proceeded to open the gate and the door to let us in.

"Why have you travelled such a long distance?"

"I come seeking Utnapishtim, my ancestor who joined the assembly of the gods and has been granted immortality."

"No one has crossed the sea for a long time since memory. Only the God Shamash can cross the sea. It is treacherous and you could die attempting it. Go back," Siduri said. her face still veiled.

"No! I will not go back. I would rather roam these woods and die here than go back."

I was watching this fascinating conversation between probably the most powerful man on earth and a tavern keeper along with others. "Well, in that case, go and see Ursanabi, the ferryman. He is the only one who goes to see Utnapishtim. But beware of the stone beings who devour humans."

"How do we recognize the stone beings, tavern keeper? How do we overcome them?" I asked.

"You will know them when you see them. You have to figure out how to fight them. I cannot help you there." And she turned back into the tavern. I thanked the tavern keeper for her help and we left looking for the ferryman, Ursanabi. It was not long before we came across these "stone beings".

"Wait! I can hear something!" It was Parthava with his keen hearing. Sure enough, there was a grinding and rustling sound coming from the edge of the lake. What happened next took us all by surprise. I had never seen anything like that. I had heard tales from travelers of far away lands telling about these magical beings who roamed the forest. There were massive creatures at least twice a man's height coming towards us. They were not walking, rather shuffling their torso. The amazing thing was that they were made of stone! I had never seen stone move that way before. I had never heard of stones move on their own! They had long heads nearly half their height, expressionless faces, with a stubby torso and no legs. All of them had flat-topped caps which were brightly coloured in red, yellow, purple and ochre. We were all so shocked that we kept staring at them and did not move until they were almost on top of us. It was again Parthava who moved first. He threw his axe at the nearest stone being. His aim was perfect and hit the head in the middle and split the idol in two. Soon all of us were doing the same. All of us tried to hit the on comingstone idols.

Gilgamesh went into some sort of rage and started a massacre, if you can call smashing half a dozen stone idols that. Just when we thought we had all of them, the hacked off pieces joined themselves and came back at us.

"They are magical! Let me handle this." It was Budii who reached for his ever-present satchel and took out tiny mud pots. He recited some Avestan hymns before chucking those tiny pots at the idols. "Don't stop your attack. My potions can only stop them reforming."

We had all of the stone idols on the ground in pieces in no time with Budii's magic potions and our axes doing the trick. As we were patting our backs on a successful attack, a gravelly voice said from behind us,

"You did not do good. They were my assistants. You have killed them all."

He was a tall, gangly, rather unkempt man with a long, scraggy beard. He held a long staff in his hand. His head kept nodding as he spoke.

"Who are you? What are these stone beings?" I asked, staring at his nodding head. That nodding head was disconcerting.

"I am Ursanabi, the ferryman of Utnapishtim," he replied and turned to Gilgamesh. "... And I know who you are. Now tell me why you look so emaciated and sad?"

Fascinating! His questions were exactly the same as that of the tavern keeper. Gilgamesh went into his rant again and explained why he was the way he was despite being the most powerful emperor and more god than human and why he was here with all of us.

"Now I want you to take us to Utnapishtim, the sage who joined the assembly of the gods."

"I cannot. It is your hand that prevents us from crossing the sea," Urhsnabi replied.

"What do you mean, my hands?"

"You smashed the stone things and pulled out their retaining ropes. We needed them to cross the sea."

"There must be other ways of crossing the sea, surely?"

"Go to the forest and cut down 300 punting poles, each 60

cubits in length, strip them and put caps on them and bring them to the magillu-boat."

Gilgamesh turned to us and said,

"You heard what he said? We don't have time to lose. Come, to the forest we go." And he started towards the cedar forest. We looked at each other.

"300 punting poles and 60 cubits each? That will take us a long time to do," I said with some doubt. "And what is a magillu-boat?"

"Yes, it will take a long time. But we can do it. I did it with my friend Enkidu in the mountain and now we have six of us. We can make it." He just stormed off. We spent most of the day chopping down tall cedar trees and carrying them to Ursanabi the ferryman. He measured all of them and made sure they were the thickness and the length he wanted. He turned out to be a very finicky character for accuracy of the size of the punting poles. Finally when he was satisfied that he had 300 poles of the right size and thickness, he said,

"We will leave first thing in the morning, before sunrise." When Parthava started to protest, he continued, "We need the protection of the sun god, Shamash, when we reach the waters of death."

We did not understand that logic. But it quietened Parthava for the time being. I could hardly sleep that night, thinking about the voyage across the "sea" as they were calling the lagoon. I could not understand why such a big deal was being made of the voyage. The waters looked so quiet and peaceful from where we were at the ferry stage. But the images of the waters of death the sage had put in my mind were terrifying. I tossed and turned throughout the night, lying under open skies and woke up before dawn. I went into the garden-like forest and collected lots of fruits. Apples, pears, apricots and grapes for breakfast. I knew everyone would be hungry when they woke up. I started waking everyone up, much to their irritation. All of us were extremely tired from the physical work of the day before, after the emotional stress of travelling in pitch black through the tunnel the night before.

"Is it time already? I had just dozed off this minute." Surprisingly, it was Lopa who was complaining. I leaned forward, kissed her on the forehead and said,

"I am afraid it is morning, my love. You heard what Ursanabi said. He wants to start before sunrise. Something about Shamash."

She smiled and was awake in an instant. When we reached the ferrystage, Ursanabi was already there on the boat. The boat looked oddly familiar. It was Lopa who recognised it.

"It is a Harappan ship!" she exclaimed. "So, that is what a magillu-boat is."

"Yes. It is a Meluhhan ship. They are the only ones who can withstand the journey through the waters of death," Urasnabi replied. "King Shuruppak acquired it a long time ago from one of the Meluhhan merchants for Sage Utnapishtim."

Fascinating, again. I did not know that our merchants had been traveling to Sumer for so long. It would be interesting to see if the ship had aged well. Another surprise was that all the punting poles were already on board the ship. Shushun looked at me and said,

"I know what you are thinking. How did he get all those heavy poles on board the ship on his own?"

"Yes, that too," I replied. "Do you think we should ask him?"

"Certain things are well left unanswered for our own good," Shushun said philosophically. Having seen the behavior of Ursanabi the day before, it was sound advice. We were on the "sea" well before sunrise. The waters were quite still and the sail on the main mast was barely moving. But the ship was gliding smoothly on the water without any effort. The ship was familiar to me and typical of our ocean-going ships with a large central mast, two sails attached to side riggers and a facility for rowers at the bottom. There were several signs of it being from Bharata, including a frieze on the inside of the deck showing the scenes of the flood and Manu saving mankind. Another strange phenomenon happened. The island, which we could see quite clearly from the shore, started to recede in size as the ship moved forward towards it. The farther the ship went, smaller the island became and eventually by the end of the first day, the island was a mere speck over the horizon. All of us were baffled by this occurrence except Ursanabi. He shrugged his shoulder and said laconically,

"The more you want something, the harder it becomes to attain it."

He was looking wistfully at a distance when he said that and, turning to me, he continued, "So stop thinking about the island and we will reach the end."

Well, it was easier said than done. I could probably force myself to stop thinking about the island and Ziusudra in the island. But Gilgamesh was simply obsessed with meeting the sage and getting an answer to his question about immortality. It worsened when we woke up in the morning. We could not see either the island or the shore we had left the day before. Seeing this, Gilgamesh became even more desperate.

"What am I going to do? Will I be left to roam the world like a tramp for the rest of my life? God Shamash, take pity on me. Am I not your son? Don't you want me to succeed?"

It was rather pathetic to watch such a powerful man on his knees, sobbing his heart out staring at the sun. He was looking more tragic than ever. I had better do something to stop this. Otherwise, we would be circling the waters of the lake forever. Now I knew why they called it a "sea". It looked vast now and the waves were slowly picking up, imperceptibly at first but growing in strength by the hour. I should try and get hold of one of our sages and ask for help. I sat down in the cabin under the deck and concentrated, trying to reach Sage Vasishta.

"Upaashantha, son. I can see that you have problems. You need to control your desires and teach others to do the same."

I am sure it must be dead easy for these sages to do such things. Not so simple for us mere mortals.

"But how, Sage Vasishta?"

"You appear to have forgotten the power of the yogic *asanas*! Remember them, use them and teach them to the others." There was a slight hint of irritation in his voice. The whole thing became clear to me. Why had I not thought of it before? I thanked the sage and went outside.

"Your Highness, we have to control our senses and desires. Only then will we be able to reach the island. Ursanabi is right. The more we want something, the more difficult it becomes to achieve it."

"And how do you propose to do that? I am sure it must be an everyday thing to you Meluhhans to control your minds and desires," Gilgamesh replied, with undisguised sarcasm. Shushun came to my rescue now.

"I am sure Upaas is talking about yogic *asanas*, Your Highness. Once we master the technique, it is not that difficult to control one's mind."

"Let me see what you have. I have nothing to lose now."

I had better teach him the *asanas* before he starts lamenting all over again, I thought. It was not easy teaching people who are not from Bharata the intricacies of the *asanas*. I spent the whole day working on the yogic *asanas* which are used to control the mind. By nightfall, we could see that the sea had calmed down significantly, but it was not quite the calm, still waters we had seen on the first day. Just before sunset, Ursanabi pointed towards the eastern horizon at something. Lo and behold, the dot (that was the island) had reappeared again. If we continued the same way throughout the night, I was sure we should be quite close to the island by morning. I went to sleep that night, happy and satisfied.

The next morning saw Ursanabi tying stone caps to the ends of the punting poles. The sun was shining brightly on the eastern horizon and we could not see anything on the horizon. I was quite disappointed at not being able to see the island again.

"Don't worry, it is there," Ursanabi said, looking at my disappointed face. "We are nearing the waters of death. We will need these punting poles because you and your friends destroyed the stone beings. Better get going and tie these stone caps to the poles. We'll need at least 60 of those."

He showed me how to tie a flat piece of rock with a slot cut in the middle to the end of each of the punting poles we had cut a few days before in the cedar forest. Soon others joined us and the job was finished before the sun was up to our shoulders. Parthava pointed to something in the distance and shouted,

"I can see the island. We are nearly there!"

"Not quite," Ursanabi said. "We still have to go through the waters of death before that."

"What do you mean? I can see the island quite close by. It is so close that I can even swim across to it."

"I would not advise you to do that, my friend." Ursanabi replied with a dour voice. "We are in the waters of death and you will be consumed before you take two strokes."

I could not understand his worry. The water was crystal clear and was absolutely still. Another thing struck me. So was the ship! It was not moving. The ship had come to a complete standstill. The sails were sagging and there was no breeze. There was no sound either. It was eerie.

"What is happening? Why is the ship not moving?" Gilgamesh was getting agitated again. I had to convince him that being scared would only take the island farther away. Ursanabi called us over to where he was busy with his poles. He dipped the first pole into the water on the side and tied the second pole to the end and so on until the cap of the first pole hit the floor of the lake. He asked Parthava to do the same on the other side. The lake was about twelve poles deep. We had to do the same in two places towards the back of the ship.

"Now we have to move the ship forward using these punting poles until we get out of the waters of death," Ursanabi said and started to push the pole down and back. We started to do the same with all the four punting poles, and the ship slowly started to move forward. It was hard, back-breaking work and we were sweating profusely before long. Even Lopa took her turn on one of the poles for a while. It was late afternoon when a slight breeze picked up and Ursanabi asked us to stop punting. The sails start to fill out and were soon billowing out, pushing the ship along at a decent speed. We were finally moving rapidly towards the island and we could see someone standing at the landing jetty, looking out. Ursanabi dropped anchor quite close to the wooden jetty and the ship gently thudded against it before coming to a stop. The gentleman who was watching the ship came down the jetty as we lowered the landing steps on to it. Ursanabi was the first one down the steps. He leaned forward and kneeled in front of the gentleman and touched his feet, the way we greeted our elders back home. He must be Sage Ziusudra or Utnapishtim as they called him. The sage lifted his hands with palm facing forward to bless him as we stepped off the ship slowly one by one.

"God Shamash bless you, Ursanabi. What happened to the stone beings? Why were you using the punting poles?"

"The stone beings were crushed by Emperor Gilgamesh and his friends, Great Sage. This is Emperor Gilgamesh who is the emperor of Sumeria, more god than human. Your descendant has come all the way from Shuruppak to meet you."

The sage was a tall, rather gaunt gentleman with a long face, full of creases with a thick, bushy mustache and a long beard. His white hair was tied in a bun at the top of his head. His eyes were a deep sapphire blue and did not miss anything. He was carrying a long, thick, gnarled wooden staff. His head tilted forward a little when he was speaking which made him look like a giant owl.

"Emperor Gilgamesh. Why do you look so emaciated, haggard and sad? You look like you have travelled a long time and look disheveled without your royal regalia. What happened to you?"

Again, a fascinating use of the same words and same expressions asking Gilgamesh the same questions! Gilgamesh came forward, knelt on one knee in front of the great sage and held his hands before speaking. He was looking at the sage's eyes when he repeated the same answer,

"Why should I not look haggard, emaciated and sad? Have I not lost my dear friend with whom I went to destroy Humbaba? We spent days together climbing mountains, killing bears, hyenas, lions, panthers, tigers, stags, red stags and other beasts of the forests. We ate their meat together and covered ourselves with their skin. We killed the giant boar sent by Ishtar. I mourned six days and seven nights for my dear friend who turned into clay." Tears were flowing from his eyes and the words were coming out in a flood. "I am fed up of living like this on my own. The gate of grief must be bolted shut. Sealed with pitch and bitumen."

The sage looked at him for a minute before answering.

"Why, Gilgamesh, do you embrace sadness? You were made from the flesh of gods and mankind, and you were molded on your father and mother. Take care, Gilgamesh. The gods are worried about you. You have toiled without cease, and what have you got? You have worn yourself out and filled your body with grief. You have brought mankind near a premature end. You have nearly killed this young and beautiful girl. No one can see the face of death, hear or feel death. Yet, death has been there as a savage ending for everyone. Anyone who can see the sun cannot deny death. Go in peace."

The sage spoke chaste Sumerian and did not just address Gilgamesh when he spoke. He was looking at all of us. I was beginning to understand the questions that befuddled my mind at the end of the war with the Avestans. Gilgamesh was not finished.

"I have been looking at you. Your appearance is not strange. You are like me. And yet you are immortal. Tell me how is it that you stand in the assembly of the gods and have found immortality?"

"I will to you, Gilgamesh, a thing that is hidden, a secret of the gods I will tell you. Shuruppak. A city that you surely know, situated on the banks of Buranuna, that city was very old, and there were gods inside it. The hearts of the great gods moved them to inflict the flood."

He paused for a moment to see if we could understand what he was saying. He went on to tell us the story of the great flood and how he was asked by the gods to "*tear down the house and build a boat. Abandon wealth and seek living beings.*" He continued the story of how he got all the living beings on his boat and sailed away to save all the living beings during the flood. After a few days, they came to rest on Mount Nimush. He stayed in the boat for seven days while the storm and flood raged outside and on the seventh day he sent out a dove which did not come back and he knew that they were safe from the flood.

He described how he built the boat with the help of his carpenter and even told us the measurements of the boat. The next bit was confusing to most of us. He went on about how the Sumerian Gods rebelled and how he shouted in the assembly of the gods about killing mankind. The god Enlil, who had ordered the flood, saw the boat and went into a rage. "Why did a living being escape? No man was to survive the annihilation!" He was told that God Ea helped Utnapishtim escape, and all the gods rallied round to calm Enlil down. They convinced Enlil to let Utnapishtim and his wife live and be one of the gods like them, and live in a faraway land in the middle of the Apsu. After hearing this long soliloquy, Gilgamesh turned around and said,

"What shall I do, Utnapishtim? Where shall I go? Wherever I set foot, there is death. There is the smell of death in my house."

"You want immortality? You have to earn it. Show me that you are better than humans like I did on that boat I built. You stay awake for seven nights and six days like I did and you can have immortality like the gods."

But as soon as Gilgamesh sat down and put his head between his legs, he fell asleep. All the tiredness of the journey and stress took their toll. The sage said to his wife,

"Look at the man who wanted eternal life and youth. He can't even conquer sleep."

"Touch him and let the man awaken. Let him return safely by the way he came. Let him return to his land by the gate through which he left."

"Mankind is deceptive, and will deceive you. Come bake loaves for him and keep setting them by his head and draw on the wall each day he lay down."

The wife baked a loaf each day and kept it next to Gilgamesh's head and marked on the wall of the hut. On the seventh day, we went back to the hut to see if Gilgamesh was successful. The sage touched him and he woke in an instant and said,

"The very moment the sleep was pouring over me, you touched me and alerted me."

The sage snorted and said, "Look over here, Gilgamesh, count your loaves. You should be aware of the marks on the wall. Only the sixth loaf is fresh. All the others are stale and desiccated. You could not even stay awake for one day."

"What shall I do, Utnapishtim? Where shall I go? The snatcher has taken hold of my flesh. Wherever I set foot, there is death. There is the smell of death in my house."

The sage stamped his long staff on the ground and turned to Ursanabi,

"Take him away, Ursanabi. Take him to a washing place. Wash

his matted hair and filthy skin with the water of ellu. Get rid of the animal skins and anoint him with scented oils. Give him a new wrap for his head and wrap him in new, royal robes fit for a king he is and that will not stain till he reaches his land." And he walked away without another word. Ursanabi did as he was told and took him to clean him with the water of ellu. Gilgamesh was back in an hour, clean and looking royal again in clean clothes and shoes. Ursanabi took us to the sage's hut on the island. He was sitting outside cross-legged and appeared to be meditating. He stood up as we approached and for the first time, smiled.

"My friends from the faraway lands of Meluhha and Elam, you have pain inside you. Have you found what you came for?"

I plucked up a bit of courage and replied, "Why do men fight? Why is there so much greed in this world? Why do men cheat and crave for things not their own?"

"Master Upaashantha, you ask questions that have troubled sages for millennia. Man is an animal unlike any created by god Enlil—never satisfied. I give you one word of advice. See others the way you want others to see you and don't grieve at things you don't understand." And turning to Shushun he continued, "There will be born a sage in the city of Ur in time to come. He will be called Avram and he will lead his men out of Ur and Sumer to the land promised by God. The gods will grant him a nation of children that will rule the world. His children and grandchildren will have followers throughout the world but they will fight each other. There will be several messiahs, but to no avail. There will be chaos and man will cause threat of the end of mankind, when the gods once again despair at his actions. There will not be another Ziusudra. Man faces death, but mankind is immortal."

I did not know what to say. It would take us a while to digest this. His wife, who had joined us, spoke,

"Gilgamesh came here exhausted and worn out, looking for immortality. What are you going to give him so that he can return to his land with honour?"

He came forward and put a hand on Gilgamesh's shoulder and said,

"Gilgamesh, you came here exhausted and worn out. What can I give you so you can return to your land? I will disclose to you a thing that is hidden, Gilgamesh. There is a plant like a boxthorn in the depths of the waters of death in the Apsu, whose thorns prick your hand like the thorns of a rose. If you eat that plant you will become a young man again."

The sage then turned around and walked away into the forest and appeared to merge with the forest in front of our eyes. All of us sat there, speechless, stunned at the spectacle.

The Fall of Shuruppak

"I think we had better go back to the magillu-ship before it gets dark," said Ursanabi. He finally broke the silence. I had to pinch myself to make sure I had not dreamt it all. Had I really seen that famous sage? Did he really speak to us? As we reached the ship, the wind was picking up and we set sail quickly. Next morning, the ship stood still again as soon as we approached the waters of death.

"I will get to the bottom of Apsu and get this plant," Gilgamesh said to no one in particular.

"I think we should come with you and help you. Ursanabi tells us that these are the waters of death. We don't know what lurks underneath," Shushun said.

"No! No one is coming with me!" His reaction was quite vehement. "I do not want anyone else's death on my conscience. I will do this on my own and if I die trying, it does not matter." He would not listen to any of our protestations. He tied the stones we had used for caps on the punting poles on his feet and jumped into the water. It was a stressful hour for us. We were sitting at the edge of the ship, waiting for him to get back. We kept looking down into the clear waters of the Apsu for any sign of trouble. He disappeared as soon as he went underwater. After what seemed to be ages, he came out with the plant tied to his waist. Parthava threw a rope for him to hang on to and we dragged him out of the Apsu into the ship.

"Upaashantha, this is the plant against decay. I will take this to Uruk and make an old man eat it to test it. If it works, I will eat it and become young again," he said, and was smiling from ear to ear. He was obviously delirious with joy that he had found the plant that would make him young again. "I will keep it with me all the time till we reach Uruk."

"I am glad you have found what you were looking for, Your Highness," I replied. "We have found answers to our questions. Our journey to Sumeria is complete and successful."

Ursanabi was busy with his punting poles and off we went again down the Apsu towards the shore. It took us a whole day to get out of the waters of death before the wind started to pick up again. The sails were billowing out very soon and the ship picked up speed. On the second day, the waters of the Apsu were so clear and inviting, we all decided to go for a swim. Gilgamesh would not let go of the plant. He had it tucked under his waistband as he was swimming. We swam for a long time enjoying the cool waters in the hot sunshine. Just as we were about to climb back into the ship, being helped by Ursanabi, there was a shout from Gilgamesh.

"My god, Shamash! The dreadful creature! Someone help me!"

All of us dashed towards where the sound seemed to come

from. He was thrashing around desperately and was quite incoherent. We managed to calm him down and took him up into the ship. He sat down on the deck and was weeping.

"Counsel me, Ferryman Ursanabi. For whom have my arms labored, Ursanabi? I have not secured a good deed for myself."

It turned out that a serpent in the water had smelled the fragrance of the plant and had stolen it from his waist. As he went after it, the serpent shed its skin and escaped with the plant and disappeared. He was inconsolable after that for a while. We tried to calm him down again and remembered the words of the sage to him. Finally he realized the futility of what he was aiming for and understood the words of the sage.

"Now I know what Utnapishtim was saying. There is no salvation for us humans unless we strive for it and earn it. I will take Ursanabi to Uruk and show him the wall I have built and show him I do mean well for my people and my work for my citizens."

And so it was that Ursanabi joined us on our way back home. I dreaded the trip back through the tunnel in Mount Mashu and the scorpion men on the other side. Budii's magic came in handy again while finding the gate for the tunnel. The journey seemed to be that much quicker this time and when we emerged on the other side, there was no sign of the scorpion men or the scorpion king. Maybe they did not expect us to return or maybe they did not really exist. Was it all a dream? Our horses were still where we had left them. We were back in Shuruppak a couple of days later to be greeted as heroes returning from war by the Lugal Upar-Tutu.

"Welcome back, Your Highness, Emperor Gilgamesh. You,

who is more god than human, and you, who has seen the face of Sage Utnapishtim."

"Thank you, Lugal Upar-Tutu. We will rest here for a few days before returning to Uruk on my ship with my friends. I have brought Sage Utnapishtim's ferryman, Ursanabi with me."

It was nice to have a proper bath and sleep in a proper bed after weeks on the road. We spent the next couple of days wandering around the city. I spent some time in their pharmacy learning Sumerian medicine. Lopa joined Shushun to explore the vast library of the scribes' college in the city. We heard that Nisaba and Shu-ilishu had left the day after we were transported by the sage at the Ziggurat, obviously very disappointed at being left out. On the third night the Lugal had arranged a grand meal for the whole group. There were the choicest delicacies the city of Shuruppak had to offer and the best wines from Nippur were flowing like water. All of us had enjoyed the evening which was accompanied by dancing girls and Sumerian music. We were woken up by loud shouts and screams coming from outside the palace walls. I woke up with a start and looked out of the window. It was bright, not because of the sun or the moon, but because the buildings next to the palace were on fire.

"What is it, darling? What is all that racket?"

The noise had woken Lopa up as well.

"The building next to the palace is on fire," I said and grabbed my sword just in case. "I will just go out and check what has happened. No need to wake up. I will be back in a minute."

"Be careful. There seems to be an awful amount of noise for

just a fire," she replied.

There was a persistent loud knock on the door just as I was about to open the door.

"Upaas, wake up. Come out quickly." I opened the door to see that it was Parthava standing at the door fully armed with a bow, a quiver and his axe over the shoulder.

"You look like you are going to a war, my friend," I said with a smirk on my face. "It is only a fire. I don't think your weapons will be required."

"Then why are you carrying your sword?" he was quick for that time of the morning.

"There was a lot of shouting going on and it is still dark. It won't do any harm to be on the safe side." I was being defensive.

"Exactly. Why should there be so much screaming and shouting if it is only a fire? It does not fit. I will not be satisfied till I find out."

I closed the door and rushed out to the gate of the palace keeping to the shadows as the fire was bright enough to light the courtyard of the palace. We were not taking any chances. The scene that confronted us as we peeked around the column near the gate was carnage. There were bodies everywhere. The building next to the palace was the armoury which had caught fire and there were several riders attacking anything that moved with spears, swords, machetes, axes and maces. Some of them were still carrying burning torches and were busy lighting up houses around the armoury. It wouldn't be long before they reached the palace. Where were the guards of the palace? What happened to the army of the Lugal?

I realized that I was standing on something sticky on the ground and my hands were sticky as well. I bent down in the darkness to see what it was and put my hands up into the reflected light. I felt sick at the sight. It explained what had happened to the soldiers. I was standing in a pool of the blood which was still flowing from the body of the decapitated soldier lying a few feet away from me. My hands were bloodstained from the bloodsoaked column. There were at least half a dozen dead soldiers around the gate. They obviously had no idea what had hit them. Whoever was attacking them must have taken them by surprise. The gate was still locked and held by brass chains. The brass plates that covered the gate obviously had saved it from being burnt down.

"We need help," I said to Parthava. "You go and alert Shushun, Gilgamesh and the others while I keep a watch here."

"No, my friend. You go and fetch them. I will keep watch here. I don't want you to be in any more risk than you already have been," he replied and would not listen to any argument. "Who is the soldier here? You or me?"

There was no use arguing with Parthava once he had made his mind up. Especially when it came to protecting me or Lopa, he would not take any chances since that night on the road from Harappa to Saraswata when we had been attacked and the faithful Pindara had been injured. I ran across the courtyard keeping myself among the shadows and knocked on Shushun's door and soon the entire palace was awake, including the cooks. Everyone was armed with whatever weapons they could find inside the palace. Lopa insisted on joining us and was ready in her warrior clothes and the trusty bow and quiver full of specially-picked arrows.

For both of us this was a new kind of warfare. In Bharata, the wars took place in fields and battles took place according to a set of rules agreed upon by the two warring parties. Here, we didn't even know who the enemy was. I did not know how to cope with this. Shushun saw uncertainty on my face and asked,

"What is the matter, Upaas?"

"Strange way to fight a war. Where is the war council? Who is the enemy? What are the rules of battle?"

He just laughed out loud and Parthava joined in as well.

"What is all the hilarity? Are we not going to fight these villains?" Gilgamesh joined us. He was fully equipped with a bronze shield on his chest, his crown and brass bracelets on both forearms and ringlets on all fingers. He looked the part of a ferocious warrior. I could understand his reputation when I saw him. He would put the fear of death into anyone looking at him at the wrong end of his sword.

"Upaas is confused. He wants to know the rules of engagement and battle regulations," Shushun complied. Gilgamesh smiled before speaking.

"I have heard of battles in Meluhha. I must admit it is very civilized if you like that kind of a war. My friend, welcome to the real world. Here the winner of the battle is the strongest and it does not matter how you do it. There is only one rule. You kill the enemy before he kills you."

Both Lopa and I found this rather unnerving. Even Parthava, who had been involved in battles with numerous peoples including the Dasyus of the south, felt a little uncomfortable.

"Do we at least know who the enemy is?" I persisted.

"We will soon find out when we go outside," Gilgamesh replied and stomped down the corridor into the courtyard. All of us marched to the gates of the palace courtyard without being noticed by the enemy, whoever they might have been. As soon as we reached the gates, Shushun peeked out from behind the column onto the street and hissed,

"Gutians! They are Gutian bareback riders. They ride bareback to silence the noise from the saddle whenever they want to raid houses."

"I should have guessed it would be the uncultured barbarians from Gutia who would do something like this," Gilgamesh snorted. "We have to hold them back and send word to the Kengi to get our army back in here."

"There must be at least twenty riders out at the front causing the damage. If a couple of us can climb up to the tower on top of the palace, we can hold a covering fire until the rest of us can go round to the scribes' college and fire from the other side and involve them in the crossfire," Shushun had calculated the odds quite well. Gilgamesh turned to the Lugal and said,

"Send your messenger to the Kengi to bring the army across."

"I will, Your Highness. We have an underground passage to reach the city walls. The messenger can get across without being seen," Upar-Tutu replied.

"Upaas, I want you to take Lopa to the tower and start a covering fire. We will try to get across to the scribes' college," Gilgamesh continued.

It was an interesting couple of hours. Both Lopa and I hid ourselves in the tower and used the tiny little portholes to fire arrows at the group of riders on the street below. It did not take long for the Gutian riders to pinpoint where the firing was coming from and we were hit by a barrage of arrows. But what followed was entirely unexpected. They started to shoot arrows dipped in bitumen and set on fire. Soon the entire tower was on fire. That was that and we had to run for our lives down to the bottom of the palace. Luckily the others had managed to go over to the scribes' college and started firing from the other side. Suddenly all firing stopped. There was utter silence apart from the fire raging in the armoury with the crackling of dried wood that was used in the construction of flooring and roof of the aromoury. The entire building was on fire now and beyond rescue.

As there was no sound coming from the street and the firing had stopped, I plucked up enough courage to go across the courtyard again to the column near the gate. The street was empty apart from the bodies of dead soldiers. I waited until I saw Shushun and others walking across the street towards the palace gates. The Lugal opened the gate from inside and we walked out onto the street. I ran across to the soldiers lying on the ground to see if I could help any surviving men. It was too late for most of them, except a couple who were merely unconscious and were coming around when I reached them. About twenty of Shuruppak's soldiers and three of the Gutian riders had been killed.

"You do realize that this is not the last of their attack?" Shuhun was speaking to the Lugal and Gilgamesh. "This is only a probe into the city. They will be back soon with a much larger army."

"Yes. You are right. We don't know how big their force is. It is imperative that the armies from the garrison at the Kengi get here as quickly as possible."

And turning to the Lugal, he continued, "Have any of your spies brought any information, Lugal Upar-Tutu? Do you know where they are and how many of them might be there?"

"I am sorry, Your Highness. But our army has been infiltrated by the Gutians and the information provided is not very reliable. I knew letting them settle in our city was a mistake. They have been quite active, what with the hit and run attacks in the city as well as on travelers from and to the city from the south. Some of the Gutians living within the city are obviously helping them with information," the lugal replied, looking rather glum.

"That, I am afraid, is not very useful. I will send word to Uruk and get my army to join here," Gilgamesh replied. "Come, let's get some rest when we have the time. I don't know when the next attack is going to be."

He turned and walked briskly back into the palace. We walked back behind him not quite sure what to make of the situation. Once we were inside the palace, Parthava turned to Shushun and asked him,

"This may sound selfish, but do we need to get involved in their fight? Have we not had enough fighting for a while?"

"I understand your reticence, Upaas. But, unfortunately, I

don't think we have an option here. For one thing, our hosts are in trouble and it is only right that we should help. Secondly, as long as there are threats of a Gutian attack, it is not safe to be on the road outside the city.

"Well, in that case, there is nothing much we can do apart from getting as much rest as possible before the next attack," Parthava was being rational once again. The armies started to arrive late that afternoon from Kengi. The captain of the guards who had accompanied us came over to see us and said,

"The battalions of Uruk and Lagash are both here now, along with the army of Shuruppak. You should be safe now. I would be surprised if the Gutians are brave or stupid enough to attack the city with a such a large army presence."

It was really comforting to see the streets full of Sumerians soldiers armed to the teeth. They had managed to douse the fire in the armory and had salvaged some weapons which were not burnt. We went to bed that night feeling much safer at the thought of the hundreds of soldiers just outside the palace.

What happened next can only be described as hell on earth. We were woken up around midnight by explosions. The Gutians had come back with a force never seen before and they had brought weapons none of us had come across before. We could not see them. Balls of fire were raining from the sky. They were stationed at a distance and were firing these bitumen-covered balls using huge catapults. Some of the balls contained explosive sand they exploded on contact with anything solid. Practically every building was on fire. We grabbed whatever we could and ran outside into the courtyard. We could not see who was firing these and how. They kept coming at an incessant rate and some were coming from the direction of the city itself.

Soon the palace was burning out of control. The upper storey came tumbling down in front of our eyes. There was nothing we could do but stand and stare. The captain of Gilgamesh's guard came running to us. Most of his clothes were burnt out and his skin was burnt in places. He was waving to us frantically and asking us to stay down.

"We have to move towards the dock and get into our ship before the ship is set on fire. The fire has not reached the dock yet," he had to shout over the noise of the explosions for us to hear anything.

"How can we desert the city? What will happen to the people and where is the Lugal?" Gilgamesh asked.

"I am sorry, Your Highness. But the Lugal is dead. He was one of the first people to be killed along with his Ensi and the commander of the Shuruppak garrison. The army is on the run. We cannot hold them for much longer. There does not seem to be any let up of firing. Most of the city is on fire and the army is either dead or have fled the city by now."

I was shocked to hear that. To cause such a loss so quickly, the Gutians must have been a large force. It turned out that the Gutians had attacked the Kengi and the city at the same time. There were not going to be any more reinforcements coming from there. They had attacked from the outside, sitting on top of the hill wherewe had stopped on the way to Mount Mashu, and fired their catapults. It was the attack from inside the city that surprised us all. At the same time as the attack starting from outside the city walls, there was a firing of fire arrows from inside the walls mainly coming from the tops of some of the large buildings within the city. The Gutians had infiltrated the city with a force that the Lugal had miscalculated. It was not just his army they had infiltrated. They had infiltrated the large houses and the biggest building in Shuruppak—the scribes' college. The rooftop of the scribes' college was a vantage point from where they could fire down at everyone all night with impunity. It was one of the highest points in the city after the ziggurat and no one was allowed to go on top of the ziggurat. By the time the soldiers realized this, it was too late to climb the ziggurat because it was one of the first buildings to be set on fire.

"I think the captain is right. We better make our way to the ship and save as many people as we can on the way," Gilgamesh said, turning to the captain. "You lead the way, captain, we are right behind you."

We were running from one intact building to the next, trying to stay in the shadows as we made our way towards the dock. The main street, which was quite wide, was littered with burnt carts and several bodies. Both Shushun and I tried to see if any of them were alive without exposing ourselves. We found several men and women struggling within the burning houses. Parthava and a couple of soldiers from Gilagamesh's guard rounded up as many of the people as possible and headed towards the dock. It was like a scene from the inferno in hell. Hundreds of men, women and children, some limping, some being carried by others and some crawling on all fours were creeping towards the dock, hoping that the ships in the dock were not on fire yet.

Luckily for us, the dock was on the western side of the city with the huge city walls protecting it from inside the city and the river Ulaja on the other side. When we reached the dock, I breathed a sigh of relief to see that it was still intact as were three of the large ships. Shushun had asked his captain to sail his ship up the river Ulaja from Ur to be in Shuruppak for our return journey. The captain saw us coming through the gates of the city wall and came running down off the gangplank and the dock to help us. The sailors on the ships saw the army of refugees coming down the dock through the massive gates and ran across to help. Gilgamesh's ship had the gangplank already down and ready to take care of casualties. The third ship was a Harappan merchant ship. It was a large cargo ship flying the saffron colours of Bharata and was lying high in the water. A thought occurred to me. If it was lying high in the water, it must be empty. It could accommodate hundreds of people in its hold. I went across to speak to the captain of the ship and ask for help. The captain was more than willing to help. He had emptied the ship a few days ago and still had not loaded any new cargo. The sailors of the three ships loaded everyone on to the ships as quickly as possible. The wounded were being carried on bamboo stretchers and some of them were being carried on bare shoulders of other men. It was a remarkable show of spirit. Everyone was trying to help the injured and the sick.

The load was too much for the ships to take and they groaned under the weight. But, the captains refused to stop loading until the ships sank so far into the river that the water line was threatening to sink the ship. Finally they had to pull the gangplank up to stop the people boarding the ships. Gilgamesh stood on the brow of his ship and raised his hands to the sky.

"Oh God Shamash! Have you not finished testing me yet? What more do you want of me? I did not succeed in the Apsu and you stole the plant of eternal youth. And now the city that gave me food and shelter is being destroyed. What else is there for me?" Gilgamesh turned to the people still on the dock and continued,

"My people, listen to me. Try and use the smaller boats and get away from the city as far as you can. Once we find a safe place to get the sick people off, I will come back for you. As God Shamash is my witness, I will get rid of the barbarian Gutians from your land and help rebuild your city. Have faith in me. We are not deserting you."

It was an emphatic speech and I was quite impressed by it. I looked back at the city as the ship sailed down the river Ulaja. The entire city was burning, the flames almost touched the sky and the smoke was covering the countryside far and wide. The sky had turned blood-red by the flames licking the low-lying clouds. Normally, at this time of the night a chill lands on Shuruppak. Tonight it was so hot from the flames that sweat was pouring down our backs. We stood on the deck, watching the city burn for a while before forcing ourselves back into the ship to deal with the casualties we had picked up. I hoped we could find a landing place soon and he could bring the ship back. In the meantime, we got busy treating the victims of the fire. They were too many to for the two of us to treat. Both Lopa and Parthava helped, but to no avail. I wanted to know if there were any Sumerian physicians on board and went looking for them amidst the chaos of the ship.

There were people lying on the deck everywhere, mostly sick people groaning in pain, holding broken arms and legs. The deck was awash with blood and my feet made squishy noises as I walked up and down the deck calling for any Sumerian physicians on board. After going up and down both the decks, I managed to find a couple of Sumerian physicians who were not themselves ill or injured. We headed back to the upper deck where Shushun and his captain had managed to set up a makeshift hospital. Lopa was acting as a nurse and she had managed to find a few helpers as well. We spent the next few hours patching up people with broken bones and severe burns. I was quite sure that some of them wouldn't make it through the night. We worked for several hours non-stop. I lost count of how many broken legs I splinted and how many total body burns we dressed. Soon we ran out of medical supplies and had to make do with tearing up clothes and breaking some of the furniture in the ship for making splints. Parthava was amazing. His strength seemed to increase as the night progressed, and he got stronger. He managed to break almost all of the tables and chairs on the ship to make splints and was always busy doing something or the other. If he was not making splints, he was cleaning the mess we made while treating the patients. We were washing our hands after treating every patient. But soon we had to stop that as we ran out of fresh water. We had to keep some clean water for drinking and rehydrating burns victims. The sailors kept taking water from the river constantly. But, that was not sufficient to clean the blood from the decks and gore as well as cleaning our hands and drinking.

Budii was a revelation to me. I will take back everything

bad I said about the magi before. He was amazing. He worked tirelessly, treating sick people through the entire night. He appeared to know how to deal with the injuries, especially burns. He was using his potions and powders to good effect. He was feeding the patients with some liquid which made them forget the pain and appeared to keep them happy. Of course he ran out of everything he had in his satchel very soon. He had to improvise and do what I was doing for the fractures and burns—splints and dressings. Shushun came up to the place where I was working and put his hands on my shoulder and said,

"Upaas, we cannot continue doing this anymore. There is no wood left for splints and there is no cloth to dress. We have even used the sail of the ship for dressings. You have to stop and hope for the best."

"You have been going at it for a long time tonight without rest. Your body will be tired and you will start making mistakes."

It was Lopa looking concerned. "You have done all you could. Now leave it to the God Ashwin. You will not be of much use if you fall ill now." She had her arms around me and despite the fact that I had blood-stained clothes and my face was filthy, she kissed me. I must admit I was just beginning to wane and my eyes were drooping. But her kiss woke me up and I was ready to go on for a few more hours. The look on Lopa's face saida firm "no." Parthava joined us just then and said,

"I have run out of wood to chop and clothes to tear up for your dressing. I don't know what you are going to use for splints and dressings."

"Come and sit down, Parthava," I said, pointing to the space next to me on the deck floor. "There is not much we can do now. We have to leave it to the god Ashwin to look after the rest. We have to wait till we reach Uruk for more treatment. The physicians there are going to be busy for months."

I just remembered Gilgamesh's last words about him going back for the rest of the people on the dock. I turned to Shushun and asked,

"Do you know if Gilgamesh managed to go back and get more people?"

"I saw his ship dock at a small village on the way. I am hoping he might have been able to go back for more of them. We could not dock there as this ship is too big for the little jetty they had," Shushun replied.

"When are we going to reach Uruk?" I asked. I could see question marks on all the four faces. "I want to go back and see if we can help anymore of them."

They looked at me as if I was mad. They all started to talk together, protesting. The gist of their objections was that I was completely mad even to suggest such a move at this time.

"We owe it to the city of Shuruppak to do the best we can. Our scriptures say that the hand that feeds us is like God. They have looked after us, they have helped us to go to the Apsu to see Sage Ziusudra. We cannot abandon them. I am not suggesting that we go back right away. We will wash and refresh ourselves in Uruk before leaving. We can rest in the ship. We can stock up the ship as well in Uruk."

Shushun looked thoughtful for a minute before replying,

"It makes sense. We should be reaching Uruk by sunrise. My captain and his crew can stock up with medical supplies and food, while we refresh ourselves and get some rest and food. We can leave before sunset, sleep during the journey and reach Shuruppak next morning."

They all nodded in agreement. Lopa was looking at me with part admiration and part worry. When we were alone, she whispered, "I am thrilled at what you are doing, darling. I am moved by your concern for other humans. But, I don't want you to fall ill."

I kissed her warmly and replied, "Don't worry, darling. Your Upaas is much stronger than he looks."

She just giggled and leaned against me, closing her eyes. We must have dozed off against the deck only to be woken up by birds chirping away loudly and the early morning sun burning our faces. We had reached Uruk.

There was a lot of activity on the dock. Gilgamesh must have sent a message to Uruk. There appeared to be a whole army of people on the dock waiting for the ship. We were the first ship to dock. As soon as the captain lowered the gangplank, the ship was crawling with soldiers, orderlies, nurses and physicians. It was a very efficient operation and within an hour of docking, all the patients had been removed to the hospital in the city. A small platoon of soldiers was waiting to take us to the palace and guest quarters. Shushun was busy giving instructions to the captain to get the ship stocked up and turned around.

We spent the day recharging ourselves and resting. I went down to the pharmacy to stock up on medicines for the journey back to Shuruppak. Budii had disappeared somewhere and came back beaming ear to ear with two sacks full of powders and potions. Gilgamesh must have returned a couple of hours after us, judging by the noise in the palace with the guards and physicians running helter skelter. There was a knock on the door that afternoon just as I was dozing off after a heavy meal.

"Who is it?" I asked.

"It is I, Gilgamesh."

I immediately jumped to my feet to open the door. He had obviously spent some time cleaning himself up as well. He looked refreshed, but there were lines of worry on his forehead and dark circles under his eyes.

"I hope the journey back was not too taxing. I have just returned from the hospital and they told me about your yeoman service. I am eternally indebted to you and your friends for your help towards my countrymen." I could see he was genuinely grateful. "I would like to reward you for your service. Please name what you want and you can have it."

"It is extremely generous of you to appreciate our little work, Your Highness. We did what we could do to help our fellow men. Our scriptures tell us that to serve a fellow man is service to God," I replied. "I do not want any reward, Your Highness. It would be wrong of me to accept anything in return for what we did in Shuruppak or on the ship."

"That is very noble of you, kind sir. I have always held the Meluhhans in high regard and my belief was not wrong. You are a worthy representative of all Meluhha." He bowed his head down to the waist and withdrew, walking backwards through the door and touching his forehead just as he passed the door.

We were touched by his behaviour. Lopa said, "He has shown why he is an emperor in his actions."

"Well... We cannot sit here congratulating ourselves all day. We have work to do. We have to get back to Shuruppak and see what we can do to help."

As we walked out to the corridor, the others joined. Shushun was looking very thoughtful.

"What is the matter, Shushun?" I asked.

"Did you see Gilgamesh?"

"Yes, he came to say thank you. What is the problem?"

"There is no problem. The news from Shuruppak is not very good. When Gilgamesh went back to the city, most of the dock was destroyed and hardly any survivors were there. His ship came under attack and he barely escaped with a few survivors," Shushun replied. "He has offered to send an emissary to my father's court for discussion of peace and trade agreements between the two countries."

"Something positive has come of this disaster after all," I said. "Do you think there is any point in us going back now?"

"Yes. I think we should at least make a final attempt. I want to see if the old sage at the ziggurat who helped us, has been spared. We owe it to him."

I had completely forgotten the old sage in all the confusion and hectic activity. I hoped he was safe. He did manage to transport the six of us quite easily from the ziggurat. I hoped he had managed to escape in the same way.

"What are we waiting for, then? Let us go!" I said and set off towards the gate of the palace. As we reached the gate, the captain of the emperor's ship was coming in.

"Good day to you, Master Upaashantha. I hope you have recovered from the travails of your journey and the battle of Shuruppak."

"We certainly have, captain. We are actually on our way back to the city of Shuruppak."

He looked a bit shocked and said, "Is that wise? We barely managed to get away from those balls of fire. Why do you want to go back?

"With any luck, they would have quietened down or left. They are not known to be organised and so far, they have not shown any leanings towards ruling a city. Anyway, we would be flying a Meluhhan flag on the ship. I am sure they will not attack a Meluhhan ship," Shushun replied.

He mumbled something under his breath, wished us luck and left. We made our way to the dock to see that Shushun's ship was busy with many men running around the dock as well as the top deck loading and stocking it up with supplies. I could hear carpenters busy repairing all the furniture that we had broken off for splints. There was a brand new sail and the saffron flag of the Harappan navy showing a fist holding a bolt of lightning was flying high on the mast. There were some white flags of Harappa with the rising sun flying from the top deck. They had gone as far as naming the ship "Marut" in Sanskrit to give additional authentication of a Bharatan ship.

We were about to set sail just before nightfall when there was a commotion on the dock. It was Gilgamesh with his guards on horseback. The guards were fully armed with shields and spears along with their customary bows and arrows. He stopped next to the ship and raised his right hand towards Shushun standing next to me.

"Hail Shushun, prince of Elam. Lower your steps, I would like to come aboard."

I was not sure what was happening. I hoped he was not going to come with us. It would complicate matters. We would have to fly the Sumerian flag and that would not be welcome in Shuruppak now.

"Prince Shushun, I have been told that you are going back to Shuruppak to help any survivors. Is that true?"

"Yes, Your Highness. We feel obliged to the old Sage Ishme of the ziggurat who helped us get to the Apsu and meet Ziusudra or Utnapishtim as you call him. I want to know if he is safe," Shushun replied.

"You do realize that it is dangerous. I know the Gutians don't stay in a place where they attack for long and leave once their pillaging and looting is done, but they may still be there in force. It has only been three days now."

"We fully understand there are risks, Your Highness. We are taking as many precautions as possible. We are going there as a Meluhhan merchant ship and crew. I want to at least try and find the sage for myself. It is the least we can do for the old sage," Shushun replied. All of us nodded in agreement. When he saw that we were determined to go at whatever cost, he gave up trying to persuade us and said,

"At least take my platoon of guards with you. That will give me some peace of mind as well. They will be disguised as a Meluhhan ship crew."

We looked at each other and finally agreed as long as someone could find enough clothes to dress them like Meluhhan sailors. There were twenty Sumerian soldiers dressed as men from Sarsawatha within the hour. I didn't know where they found the clothes so quickly and I was not going to ask them. Before long, the pacemaker was on his drums and the ship was moving back up north on the river Buranuna and it joined Ulaja just after sunset, towards Shuruppak. We used the time to get some well-needed rest and more sleep. I was woken up by Parthava, with a gentle knock on the cabin door. The ship had come to a standstill and there was a racket of heavy rain pelting down on the wooden deck. When I opened the door, Parthava stood there with his head bent down and looking glum.

"I think we are too late, Upaas …" A thunderclap drowned the rest of his sentence.

"Why, what has happened?" I had to shout to make myself heard.

"Come and have a look yourself."

I ran out of the cabin onto the wet deck flooded with rainwater and went to the ship's side. I was shocked to see nearly half the dock was destroyed and burnt ends of the jetty were hanging down into the river. The magnificent, massive wooden gates of the city wall were half burnt and hanging on at the hinges. There was burnt out carts and furniture lying on the broken dock and what was left of the jetty. It did not look safe enough to land on to. The captain had stopped the ship in the middle of the river. The river was brown and a raging torrent with heavy rain was pelting down.

"It is not safe to dock the ship. We have to take the boats to reach the dock." It was Shushun who had joined us, shouting in my ear. There was another bolt of lightning striking the city somewhere in the middle, soon followed by a heavy clap of thunder. There was no sign of life on the dock or in the city from what we could see from the ship through the broken gates. Looking at the state the river was in, it must have been raining like this for a while. One good thing was that it was most likely that the Gutians would have deserted the burnt city behind.

There was a lot of discussion as to what should be done next. The captain of the guards felt that we should just head back towards Uruk. I was not going to go back empty-handed after coming all this way.

"No. I think some of us should take the two lifeboats and land. Each boat can take up to twelve people," I said, looking at the captain. "We have to make an attempt to see if there is anyone alive needing help. Chances are that the Gutians would have left by now amidst all this rain and thunder and lightning."

Shushun and Parthava agreed with me. It was finally decided that six guards would accompany us in the two boats for a reconnoitre of the city. The captain of the ship would stay behind with the rest of the armed soldiers on the lookout on the ship. The second boat would be ready to be launched at the first sign of trouble with the rest of the soldiers. We left Lopa behind to spearhead the rescue operation if one was necessary and the rest of us boarded the boat with guards disguised as sailors. The water was choppy and the river was fast and turbulent. It was difficult to control descending into the river and then holding course to the dock. We were being pushed south by the strong current. It would have been impossible without the strong arms of the guards to make it across the river. We tied the boat to one of the heavy poles sunk into the river bed holding what was left of the jetty, and climbed up with a lot of struggle. We nearly lost one of the guards when his hands slipped. Luckily he fell back into the boat and was saved.

As we walked across the broken and burnt-out dock, stepping gingerly around burnt out carts and furniture and even some half burnt-out bodies of men, we had to hold on to each other to avoid being blown over into the river by sudden gusts of wind. We reached the relative safety of the massive city wall to take a breather when I noticed something odd. The burnt out bodies made a pattern on the dock. A lot of them were clumped together near the edge of the dock and several bodies were scattered in a half circle. It was as if something had exploded in the middle throwing them out in a circle, one half disappearing into the river. I felt sick at the thought of all these desperate men, women and children trying desperately to get into a boat or a ship to escape the horrors of fire, being blown away in an instant.

None of us spoke a word as we made our way through the

half burnt out gates into the high street. It was only two weeks ago that this street was bustling with happy people going about their business, gaily painted carts selling toys and sweets, shops thronged by colourfully-dressed women and children— Sumerian, Akkadian, Gutian, Egyptian and even some from Bharata. Now it was completely deserted with burnt-out carts on their sides and shops empty and bodies lying everywhere. Apart from the sound of raindrops on the pavement, it was silent. We tried going into some of the houses which still appeared intact in the front only to be faced by scorched interiors. There did not seem to be any building which was not burnt down. The magnificent scribes' school building was in ruins and appeared almost completely flattened, apart from some walls that were still standing up. The palace, where we had spent the night only a few days ago, was also in ruins with charred remains everywhere. When I looked across the city from the front of the palace which was the highest point of the city, even part of the city walls had collapsed on the east and north. I looked to the right at the ziggurat. It was mostly intact except the temple at the top which looked to be in tatters, but was still partly intact.

"The temple is still intact. Come on, let's go up there quickly." It was Parthava who was running towards the ziggurat before he finished the sentence he started. We all ran up the long stairs of the ziggurat. I was out of breath by the time I reached the temple doors at the top. The guards were there before us. The temple door was broken down into pieces and one of the doors was still hanging on its hinges. It fell off when we tried to push it open. It was again deathly quiet, which got me worried. The temple was empty. The idol of the city deity, Ninlil, was missing as were all the gold and brass prayer utensils. I called out in my best Sumerian,

"Hello! Is there anyone there? Sage Ishme! Are you there Sage Ishme? It is I, Upaas."

The others joined in shouting his name. No reply. It did not look good.

"The secret chamber! Where was it?" I asked. None of us had actually seen the door of the chamber he had taken us into. There were just walls all around except the front door. No sign of a door. All of us started to feel and probe the walls all around us. Parthava must have touched a prominence on one of the walls which he pushed to reveal a narrow door which we all remembered. We rushed in with great hope only to find it empty. We searched the other chambers of the ziggurat and the temple again with no result. There were no bodies and there was no sign of any fire anywhere either. It meant only one thing. That Sage Ishme had transported himself out and the priests had run away at the first sign of trouble.

We came out of the temple half disappointed. The rain had worsened and we could not see the ground from the top of the ziggurat. It was so heavy that a small stream was flowing down the steps of the ziggurat. It was substantial enough to peel off the bricks from its sides. As we came down the ziggurat, we saw that the road itself had disappeared and had been replaced by a raging torrent of water.

"I think we should head back to the ship. I don't think there is anything we can do here." I had to shout to be heard over the noise of rain. It seemed to be quite unrelenting and was getting worse. "I am sure Sage Ishme must have transported himself out of the ziggurat before the Gutians came."

"I hope you are right about the sage," Shushun replied. "Maythe God Varuna look after him."

We struggled to get across the high street which was sloping down towards the dock. We had to hold on to each other to stop being flushed down the street and into the river. The river had risen so high that we had to climb onto the boat rather than climb down. The journey on the boat to the ship was again a supreme effort. We were buffeted by the wind, the rain and the rapid current of the river which had swollen beyond recognition. It had reached the city walls and the entire dock was under water by now. When we reached the ship it took the strength of all of us to hold the boat from hitting the ship and be blown into smithereens. The guards and the captain pulled us on board quickly and as the last one got on board, there was no one to hold the boat out and it was thrown out into the river. It came back with the next wave and hit the prow of the ship and shattered into thousands of pieces. The captain signaled for all of us to get under cover. No one could speak as the noise was deafening. Once we were under the deck, Lopa was waiting for me and ran across and threw her arms around me and held me tight for a long time before saying anything.

"We saw several bolts of lightning strike the city. It was frightening. There were so many that we thought one of them surely must have hit you. I thought I had lost you." There were tears in her eyes and we just stood there holding on to each other for a long time. There was no necessity for words. We knew how we felt and were glad to have each other again. I heard the faint clanging of the anchor chains being raised and the pacemaker's drum against the noise of the storm. The captain dared not use the sail to go down the river in this storm. He again used the oars to go down the river.

"I think once we reach the Buranuna, we should be okay," the captain said. "It is a much larger river and it never gets this rough and rapid."

We reached the river Buranuna fairly quickly as the rapid current of the river just pulled the ship along at some speed. But there was no respite. The large river Buranuna was also in spate and the rains were heavier than before. Visibility was almost nonexistent. The captain was navigating the boat by instinct rather than by vision. If we crashed into any of the rocks or little islands that dotted the huge river, the ship stood no chances of survival, I thought. As the day wore towards the afternoon, there was a brief respite from the heavy rain. We could actually see the water, but we could not see any shore! The river had swollen to such a size that it had become an ocean. But it was much calmer and the ship was not being tossed around like a toy. We could hear each other speak. I turned to the captain and asked him,

"Do you know where we are, captain?"

"We have reached the river Buranuna and should be reaching Uruk anytime soon," he replied. He did not sound very convinced.

"How do you know where we are?" Shushun asked this time.

"Aah! Well, it is like this..." And he looked completely blank and kept staring at the sextant he had in his hand and the little mechanism that was mounted on the wall of the cabin.

"Yes, go on. Tell us how you know where we are. I cannot see any shore anywhere to tell us where we are," Shushun continued. " For all we know, we might have reached the ocean."

"No, Prince Shushun," He looked rather apologetic and also a bit sheepish. "My calculations based on the speed at which we were travelling and the direction the ship was going tell me we should be in the vicinity of Uruk soon. But you are right, I cannot be certain."

"Thank you for your honesty, captain. We will keep a lookout for you."

"Thank you. I posted a lookout on the central mast when the wind calmed down," the captain replied. "He should be able to see for miles around."

The rain had dropped to a drizzle and the sun was out. There was a huge rainbow in the western sky. We went out on to the deck to get a better look at the rainbow and the cooling rain was good as the sun was beating down on us with some ferocity. Strange country, I thought. We were nearly drowned in a heavy storm not long ago and it is boiling hot now, albeit with a small drizzle. Just then the lookout on the mast shouted,

"Land ahoy!" He was pointing in a southwesterly direction. We all ran to the side of the ship to get a look. Still no sign of any land. The captain shouted some instructions to the sailors.

"I can't see anything," Parthava voiced what we all thought.

"You will have to wait a while, Master Parthava. I have asked them to change the course slightly and head towards where the lookout is pointing," the captain replied. "We'll be able to see land soon enough."

We could feel the ship groaning as it changed course in the middle of the river and kept up the speed. We stood there glued in the direction of where the lookout had seen land. It was Lopa who saw it first.

"There it is!" she said, pointing in a direction slightly off where we were looking. All of us saw it and the captain shouted more instructions to change course again. It was only a dot in the distance at first and it soon grew in size and it was not long before we could recognise it as the massive walls of the city of Uruk. The ship steadied its course as we got closer to the walls of the city. The water level here had also risen quite high and the entire dock was under water and the river was lapping at the massive cedar gates Enkidu had built for Gilgamesh in his last days. I could see the tops of the palace and the ziggurat in the distance within the city walls. There were a couple of ships still anchored at a distance away from the walls along with the smaller boats. There did not appear to be any activity in the dock area. The ships and boats appeared deserted.

"What do we do now?" I asked, looking at Shushun.

"I am afraid the sky does not look good," the captain said. "Dark, heavy clouds are gathering again and coming down from the north. Our safest option is to head south towards Ur and the ocean."

"The only thing we can do now is let the guards off with the boat and two of us should bring the boat back to the ship,"

Shushun replied. "If all of us get off the ship, we may have difficulty getting back on the ship and there is a good chance we may lose the ship in a storm if it is left anchored here."

"I think the captain is right. It is time we head back to the ocean and back home," I replied. "It will be a year next week, since we left Harappa. I don't think we should tempt fate."

"Has it been a year?" Parthava was the only one who did not look worried. There was a brief discussion and we finally decided that we should head back to the ocean and then to Susa, the Elamite capital and Shushun's home city. Shushun turned to the captain and said,

"Take us as close as you can to the city gates, please. We will have to make a couple of trips to get all the guards into the city."

The captain showed his navigational skills again by taking us really close to the gates of Uruk. I could see the guards in the bastion at the top of the walls and we waved our hands at them. They waved back. The captain signaled to the soldiers what we were planning to do. We did not want them to start firing arrows at us in the little boats. We lowered the boat down with ten of the soldiers and the three of us—Shushun, Parthava and I—went down into the boat. The waters were much more stable here than at Shuruppak and it was not hard to row the boat to the gate. As we reached it, we saw that the soldiers had opened a small opening in one of the doors of the wooden gate. They dared not open the gate for fear of flooding the city. The guards got off one by one and climbed through the opening and into the city.

The second time we went down to the gate, the captain of

Gilgamesh's ship who we had met on the way out of the palace was at the door.

"Thank you, Master Upaashantha. I am very grateful to you for bringing our soldiers back to us," he said. "Were you successful in your quest? Did you manage to see the sage you were seeking?"

"No, captain. Unfortunately the city is in ruins with no survivors. The Gutians have destroyed everything in the city and looted everything. There was not a single building standing and the storm did not help our search," I replied. "But, we did not see any remains of Sage Ishme either. I am hoping he has escaped and not been taken hostage by the Gutians."

The captain gave a wry smile before replying, "That is unlikely, Master Upaashantha. The Gutians are afraid of touching priests and sages for some reason." Then the last of the guards climbed through the opening in the door.

"We will say farewell here, captain. We are heading back down the river to Ur and then back home," I said. "Please convey our wishes and grateful thanks to your emperor."

The captain saluted us and closed the door as we turned around towards the ship. We stood on the deck watching the massive city walls of the city slowly diminish in size as we sailed down south, until it became a small speck and disappeared altogether. I sighed a deep sigh and said,

"We better get back inside. The storm clouds are gathering and the wind is picking up speed again. We are in for another battering."

Parthava smiled and replied, "We are getting used to the storms in the waters by now. We have so far lost several ships in these storms and we have survived every one of them."

"I would not joke about it. You would be tempting fate," Budii said, looking very serious. He was partly right. The storm picked up again and hit us hard. It was the skill of the captain and his crew which kept the ship afloat. As the sun went down, the storm was still raging with rain pelting down heavily. Thunder and lightning appear to follow us. None of us could bring ourselves to eat anything that night and we went to try to get some sleep in the rocking ship. The ship was being buffeted so hard that it was difficult to stay still long enough on the bed to get any sleep. The storm raged for two days, almost non-stop as we sailed down south. The oars were used along with the rudder only to control the direction of travel. The ship was being pushed forward by the raging current of the river Buranuna— whether it was going in the direction we wanted was another matter. The captain looked increasingly worried as the days passed. He spent more and more time with his instruments, and looking at the stars in the sky. Unfortunately, we could not even see the moon on the first two nights, let alone stars. I was quite sure we were lost. Even Shushun voiced his suspicions once or twice. We saw the shore only on a couple of occasions during those couple of days. The river had swollen so much and the width was so vast that the shore was beyond the horizon.

The storm subsided on the third day and almost stopped. The captain sent the lookout tothe top of the mast. The sun then started beating down on us and burning wherever we stood. We tried to keep in the shade as much as we could. It was important that we reach the port of Ur before we proceeded to the sea for supplies. We would be running short of supplies such as fresh vegetables and water soon. Parthava went down to the hold of the ship and came back looking glum.

"We probably have enough supplies to last us ten to fifteen days at best."

"You are was always worried about food, Parthava," I said smiling.

"No. Honestly. We have to find the port of Ur soon for supplies before we cross the sea."

The captain just walked onto the deck, smiling.

"I have good news for you, friends. The lookout has spotted land and I think it is Ur, by my calculations." He sounded very positive. "Come to the other side of the ship—we can see the city come into view."

We trooped across to the other side of the ship. The water was really calm with hardly any waves or current. I found it difficult to believe that we were still on the river Buranuna. The river looked just like a sea. There were no visible shores, as far as my eyes went. But the captain pointed to the eastern horizon and said, "That is where the city of Ur is."

We strained our eyes to look for the port that the captain promised was there. After travelling about an hour, we saw a speck appear on the horizon which grew quite quickly. All of us were standing at the side of the ship eagerly watching the appearance of the city. The first thing we saw was the top of the ziggurat which was shining brightly in the sun and the reflected sun made it look as if it was on fire with an orange glow. Soon, we saw the massive walls of the city. These were huge, not quite as big as that of Uruk's but much bigger than that of Shuruppak. As we approached the city, we could make out the tops of some of the bigger buildings such as the temples and the granaries. I could even recognise the tops of some of the temples. The tall stone columns of the necropolis could be seen. But there was something odd about the whole thing. It looked like the whole city was floating on water. Where was the dock and the landing jetty where we had seen so many Harappan merchant ships?

"What has happened here, captain? Where is the dock?" Shushun asked the captain. The captain looked at us quizzically before answering.

"I have been to Ur several times in the past and I have never seen water level get so high. It looks like there has been a flood after all that rain we have been watching upstream."

"Oh my God. We better get there and see if we can help," I said.

"Captain, try and get us as close as possible to the city, please."

As we got closer we could see that the wall was breached at one end and the massive wooden gate was floating on water. The dock and the jetty could not be seen. The stain on the wall showed that the water level had reached nearly half way up the perimeter wall. The captain was not sure of the depth and anchored the ship away from the gate. We put the only boat left on the ship down to the water. It was the repeat of the episode in Uruk except we were not struggling with the boats. The water was calm. The five of us went along with a couple of sailors. As we neared the gate, we could just make out the dock and jetty under a couple of feet of water. We managed to row past the gate into what was the high street only a couple of weeks ago. We were all quiet in the boat and there was silence in the high street which had been bustling with traders and customers haggling for wares. I could just imagine the fisherman arguing with the housewife about the price of a haddock and in another shop, the little boy tugging at his mother's sleeve was asking her to buy him the little toy cart. But there was nothing now. It was deathly quiet apart from the sound of the water lapping against the walls of the houses and shops and sea gulls chirping low in the sky. The inn we had stayed in only a couple of weeks ago was in ruins with the top half of the building having collapsed down the side, blocking the alleyway where Parthava had kept his special cart with all the weapons in the secret hideaway under the floor boards. Most of the surrounding buildings had also collapsed into rubble. The whole scene showed that the once thriving metropolis was now just a pathetic pile of rubble. We were nearly at the intersection of the high street with the main street when we heard it.

"Help! Please help us!" It was the emotional voice of a woman. We scanned the buildings to see where it was coming from.

"There. She is there on top of that house." Parthava was pointing to a house on the main street just off the high street. There was a woman standing on top of a house which was tilting precariously to one side, holding on to a little boy with one hand and waving a piece of cloth with the other. We moved towards the house quickly and one of the sailors jumped off the boat and started to swim towards the corner of the house. Parthava followed the sailor. Both of them clambered up the sloping walls on all fours and reached the woman. The woman gave her son to Parthava and pleaded,

"Please take my son first. It does not matter if you cannot save me. Please save my son." She was sobbing her heart out and the words came out in stutters. Parthava took the little boy in his arms and said,

"Don't worry. You are safe now. We are not going to leave you here. My friend here will help you."

He managed to climb down the wall with a lot of difficulty, scraping his knees in the process. The sailor held her hands and tried to help her onto the side of the leaning wall. She was petrified and refused to budge.

"No. Leave me. You save my son. I cannot climb down that wall."

The sailor was not sure what to do. He kept trying to cajole her into getting off the roof of the house without any success. By now, Parthava had reached the boat with the little boy.

"Can you hear something?" Shushun said, cocking his head to one side. There was a low rumble, like an unending thunder in the distance. We had not noticed that the wind had started to pick up as well.

"A flash flood!" Parthava screamed. " I have seen this on the Saraswathi several times. It is lethal. We need to get out of here and to the ship quickly."

"We cannot leave the poor woman here," I said and turned to the woman who was still on top of the house. I shouted, "Can you swim?"

She nodded her head and jumped past the sailor into the water. Immediately we could see she was struggling. Obviously, she was not a very good swimmer and the current had picked up and we were struggling to keep the boat steady as well. Parthava jumped back into the water and with the sailor, helped the woman reach the boat.

"I think we should forget the rest and head back to the ship before the flood hits us," Shushun said. We started to row as hard as we could and by the time we navigated around the broken gate and reached the ship, the wind had picked up and so had the current. It took immense effort for us to climb back aboard the ship and even harder to get the boat back on to the ship. All of us were out of breath and panting by the time we reached the deck. The captain had noticed the wind and current as well.

"The storm appears to be picking up again. We better get away from the city as quickly as possible or else the ship might land up against the walls."

The sky had clouded over and it had become quite dark. The rumbling sound had also increased in intensity.

"Is that the sound of the storm?" I asked. The captain obviously had not noticed the rumbling sound. It was getting louder by now. He stopped and listened carefully and his face went white,

"Oh my God! That is not a storm. That is a flood heading this way." He turned and ran down to the rowers shouting orders as he ran. The drums of the pacemaker joined the sound to make it feel even more menacing. The ship groaned as it turned around to face south and away from the city walls. We had not even gone a few yards when it hit us and the walls. A huge wall of water coming down the river hit the city walls and completely submerged the city. The city wall was crumbling down into water and it tossed the ship about like a toy. The ship was taken high up on the crest of a wave where we could see almost the entire city. The city was already in ruins and the new wave of water quickly submerged the city. The only thing that was still visible was the tip of the massive ziggurat. As the wave moved down, we could see that most of the massive city wall had collapsed as had most of the buildings. We soon lost sight of the city as the ship was being taken down along with the wave of the flood at some speed. It was a long time before anyone could speak. We were trying desperately to hold on to whatever we could, to stop us going overboard.

The woman sobbed her heart out and thanked us by kissing each of our hands repeatedly. "I will never be able to repay you for saving my child. I will be in your debt till I die."

"We only did what any human being would do, madam," I replied. "We are only sorry that we could not save more people. Tell me what happened to everyone."

She poured out a story of devastation caused by the storm raging for days followed by a great flood which destroyed anything that stood in its way, and killing most of the population. Some had escaped by leaving early in the ships that were in the harbour at that time. She told the story of mothers trying to save their children by clinging on to anything that was floating only to be drowned by the raging torrent of water. She told the story of how the horses and all the farm animals had drowned as they could not swim away from where they were tied in the enclosures. There were heroic stories of men dying trying to save others. Her husband had gone to help the aged people living next to her and had never come back. She had managed to climb to the roof of the house and we had reached her just as it had started to tilt to one side. She did not think that there were many people still alive in the city. Well, if they were, they would not be now.

"What are we going to do for supplies now?" Parthava was thinking about food like always.

"Don't worry, Parthava. Now that the sea has encroached further on, we should be able to get to the river Gihon soon and reach my city of Susa within ten days. You can get as much supplies as you want there," Shushun replied, smiling.

"What an end to a magnificent city…" Budii was reminiscing. "So much for Sage Ziusudra or Utnapishtim's forecast of its future."

"What do you mean, Budii?" Shushun asked.

"Remember he had foretold that someone called Avram would be born in the city of Ur, who would lead a nation of children out of the land of Sumeria to God's promised land?"

"I would not write the city off yet, Budii. Floods in the rivers of Buranuna and Hidekal are not uncommon," Shushun said. "Cities like Ur and Shuruppak have an eternal life. They cannot be destroyed. From what we have learnt from being with Emperor Gilgamesh, he will not let the city go down without a fight. I am sure he will rebuild it once the flood recedes. Sage Ziusudra cannot be wrong. I am as sure as I am standing here that there will be a man called Avram born in the city of Ur, once it is rebuilt. He will lead the people of his city to the promised land of the Gods. What is disturbing is what he said about the followers of his children and grandchildren. I can only wish that he is wrong and that they don't bring mankind to near extinction."

Glossary

1. Lugal: Sumerian king, leader or general

2. Zigguratt: Temples in Mesopotamia/Sumer

3. Enkidu: Wild man of forest living with animals, becomes a close friend of Emperor Gilgamesh and helps him in his fight against the demon Humbaba of cedar forest, part of the legend of Epic of Gilgamesh

4. Buranuna: ancient Sumerian name for river Euphrates

5. Meluhha: Sumerian name for Bharata. People of Bharata were termed Meluhhans

6. Shamash: God of Sun in Sumer

7. Marduk: Sumerian god.

8. Saraswatha: The port city of Lothal

9. Varuna: Ancient Vedic god of wind and water also Avestan and Elamite god

10. Indra: The chief god of Vedic period. Majority of hymns in Rigveda are composed for him

11. Susa: Capital city of ancient Elam on the banks of river Karun

12. Panis: One of the ancient tribes during the Vedic and puranic times

13. Matysans: Another one of ancient tribes of Vedic times considered uncouth and like "fish" or Matsya

14. Dilmun: Ancient city of Mesopotamia currently recognized as most probably the island of Bahrain. Some historians believe it to be the land Gilgamesh goes in search of immortality in the epic of Gilgamesh

15. Sindhu: Fictional name of current Mohenjodaro

16. Gihon: Ancient name of the river Karun in present day Iran, also mentined in the Bible.

17. Urpak: Ancient city of Sumeria known to have many Meluhhans living

18. Bharata: The name of the ancient empire of the Harappans

19. Lagash: The city of the Sumerian translator Shu-Ilishu

20. Nineveh: One of the major cities of ancient Sumeria? First wines are said to have come from here.

21. Elam: The ancient empire of present day Iran

22. King Awan: The king of Elam who fought against the Sumerians and won independence for the Elamites

23. King Ur-Nanshe: King of Shuruppak

24 Zubi: Ancient name of Zagros mountains

25. Akkadian: The language of Sumerians

26. Shu-ilishu: Translator of Lagash, who was also reputed to be the king of the city state

27. Aratta: ancient mountain country in Zagros range

28. Sumeria: Country of Sumerian who later were the inhabitants of Babylon

30. Gutians: Very little is known of this warlike tribe who were reputed to be constantly at war with their neighbours – Sumerians.

30. King Vishtaspa: Avestan king who was taught by sage Zarathustra and considered to be one of the first Avestan Kings

31. Mundigak: capital city of the Avestans

32. Bhrigus: Descendants of one of the seven Maharsi's of the Vedic period – sage Bhrigu also considered to be present day Persians by some authors

33. Magus: Magician or a witch doctor during ancient times in Sumer, Egypt, Syria and Greece

34. Gedrosia: One of the main Avestan states

35. Ariana: An Avestan state to the west of the country

36. Haoma: Avestan name for Soma, exact identity of the plant unknown

37. Yasht: It is a collection of 21 hymns written in Avestan language. Each Hymn is in praise of a Zoroastrian divinity. Similar in context to the Vedas of ancient India.

38. Yajna: It is ritual of offerings to a fire altar accompanied with chanting of vedic hymns.

39. Haozdar: Ancient city of Avesta, now a ruin in Afghanistan

40. Abjo: ancient name for the country of Abydos

41. River Ulaja: Ancient river in the southern Mesopotamia

42. Ziusudra: Also called sage Utnaphistim, one of the central characters of the epic of Gilgamesh. He was the king of Shuruppak who saves his people from a devastating flood and was given immortality by the gods.

43. Shuruppak: Ancient Sumerian city said to have been devastated by a huge fire and then by a massive flood

44. Kengi: name given to a central army camp from which the soldiers lead out to protect the country in Sumer

Further Reading

This is a collection of books I have used for my research while writing the Harappa series. It is given in no particular order. If this book has stimulated interest in people in finding out more about one of the greatest civilizations the world had ever witnessed, I would strongly recommend the following books and websites.

Underworld: The Flooded Kingdoms of Ice Age by Graham Hancock.

The Moses Legacy: The Evidence of History by Graham Phillips.

Gods, Sages and Kings: Vedic Secrets of Ancient Civilisations by David Frawley

Babylon: Mesopotamia and the Birth of Civilization by Paul Kriwaczek.

Mesopotamia: The Invention of the City by Gwendoline Leick

The Epic of Gilgamesh by Andrew George.

The History and Culture of the Indian People: The Vedic Age Vol.1 by R C Majumdar et al.

In the Search of the Cradle of Civilisation: New Light on Ancient India by Georg Feurstein, Subash Kak and D Frawley.

Ancient India by R C Majumdar

Early India by Romila Thapar

The Rise and Fall of Babylon: The Gateway of the Gods by Anton Gill

Ancient India by Palaksha

Advancements of Ancient India's Vedic Culture by Stephen Knapp.

An Introduction to the Modern English Translation of Rigveda Samhitaa with Mantra, Pada Pata, Anways, Meaning ... by Prasanna Gautam

Web sites of interest

http://www.Harappa.com

http://www.indiahistoryonline.com

http://www.archaeologyonline.net/

http://www.ancientindia.co.uk/

http://ajaonline.org/

http://asi.nic.in/

Other Books by the same author

1. *A Kangaroo Court: Triumph of Mediocrity* - http://www.amazon.com/Kangaroo-Court-Triumph-Mediocrity/dp/1468081330

2. *Harappa: The Lure of Soma* - http://www.amazon.com/Harappa-Lure-Shankar-N-Kashyap/dp/8192226670

Websites: www.shankarkashyap.wix.com/harappa-series

BLOGS: shankarkashyap.wordpress.com

harappaseries.wordpress.com